By Frederick Busch

I Wanted a Year without Fall (1971)
Breathing Trouble (1973)
Manual Labor (1974)
Domestic Particulars (1976)
The Mutual Friend (1978)
Hardwater Country (1979)
Rounds (1979)

Rounds

ROUNDS

Frederick Busch

FARRAR, STRAUS AND GIROUX | NEW YORK

Library of Congress Cataloging in Publication Data
Busch, Frederick   Rounds.   I. Title.
Pz4.B9767Ro   [PS3552.U814]   813'.5'4   79–19470

To Dick and Peggy Hosbach

Rounds

From the edge, near the road, looking to the fenced end of the graveyard, where pasture began, Silver saw his son's coffin. It was a metal lozenge. It was an oblong medicated tablet. It was going to be swallowed, he thought.

Eli Silver, M.D., practice restricted to the treatment of infants and children, stood near his car, which was parked at the side of a narrow road outside his town. The sky stared. He leaned forward but didn't walk. Cattle, beyond the far fence, ignored his dead child and his wife, Gwen, who looked at the coffin and then up the graveyard toward Silver. Her face was the coffin's gray-bronze; it glowed with sickness. Between them were thirty rows of gray stone markers, beginning with 1756 and 1786, and marching through years to Gwen, and the small gray-bronze box, and the shockingly small hole in the stony unwilling soil of northern New York. The cattle stood in a little curving stream, the hard summer sun pressed at their heads and on the box and on Gwen, who slowly fell beneath its weight to her knees, then to her hands, and who didn't look toward Silver again, or any more. When he walked down the right-hand lane to the back of the graveyard, Gwen walked up the left-hand side to the car in which she had arrived.

No clergy were to come. No one was to come. But the old man who patrolled the graveyard on a miniature John Deere tractor, its mower spitting as he jerked along more slowly than he might have walked, was emerging from a little shed, tall and as disdainful of the ground as if he drove a combine over endless acres in Nebraska. He arrived as Silver did, as Gwen drove off. The old man put the tractor in neutral and watched. Silver, on his knees, picked the box up. It was too heavy to hold like that, and though he meant to slide it slowly, he threw the box an instant before he had wanted to let it go. It lay crookedly in the hole. Silver, at the edge, his hands hanging in, pushed at the box until it was level. When he stood and stared in, the old man turned his motor off. Silver looked up, and the old man nodded. He told Silver, "That'll do it."

Silver looked at him until the old man shrugged and pointed to the shovel lying beyond the other edge of the hole. The old man started his motor and backed away. Silver buried.

And now, as his plane bucks and hisses, returning from European airports to the hot gray air of JFK, New York, Silver, who takes care of babies, whose boy was killed, whose wife could not live with him again thereafter, Silver, despite his efforts, thinks: of miscarriages, stillbirths, hydrocephalus, ectostoses and renal tubular defects. Doesn't he take care of babies?

All the time. So: pneumothorax asymptomatic, impacted meconium, transplacental hemorrhage, parotitis. He returns to the earth, his enemy, and sees a year of medical practice in the butterfly rash of systemic lupus puckering over a child's pale face, and the ghost-house X rays of a square enlarged skull, and the walleyed stare—she looks up and into her brain—of a girl with convergent strabismus, and a tongue bitten halfway through, and blue lips, and bloody vomit, and the broken nose of a battered one-year-old, and more, he sees more, he sees too much more, and more than that, but they are rolling slower toward the landing ladder and he has to claim his baggage, tell them at Customs who he is: Eli Silver, M.D., a man from the state of New York, who is home.

Eli Silver is large. His feet are long and the leather heels of his cordovan brogues sound like pony's hoofs when he walks in echoing halls. His suit jacket flaps, his thin wrists hang from his cuffs, his long back is stooped although he isn't old, and he is a foot taller than most of the men and women who wait with growing hopelessness for their luggage to tumble from someplace onto the revolving belt. His narrow face is pale and bald. While many sweat in the heat of JFK, underground, his flesh is dry, the pores transsected by the seams of squinting and frowning and holding conclusions clenched. If he wore a bandage, if he carried a cane, his awkward motions would seem reasonable. As it is, he looks frail as a vegetarian looks in a butcher shop. He looks like a man with an obsessive indoor hobby, or a man with no interests at all. He stands out among his fellow passengers, in other words, but no one likes to notice him for long.

He consults several papers stapled together—his passport case is neatly packed, his canvas suitcases don't bulge, his clothes are loose but unrumpled—and then, looking away from a child in a stroller whose long gagging bellows are the signs of recent bronchitis, he enters a cab and asks to be taken to LaGuardia, where he will board a four-seater for the flight upstate. The airport he will land at there is the airport Gwen flew from, fleeing accident and random survival, and every other fact of Silver's life.

The roadways in harshest sun and cruelest reflection are bleached from black to white. They are X-ray plates of expressways, but he doesn't want to think of X-ray pictures, or the hoarseness of a choked larynx, or elevated white cell counts, or the whispering hiss of a heart's leaky valve. With his eyes closed and his breath shallow, he leans against his taxi seat and suggests to himself—The Flask, in Hampstead; the ride up the Thames to the *Cutty Sark;* the tall and sad slender woman, wearing a Southern Comfort sweatshirt, carrying a sketch pad, followed by a giant shaggy yawning man who chews his mustache hairs as she points to the Charing Cross; the smell of spices and the cries of drunks off St. George Street at the London docks—that he think of something else. But there isn't anything else. Not the underwater almost-green of Venice, nor the *grappa* at the Lido, nor the dungeons of the Doge Palace, where the same woman in the same Southern Comfort sweatshirt led the same shaggy man, nor the awful furnaces of Murano, where glass was blown and German tourists applauded the fires.

There is beta hemolytic streptococcus, pulmonic stenosis, antihistamines in suspension, popsicles for the dehydration of fever, sweaty casts on small arms, thickened intestinal mucosa, and the sound of his voice saying, "Daddy'll be right back." He haunts himself. He pays the cabbie. He waits for his flight. He flies.

He will land, go home to the house and adjacent clinic, waken next morning to his voice—Daddy'll be right back—and take care of other people's kids.

1 | Manual Labor

They had moved through New England, owning land and bringing houses back to health from swayed beam, staggered sill, rot and roof leak. And here they were now, in upper New York State, not all that distant from New England and yet a place somehow more exhausted, a countryside of oxbow rivers and Indian mounds, more scabrous than New England, with a dull shimmer of what has failed.

Phil and Annie Sorenson, late of the state of Maine, here in Oneida County to comfort one another and work and turn forty. Phil, as he'd done before, had gone ahead to look at land and this time talk with employers, a dean, an assistant dean, an associate dean, a department of English, all of whom had hired him—because, he claimed, he was bigger than they were, and had on his beaten-up legs outplayed the associate dean in a basketball game with students—to teach grammar and reading to freshmen from Bedford-Stuyvesant and New Rochelle who were classified by the college as Reading Disadvantaged. In fact, they were illiterate, and because he was large and had worked with gentle animals as well as high-school students, Phil was to make them eligible to enter college within a year of their having entered college. This procedure was called Affirmative Action, and while it was intended to redress ethnic imbalances, it in fact guaranteed that the school received federal grants for telescopes and lab equipment.

So they'd sold the house and acres of land in Maine and during early June they had traveled in Europe, spending money, looking around. Annie was recovered from miscarriage and the long healing—itself a state of wound—and she was again tanned nearly brown, tall and slender, looking almost-thirty instead of almost-forty. The lines on her forehead had not disappeared, but they no longer looked like furrows from talons or barbed wire. And they didn't talk about fertility, or babies, or the need in their house for extra rooms for anyone but themselves.

At the end of June they arrived together in a rented truck, and then Phil went back to Maine for their dented four-wheel-drive truck, which he drove down loaded with last-things: old roofing ladders; their Ouija board, found behind a bureau in the Maine house; the handmade wheelbarrow Phil wouldn't part with; his three axes, and the adze he'd recovered from the boathouse in their back field above the bay; Annie's chest of paints and her portfolios kept in the woodshed next to the kitchen and unused for years; the poems Phil hadn't worked on since the first miscarriage; the journal he'd kept since the second, when he had cut off his right thumb with a Briggs and Stratton self-propelled lawnmower; the five-dollar hand-powered mower Annie had bought him at a barn sale, eighteen months later, to signal that they might start recovering; old photograph albums, and textbooks from twenty years before; a very old long-handled scythe; and Phil's reeking sweatsuit, which Annie made him hang in the shed and which he wore to slowly pound along single-track rutted roads and through high brush, not really running away or toward very much, but offering, he said, a moving target just in case.

They spent July 4 walking around their new house, which was an old one made mostly of octagonal stones, to which a wooden wing had been added. It sat by itself at a crossroads on a hill of pastureland; farm trucks went by, and some tractors, the occasional bright fast car of a student, some motorcycles, but it was most often quiet, and you could see what was coming. Below them, to the south and east, was a huge bowl of hill land in which a swamp had taken over an ancient forest, and sometimes in the early morning or at dusk a great blue heron, clumsy wings creaking, would struggle past to settle in one of the bare leaning beeches in the green marsh soup.

They made a fire in the hibachi and Annie cooked four hot dogs. Phil walked into the house and brought out another pound. So they fought about money on the fourth of July, and Phil worked until eleven that night, scraping floors with a large rented machine that bellowed so harshly that birds flew up, confused. Annie sketched the motion of their darkened panicky flight, using a ballpoint pen on a legal pad, and when Phil, sweating, blowing, covered with sawdust, came into the kitchen and saw her, she tore the sheet from the pad, turned it over, and, speaking as she wrote, said, "Now, seven pounds of hot dogs and a keg of beer. Better make that *eight* pounds, so they don't think down there at the Grand Union that we're worried about having enough *money.*" The sander started screaming again.

They did what they'd done before: jacked beams up nearly level, tore out old powder-post logs and replaced them with four-by-fours spiked together to help the cellar support the house, reframed windows, knocked down plaster walls and laid in fresh sheets of gypsum board to plaster over and paint, puttied in glass, tore out linoleum, sanded and scraped and nailed and drove screws, carried loads of shattered lath to the dump a mile away, bought nearly more material than they could afford, and argued about money, drank beer in the sun on the lawn, which sloped away to the swamp an eighth of a mile distant, walked slowly through the remnants of an apple orchard behind the house, leaned together or looked at each other over stretches of high-grown field or short lawn, and, working, tried to keep the peace.

It was during the week after July 4, celebrations were officially over, but kids in the hills below theirs, and on the long stretches of meadow to the south, were firing off cherry bombs and pinwheels. The colors were daunted by the intensity of clear sky and bright sun, but the reports rolled around them like the shots of deer guns. Annie was on the front porch, scraping its blistered white wood very slowly and carefully, her long legs in paint-smeared jeans twisted beneath her and still; nothing moved but her hands and arms, and her eyes, which studied the edge of the metal scraper as if every new margin of corruscated paint were another suture to be taken thoroughly away. A steady breeze blew, but her heavy hair hung behind her, and her light-blue work shirt didn't ripple. A small portable radio beside her played frantic music; her rhythms were unaltered.

Upstairs, in the loft above the second floor, under the shallow eaves, on bright-yellow ragged spruce runners, Phil was laying down a six-inch carpet of insulation for the winter. He was barechested in the heat of trapped, exhausted air but wore white cotton work gloves to protect himself from the almost invisible short spears of spun glass which the insulation shed. He opened a roll, stapled the near edge into place, then, on his hands and knees, as if making his humble way toward something mighty, pushed the roll so that it fell out straight. Then, backing on his hands and knees, he stapled, and then he hefted over another roll and laid it parallel to the first, fastening.

His neck and armpits ran, the graying blond beard and short hair sparkled with trapped moisture and oils, his long arms and fleshy belly became wet and then red as needle fibers of glass became embedded in the skin. As he did the second row, he began to brush at his arms and chest; their flesh, though, picked up more fibers from the work gloves and soon, on his knees, like someone with an allergy that must not be scratched, he held his arms before him, clenched his fists, moved each shoulder as if against something solid, then went back to rolling the carpets of insulation out and moving on all fours.

The loft smelled sweet because of the light-brown insect shells, empty—shed, or hollowed out by decay—which littered the two small windowsills and the wood along the walls. In the light of his hanging work lamp, moths stirred, then subsided. Flies hummed and buzzed, the firecrackers on the hillsides echoed around, his knees scraped on insulation, the staple gun banged, and Annie's radio brought up through the walls a jiggering music to which neither of them moved.

Phil, as he crawled back and forth above her, was seeing Annie in the hallway of a house they'd owned in New Hampshire, the bloody slush from her womb on her thighs and on the floor. When he'd cleaned the house, next morning, while she was in the hospital, he'd found their footprints in the drying blood. He saw footprints this morning on the pink spun glass he fastened into place. He decided to tell himself the correct use of the gerund, but he couldn't remember what a gerund was for, except that it had to do with what was going on, and that was no help yet, they would have to wait and see, and so he finished crawling for the sake of coming cold and went downstairs.

Annie's radio still played on the porch, but she was in the kitchen, washing her hands with steel wool and scouring powder. "Hey," he said, shaking his arms to signify his little wounds, dripping sweat, waiting for her to turn from the sink.

Her back was narrow and strong, but her shoulders were down, and she looked weak as she hung her weight at the sink on her forearms, holding her hands beneath the tap. She said, "I don't know if I can do one more house, Phil. If I want to. There's so much dumb work, and then we'll move."

He sat on a stool near their round wooden table and his shoulders slumped too. "Want a beer?"

"No."

"Want lunch?"

"It's only ten o'clock."

"Want sex?"

"Not if that's you I'm smelling."

"Want to go to town? Let's go to town and do a wash and then I'll have clean clothes to change into so I'll have to come back and take a shower and then—"

"No doubt sex."

"No," he said, "we could talk about God or the Horn of Africa if you like."

"The horn of Sorenson," she said, with her back to him still, the gladness in her voice only custom and friendship.

"Are you sad?"

She turned and gave him a large smile—white teeth and tanned face and the eyes moist and sealed-away, their moisture a membrane; she wasn't protecting herself from him, but she was hiding in there for her own reasons and he knew enough to make a face and, leaving his gloves on the stool, fetch the sack of filthy clothes and take it to the truck, where she would wait.

Bailey was down the other side of their hill from the swamp, and they raised dust on the narrow road that went to it, past brand-new antique-log-cabin homes set back in the woods, and flat white homes of the fifties which carried TV antenna masts higher than the spruce and maples on the downslope. They drove into the village, which was built around an oval public green—the colonial Bailey Inn at the far curve, an American flag at the curve they approached, large pillared homes on one side of the oval and shops on the other.

Phil carried the laundry bag, an old mesh decoy sack, and Annie walked behind him, slower, as they approached the store-front laundromat. The glass window said, in faded red serifs, TOBACCO∗MAGAZINES. And over those letters, in high uneven yellow capitals, was LAUNDERETTE. The words ran together and nearly said nothing, and under them, on the dirty unused display shelf, in front of the machines and soap dispensers, a little boy, perhaps a year old, in soft green corduroy overalls, was climbing. Phil walked in, the door shut, and Annie stood on the street in Bailey and watched the little boy harden his mouth and press his palms against the glass and by friction pull himself, wobbling, erect, to grin with achievement at the street, the village green, the pickups passing, and Annie, whose arms were crossed over her breasts, and who didn't grin back.

She walked back to the truck and sat inside, and when Phil returned to report that their wash was drying, six dimes' worth of heat, Annie requested a bottle of wine and home. Phil came back from the liquor store with a half-gallon bottle of Valpolicella, which in twenty minutes was open and in coffee mugs they sipped from as they sat in white-painted rocking chairs on their lawn, the house between them and Bailey, the swamp down the hill, steaming.

Annie wrapped her black Southern Comfort sweatshirt around her shoulders and the arms hung down, like strangers', on her chest. She rocked in slow short strokes; Phil slumped, his legs bent and planted, and he turned from the swamp to look at her. The air above the swamp danced with heat and insects, diving birds; unidentifiable objects or animals splashed in the granular pea-green surface of the water, thick as gruel, which sometimes eddied five feet up from the roots of the bare black trees which forked and reached like textbook pictures of nerves. When he turned to her, he saw the same thing. He drank wine and said, "Pretty good, huh?"

She pursed her lips and looked like a little girl, and she continued to watch down the hill as she said, "Uh-huh."

"The house and everything. It's a fancy-ass town, but that's the college part of it." He pushed the coffee mug at their sloping lawn, the bowl of swamp, the thicket of dark brush and the white birches on the far side, the hills rising away again— "It's really pretty damned good, isn't it?"

She said, looking there, "Uh-huh."

"And you're not brooding."

"Nope."

"Or going away inside."

"Nope."

"Or sad."

"Nope."

"Or making me do the famous emotive catechismal crawl."

She stopped rocking and looked at him. "Sometimes you do that anyway," she said.

"I really don't want to do it any more, you know?"

"All right, then I won't make you do it and you won't make you do it, and nobody'll do it again forever. Amen."

He was seeing her in a past winter, not far enough away in their lives, when she wore a white nightgown and wrote letters in a room she lived in alone while they worked to remain together and sane as he went off in the mornings to raise ducks for the New Hampshire hatcheries. Returning at night, not wanting to, he saw her light from the road, but often not her. When they were together, it would be in brittle wickerwork conversations like this one. Sometimes her lips were black from the ink, and she was always pale and unconsolable, often exhausted from her effort to give him some sign and durable portion—necessary proof—of the love he felt she was certain that she felt for him. That was after the second miscarriage and before she healed—before they healed together—and moved to Maine, where they lived above the bay at the edge of the country and worked together very hard to stay well.

The Southern Comfort sweatshirt was on the lawn, and so was her work shirt. The top snap of her jeans was undone, and she was standing before him, her eyes closed hard, and then—like that little girl who'd said "Uh-huh"—she was in his lap, curling on him, wrapping him in. They lay down on the grass together, spilling his wine. They worked on the lawn, bringing their house back. New Hampshire stayed where it seemed to belong.

It was a day later that Annie told Phil how much he stank, and he replied that he had in fact been bathing, and she remembered they'd left their laundry in the Bailey Launderette, spinning six dimes' worth. "Time's probably up by now," Annie said, laying identical strokes of outdoor white up and down the porch rails.

He left her at work and drove the truck in. Wearing old basketball shorts, canoe moccasins, and an undershirt of perfect ripeness, his belly jutting a little, his shoulders back, his jock's walk a delicate bounce and shuffle, he entered, and customers in the laundromat did not ignore him. A woman wearing a mini-skirt of bright pumpkins on a black ground, red terry-cloth slippers, and a red short-sleeved sweatshirt to match, slowly backed past the dryers toward the wet mop tilted against the rear wall. A very thin girl in a forest-green muumuu stared through her rimless glasses, put *The Interpretation of Dreams* mouth down on a folding chair, and said, very low, "A ninth-inning hippie off the bench." Phil waggled his eyebrows at her, made inquiries, the woman in slippers regained her courage—though once she came close, she started edging off again, having smelled him—and a consultation resulted in no clothes but an address on a Bailey back street, and the suggestion that he see Mr. Hurley, who owned the machines.

The address was away from the oval green, and Phil drove through streets of high dignity and kempt lawns, interrupted once or twice by small split-levels built in the early sixties. It was Hurley's Lumberyard he'd been sent to, a very old one of gray clapboard with grass growing high in front of it. The truck entrance to the loading docks, shut now, was narrow enough to have been designed for wagons. The front door, up some steps, was open. So was the man-high box safe against the wall behind the counter. Phil looked away from it, offering honest appearance to someone entering the store. But no one did that, and he walked through the aisles of caulking guns and glazier points and weatherstrip, then went straight through to the back, where the wood was. There wasn't much, and it was sloppily racked and it was weathering, old. He shouted hello, walked back through to the front, and stood at the counter, looking into the small office. He bellowed at the safe, the wall, the empty room, and he thought of Annie laying paint on, seeming calm.

The smell, when he finally noticed it, was high in the sinuses, sweet, like tallow. Looking at the open safe, thinking about robbery, murder, and undiscovered corpses, he went behind the counter and into the office, his right hand coming up, on its own, as a fist. But the room remained empty, a small cluttered office—desk, shelves of looseleaf invoice holders, catalogues, phone books, ashtrays—in which the occupant's life was being held by its owner for ransom.

A canvas cot lay at right angles to the desk. A blue plaid blanket was balled in its middle. On the desk were some empties —middle-range Scotch, one blended Bowery brand, and three of cheap vodka—and they weren't the worst. The worst was what were not empty, six different shapes of brown bottle containing different vitamins—B, B_1 with iron, a giant jug of C, children's multiple vitamins with fluoride, all-purpose corner-drugstore high-octane tablets, and a wax-paper carton of orange juice, its beak open, sweating in the sweaty air. It was the room of someone who had come to a final place. It was the room of someone who was not so much nursing himself as waiting for obligations toward his patient to conclude. There was care, but it had to do with terminal patients flossing their teeth.

Phil saw himself calling the police and discussing his identity and innocence. He heard speculations about the safe's open door. He took off. But at the village green, whistling, a parody of furtiveness, he went once more into the laundromat—the girl in the muumuu said, "Hey-*ho*"—and, chewing mustache hairs, pulling at his beard, bending his neck forward and down, pushing cartons with his foot, he searched behind machines and benches. Near the tilted mop and its wringer, rolled and jammed and crumpled, there were the clothes. He crushed them to his chest, stuffed a straying sock and brassiere in the back pocket of his shorts, clamped his chin down on top of the rest, and went back to the truck. The girl in the muumuu called, "*Geev-*'em!"

He drove too fast and raised needless dust and braked too hard in the gravel drive at the side of the house. Annie wasn't at the porch. He stood there, in front of the truck that tinkled and creaked as it cooled, and he roared for her. She looked out of an upstairs window but didn't answer. The borders of her face were made indeterminate by the old blackened screening, and he nibbled and leaned forward, hands on his hips, legs wide. Then his shoulders and chest let go, his arms hung, he shifted his feet, was less large. She stared. He said, "Hoo."

"Who what?"

"No: *hoo.* Never mind."

"It's okay," she said.

"That's what *hoo* means."

"I know. What'd you think was wrong?"

"They make you go to the morgue to get your laundry now."

"A clean corpse is a happy corpse. Would you wash now, please?"

"Would you come down here before I do?"

"I'm mitering toe molding."

"Would you please come down?"

"For what?"

"Romance."

"Wash." She left the screen, then her face flowed back. She said, "You have to learn about this worrying."

"No," he said, "I already know about worrying."

She said, "Forget some."

He reached into his pocket and stood facing the house. With a sock in one hand and a brassiere in the other, he said, "I am. I really am."

Annie sat cross-legged on the porch floor, her lap a spiderweb of fishing line. She cut two pieces of heavy paper she had painted, one was gunmetal gray, the other Day-Glo pink, and her scissors didn't stop; they worked as if her hands knew what to do all at once, and so the thick paper curled but didn't fold, the scissors didn't hesitate, and the delta made by the blades yielded its original white edges like the ground beneath a slow plow. She made rounded figures that dropped into her lap and the nest of catgut. Then, discarding the hollowed-out sheets and putting the scissors into her breast pocket, she drew on the gray and pink shapes with a black laundry pen, shading silly long noses and half-shut eyes, making lines beneath the eyes and the protrusions of Adam's apples, drawing belts over soft paunches and the flapping cuffs of trousers, funny shoes. She trimmed the shapes and shuffled nine soft rubbery-looking men and women who bulged and stared as if in the act of swelling. With the scissors, she punched small holes in each head. She threaded the line through each, and knotted it, cutting a six-inch length from which the characters could dangle. Then, sawing with the scissors, finally snapping approximate sizes, she cut pieces of eighth-inch dowel, tied a pink or gray person onto each, making balances, imbalances, precipice-hanging people at the edge of certain lengths, others knotted into midpoints, and she very slowly, as if she had seen the structure whole and at once, assembled the mobile she stood to hold, letting it move in the breeze from the swamp. She hung the design from the bright ugly hook she had screwed to the porch roof before she'd begun, again as if she had felt it entirely before she started, and it swayed, severally and together. Then she collected her materials and turned her back on all of it and went in.

It was a bright Sunday morning, hard in its coolness after the muggy week they'd swum through. This was a morning with resistance; the clouds snapped, going over their hill and house, like the canvas of passing boats. Annie drove the truck to Bailey for the Sunday papers, and Phil went for his run. He wore very old stiff sweatpants, equally old basketball sneakers, a dark-blue sweatshirt under an olive-green slicker, which was folded upon itself at the creases. When he moved in the sticky jacket, there was the sound of something tearing.

He pounded slowly down the hill toward the swamp, running on the grass beside the rutted road, his feet thudding, his arms controlled, head down, and with him as he went was the sound of the jacket, adhesive torn away. Down farther, and past the swamp, the road narrowed and went between jigsaw pastures, bright in the sun and serrated by the loops and staggers of an oxbow river, cutting an inch a year. And beyond the fields, at a T-junction with a road that went, eventually, to Bailey, he came to a house that was sided with imitation brick made from asbestos and tar. A section of the roof had collapsed, the windows were broken, the small barn had fallen nearly flat. It was beyond repair, should have been bulldozed and carted away and replaced with healthy weed, but he jogged in place at a burst window and, heaving, face slick with sweat, looked in at wide softwood floorboards and crazy doorframes, felt the affection he had felt before, at other broken houses he and Annie had doctored and propped.

He stopped moving in place, walked away from the house to the road, shook himself like a dog just come from swimming, gulped, and moved again, this time toward Bailey. He was two miles into the run, going past bareboard farmhouses, long narrow trailers filled with plastic insulation that baked sleeping children when fires broke out or killed them with its special fumes, past tractor wheels filled with perennials, wheelbarrows painted white and planted with big-headed bulbs that wilted in sudden chill like hydrocephalic children, past a man hauling the engine out of his jeep with a chain that hung from a low squat maple branch. He loped on tired knees and spasming calves, a slight quaver in his breathing, as he ran under a tunnel of oaks as if in pursuit of the cardinal flying low before him.

Annie, coming from Bailey, approached him, and he saw the truck and slowed. By the time she was there, he stood and panted. She was doing fifty, she drove past him doing it and didn't falter, and he turned as if they had an arrangement and ran after his wife, uphill and fast.

She was waiting for him around the bend past the oaks, the car door open, two cardboard containers of coffee smoking on top of the newspaper, and real delight on her face. He flapped in the sticky slicker, his breathing was cavernous when he stood white before her. She wore khaki trousers and work shoes and a forest-green shirt; she looked wholly possessed of secret information, and not disapproving of the man who rustled and hissed. "Another year or two," she said, "and you'll be thirty again if you keep it up."

He shook his head and grabbed breath. "I'll be forty again if I keep it up."

"You'll be forty next week no matter what you do. Did you

remember? I thought of that coming home. You'll be a forty-year-old man with an old lady who gets the reality bends, and the fourth house-in-progress in a pretty short time." He blew into his coffee cup and made a face as the boiled sour smell came back at him. Annie said, pointing at the papers, "There was this case in Florida, the adopted baby and the mother who came back?"

Phil said, "They were nuts, the adopting—"

"Adoptive."

"Right. They were crazy to hang around and take a chance like that. When the mother, the real one—"

"Biological parent, they call it."

"—came back like that, they should have taken off and you get a job in a gas station or a sardine cannery and to hell with going to court."

"They won, sort of."

"They did?"

"Sort of. Well, you can read it if you want. So what I was thinking, Phil, was what about a Vietnam orphan or a little black kid or something."

"You were thinking about that?"

She still looked happy with secrets, but she flushed so that her tan disappeared. She closed her eyes and nodded her head. "I was thinking about that."

"Yeah," he said, "but you're the person I was married to who said that was secondhand kids. You *said* that."

"I was immature. I was only thirty-seven. Now I'm thirty-nine, nearly, and I decided I would like us to have some discussions concerning the possibility of adopting a baby."

Phil walked in a tiny tight circle before her and said, "I don't know how we do that. And if they'd let us, Jesus—we're *old.*"

"We can ask someone. We can ask some of the teacher types. Teachers are always sterile in places like this. They'll know. They can tell us who we should talk to."

"Yeah. Well, I was thinking of talking to you about maybe

a *dog.* I was thinking about a Labrador retriever. To be completely honest with you—"

But she was starting the truck and hauling the papers and coffee containers inside, like a captain raising anchor. As she closed the door, he fell into step, and with the truck in first, the whine of its dry gearbox sending fast hectoring martins into the air, he plodded alongside the dented green truck and listened to Annie tell him enormous lies about the ease of middle-aged adoption, and he grinned so wide and nodded so hard that he lost his pace and stumbled, laughed.

Phil was on the roof, behind the chimney, breathing shallow and fast because his belly was shoved up into his lungs by the angle of his gargoyle crouch. The shingles threw heat up under him, and his ass and calves and armpits baked; the bright sun, red in the mist of high humidity, broiled his gray and yellow hair; his brains stewed slowly; he did bad work. He was fixing bright hot aluminum flashing between a wedge-shaped saddle of roof and the short side of the brick chimney where he'd laid in caulking. The idea was to keep the snow, which would pile here and freeze, from driving in under the shingle and between the chimney and roof; the idea was to run the melting ice off, instead of down and into the attic or under the shingles where it might freeze again and slowly burst the roofing up. The idea was to stew his brains today for the sake of the season to come.

But it was too hot, and he couldn't breathe right. So he panted and squatted on sore legs, able to move only his forearms—his upper arms insisted on clamping to his sides because they were scared of the height—and often he leaned his forehead on the oven heat of the bricks, which gave him balance and abrasions and further cut his breath. He leaned like this especially when he had to cut the flashing with the heavy two-handled metal shears. And the further he cut into an aluminum sheet, the more its knife edges tore away surface skin on his forearms, often slicing deep and clean, bringing up bright blood, which ran into his elbows and onto his khaki pants.

With his left hand working the shears, the thumbless right one spidering the metal onto his right kneecap, he had his left arm deep into the dangerous bright V as far as he could reach. He had to stop and squat farther back onto hot shingle, close his eyes and lean on his sore neck, suck in the air that smelled of tar and sweat. When he opened his eyes, the hill spun off to the swamp, and the swamp moved too, jerking away to the west and then back into place. The more he stared at it, the faster it moved, so he decided not to look any more. His arm was burning where the sweat flooded the cuts, and his fingers cramped.

He said to them, "Move."

The reflection in the aluminum sheet, blurry and red, talked silently back. He said again, "Move, please."

The fingers squeezed the shears then, and he finished the cut, let the larger piece of metal fall, gripped the shears and the small piece in the same hand, and, fumbling, shoving clumsily, teetering, began to fix the flashing into place. When he was finished, he called, "Watch your ass below!" and let tools and material scrape and turn along the steep black roof, over the aluminum gutter he'd attached, and down to the lawn. Stretching out for the first time in more than an hour, moaning with great pleasure, he lay along the roofing ladder, let himself slide slowly along it to the high extension ladder standing at the side of the house, and went down.

Annie sat on the lawn, wearing a long-billed Red Sox hat to keep the sun off and a terry-cloth bikini to keep the sun on. She popped the beer cans as he staggered to her. "That's timing," he said. "You're beautiful."

"No timing," she said. "I heard this bellowing and yelping and these little *ouch* sounds and everything falling, so I figured either we'd have a beer together or I'd use the cans as splints when you came down."

He nodded and drank, nodded the way he did when he wanted to show her that he was trying to look like he was listening but wasn't, because something serious was on his mind. He watched her note this and ignore it.

"I thought maybe this afternoon we could do the stud work on the upstairs bathroom," she said. "A small interior-wall blitz?"

"You look pretty good for an old lady," he said.

She pulled at her belly as if in refutation, but said nothing. He smiled wide and finished the beer. "Don't do it," she said.

"Huh?"

"Don't crush the can with your hand."

He dropped it onto the lawn in the diamond shape made by her loosely crossed ankles and spread thighs. "I'm not the type," he said, holding up the four-fingered hand.

"So what about the wall?"

He nodded, signaling again. He pressed his lips together, smoothed his mustache, and chewed on a long strand. "You know, we're pretty old to raise kids. We couldn't do trips any more, or whatever the hell we do with our lives."

"People with kids do what they do with their lives with kids."

"What?"

"I can't say that again. What I'm saying is, we'll do what we do with kids and that'll be what we do."

"*What?*"

"Fuck you, Sorenson!"

"No, it's all right. You're saying this is something brand new.

Something else starts now, if we decide to do it. If they decide to let us do it. They say okay, we've got this nine-year-old scaly case with flippers we've been saving for some middle-aged suckers, and you're saying the old life stops now and this *new* thing starts. That's understandable."

She crushed the beer can in her large hands and said, "That's right."

"Okay," he said, pointing at the white and blue can. "Okay. It's completely evident that you're being rational and calm and totally organized, you know what you're doing and what you think *I* should be doing. How can I complain?"

"It isn't that." And she threw the beer can at him. It bounced off his shin, but he didn't move. "It's not saying the old days are gone. We just add to them. We *move.*"

"We always move," he said, walking in closer, touching the top of her cap, reaching around it and grasping with the four-fingered hand as if he tried to hold a melon or a ball. The hand spread and pressed and stayed there, and she moved her neck so that she pushed up as hard as he pushed down.

With her neck rigid, she said, "This time we move and stand still, too. Are you jealous?"

The hand came off, then went back on top. "I think so," he said.

She said, with her eyes closed, "It's just biology."

"Oh," he said, "that."

She reached up to pull at his belt buckle and they held their equilibrium for a second, for two seconds, three, and then instead of his coming down, she went up, and they stood before each other, his hands at his sides now, both of hers on top of his pants. She opened her eyes and looked at him, all over him, a hard study. When she saw the long cuts on his forearms, she said, "You're so fucking careless with your body, you know that?"

She raised his right arm, the one with the four-fingered

hand, up to the height of her shoulder. Holding its weight with both hands, she leaned to the deepest furrow in the softness of the inner arm. Bending her long neck, closing her eyes, she slowly kissed the cut.

2 | Rounds

Waking is easy, and Silver does it. He stands beside his bed, shivering not from the early September chill but from inside, as boys quake on the first uneasily glad day of school. For Silver, it is another fourteen hours of work, of hospital rounds and then clinic practice, of seeming well—sometimes even to himself—by doing at least (with some luck) little harm.

The house is the same, though neater than when they lived in it as a family. His bedclothes seem flatter and less disturbed by his presence, clothing in the closet hangs in plastic laundry wrappers, towels in the hallway closet lie in taped brown paper, there are fewer hairs in the shower drain. The blinds on most windows are drawn, and the house has its own temperature, its own brown and black tones, separate from what happens outside. When he is standing silently, head down, receiving the hot shower like a punishment, Silver understands: his house—its thirteen rooms, its walls of prints, its fine-tuned kitchen, garage with automatic door, the annex with his clinic—his house is now a hotel. He leaves his towel on the floor to prove the point. Dressed in a blue seersucker sport coat, dark-blue slacks, polished loafers, white shirt, and bright-red bow tie, he returns to the bathroom to hang the towel in place.

He doesn't understand why he's traded in his station wagon and Peugeot—and he remembers the insurance adjuster telling him that his wife's wrecked Thunderbird had excellent tires for a two-year-old car—to drive a vintage Studebaker Hawk. He does suspect why he drives it too fast, going through the gears like a college boy with racing gloves, but he drives that way anyhow, changing down for small-town corners and revving impatiently at stoplights. He thunders into the doctors' lot at the hospital and is out the door as if summoned, leaving his keys in the car, leaving the door ajar.

He waves to the woman at the switchboard, passes the Record Room—his wife is in there, his child—and then, checking his mail and seeing nothing he wants, goes past Emergency, where a small girl writhes on a table and Cavallo, looking drunk, quite possibly drunk, calls down to her as if she were at the bottom of a well, "I'm Dr. Cavallo, Gloria, and I'm going to fix you *up.*" He doesn't look at Gloria's face. Silver nods at an assistant administrator, pushes through the swinging doors of the pediatrics ward he runs—older children in the left-hand wing, infants in the right—and seizes metal-bound charts, looking at one, then another, not recording data, just looking, trying to stand still. North, his head nurse, offers him a paper cup and three acetaminophen, but he shakes his head.

"Sober last night?" she says.

"Fuck you, Ada."

"And feisty. Want to work?"

She is sixty and fat and her gray hair falls from its old-fashioned topknot in sloppy thin tendrils. She knows as much procedure as he does, and he knows it, and so does she.

"I don't drink to excess," he tells her, taking his sport coat off and laying it over a chair. "I didn't even drink to sufficiency last night."

"You going on pills like the rest of them?"

"Who's on pills? What, uppers?"

"Lefkowitz does them both. Uppers to start his engines, barbs and booze to turn them off."

"Shit, Ada, he's been doing that for a year."

"A year and a half."

"Are we taking care of babies here, or do you want to talk about the doctors?"

"Call your wife."

He sees the orderly swabbing the floor, smells the heated disinfectant, sees the small drawing signed *William,* which a boy—"I know I'm gonna die, Dr. Eli, you wait and see"—had done for the staff three weeks before he came out of remission and kept his promise. Ada had hung it, crying, on the day of his funeral. Eli Silver tries to look around it every day, but now he stares at the slanting hand, the crooked *a,* and then the blemished sullen face of the orderly, the fingerpainted light-green walls. A small brown-skinned boy on a plastic tricycle howls down the corridor from the playroom, an infant cries in its crib, and Silver is saying—he cannot feel his jaws move—"What?"

Ada tells him, "I said, 'It's your life.' You want to waste it on practicing medicine, go ahead. You all right?"

"I'm a thing of beauty," Silver says. He sits in front of the rack of charts, Ada puts them in order, and they rehearse a night's medication, two stool samples, two batteries of blood tests, and a set of orders phoned up by Cavallo, who was presumably too drunk to write them himself. Silver reviews the chart with Cavallo's orders first: a girl, twenty-six months old, who fell down a flight of steps onto her head. He tells Ada to schedule an exam by the ophthalmologist, orders an echo-encephalogram—sound waves will be poured through the child's head, and through the third ventricle, in the center of the brain, will be photographed; if it's dead center, Silver will assume that the brain isn't squeezed by internal bleeding and, after another day's observation, will send the girl home. He looks at the chart of an infant, thirteen months old, whom he presumes to suffer an ECHO virus; the diarrhea is abating, and today the child will be fed rice, banana, peeled apple, and in another day or two released on continued medication. Walking the corridor, Silver intercepts the boy on the tricycle and squeezes him under the throat, talking friendly tough-guy talk as he palpates the cervical lymph nodes, which are down, as is the redness of the suspected strep throat; the morning's test results aren't in yet, and Silver tells Ada to phone him with the boy's ESR and CBC, although, he says, the probability of rheumatic fever, especially in light of the child's energy, is very slight.

In a private room off the other corridor, a thirteen-year-old girl watches television; she blushes when Silver walks in. Every three weeks for the last three months—Silver has missed one of these, he has, as the nurses say it, been "on vacation" for a while—Patti is admitted with complaints of abdominal pain and vomiting. This time, Silver has handled the case with the tender care he applies to her hot shying stomach—IVP to check kidneys, X rays of the paranasal sinuses, complete blood count, clean-catch urine, stool tests for Shigella and salmonella, for ova and parasites, a GI series to examine the intestinal tract. Silver has suspected pylorospasm but hasn't yet seen the little pyloric valve at the base of the stomach twitching like a frightened girl's face. He finds blood-sugar imbalances and wants to suspect hypoglycemia too, but what he thinks is that someone comes home every three weeks, or goes away, perhaps that her girlfriends menstruate and she hasn't yet performed—that her life doesn't work right and she wants it made better. He smiles and tells jokes and orders more tests, hoping that he will find chemistry the issue. Please, no minds. *Call your wife.*

Back at the nurses' desk, he writes his orders, dictates the day's conclusions, puts his jacket on. Ada watches him, silently hands him the cup of stale water and the three pills, and he silently consumes them.

Ada says, "You know Lefkowitz is popping off the girl in Radiology?"

"Popping off? Ada, you own the mind of a truck driver. How come you never say 'fucking' like the rest of us?"

"Because I don't *mean* fucking. I mean, he's shooting her up and getting sucked off in return. I think 'popping off' covers it, don't you?"

Silver whistles his admiration for the achievements of Lefkowitz, and the technician in Radiology, and Ada, and tells her goodbye.

"You take care of yourself," she says.

He wants to say, "How?" but is ashamed of himself, and he moves quickly, his leather heels banging toward the doors. He has hurried this morning because he has a clinical pathology conference at noon, but needs forty minutes on his own before it starts. He tells the woman at the telephones he'll be at Mitrano's, he makes his tires squeal as he backs the Hawk and drives in front of a panel truck whose horn he hears down the street, where he turns east, then south, then east again, into the older section of the little city where the poor people live.

Parking—he lets the car drift; this time, he wants hard to call no attention to himself, he doesn't squeal or slam, he is thinking about how he moves—he notices that the morning is clear and bright and probably beautiful. The house is not, it needs paint, the roof needs repairs, the banisters are missing from the pulpy steps. He carries his bag upstairs, moving on his toes, holding his breath against the smell he expects, then forcing himself to let it in.

The smell comes from the closed door and hangs in the stairwell, it is slightly visible as a gray thick steam. When Dolores's father opens the door, a palpable cloud issues, and

Silver wipes his face. The father is very short, he wears Bermuda shorts and a cheap cotton sport shirt, which shows leathery hard arms and pale thin legs; he is dressed for the weather in his apartment, which is special: the steam of two vaporizers set on the floor, the odor of bottled deodorizers open on a functionless mantelpiece and on two end tables, the smell of metastasizing cancer cells in the jaw of a fourteen-year-old girl who is thin and small enough to be ten, and who lies on a daybed under quilts which disguise her body. She looks like a head attached to a cloth, a puppet set aside, and her head is a crazy invention.

What hair is left after radiation and chemotherapy is a sparse collection of filaments from spiderwebs; her hairline has receded nearly as far as Silver's. Her flesh is translucent pink, as if the mucous membranes in her face were growing outside. The left side of her head is finely boned and set in pain, the left eye flickers like a bird's, she turns her face as a bird might, draws an arm—a slightly padded bone—from under the quilt to nearly wave hello to Silver. The right side of her face, between the bottom jawbone and forehead, is round, like half a pink grapefruit, and it looks hot. Silver knows it isn't. The right eye is closed, the lid stretched tight and hard. And Silver, master of ceremonies for a dreadful act, bellows, "Hello, Dolores! Hey, you look great! Doesn't she look great, Walt?"

The father grins like the idiot half of a team of stand-up comics and nods his head. He loses the grin and whispers, "She really wants to live, Doc."

"Sure she does!" Silver cries. "And she's doing wonderfully, *wonderfully!*" He picks up a jigsaw puzzle of St. Peter's Basilica and nearly screams, "Dolores, did you do that? That's *wonderful!*"

She murmurs into her own bent lips and a bone drifts at another puzzle, which Silver picks up, holds toward the dim orange-bulbed ceiling light, shouting, "It's Pope *John*, isn't it? Boy, are you *swell* at these!"

Her hand drops, and Silver sets Pope John down, looks at the nearly dwarfish father, the letter from Cardinal Cooke's secretary, which, promising everyone's prayers, is framed on the wall. Then jumping in, he sits on the daybed and runs his hands along her blistered face, shines his otoscope into her functioning eye, touches aimlessly and uselessly, showing great purpose, crying, "Ah, honey, you're working so *hard!*"

Ah, honey, Silver says inside, feeling his sinuses secrete because of what he breathes, wanting not to breathe it any more, repelled by himself because he isn't good at this, because he's too good at this, because he has looked again at the Vatican and patted Dolores's healthy cheek, because he is standing across the room with a little man whose wife has run away in order not to watch their child die, because, when Walt says, "She can't eat no more, Doc. I tried the milkshakes with whiskey like you said, I tried the pills, she can't eat no more and it *hurts* her," Silver cannot speak, can only nod his head and rub his mouth.

Dolores whispers, "Ih ur."

The father translates: "She says it hurts, Doc."

Silver says crisply, backing into the cave of his voice and faked certainties, "Give her one of the methadone when it gets bad."

"They don't work sometimes, Doc."

"Give her *two*," he growls, hating the information, the complaint, the expectation that he can offer sane answers to this insanity. He takes a deep breath, forces himself not to gag, then forces himself to place his hand on the father—Walt feels as light-boned and fragile as his child—and he whispers, "Maybe I'll put her inside in a week or so, Walt."

"They can help her in the hospital?"

"Shit, Walt. Goddamn—look, I'll come back tomorrow, I

want to think about this. Never mind. Look, I'll be back tomorrow and we'll talk. We'll see. I have to go, okay?"

So the father moves about him as if at any minute he will bow to the doctor, and Silver closes his bag while bellowing at Dolores: "You keep it up, sweetheart, and that methadone's gonna work, you hear me? You're doing *beautiful!*" and he leaves, drives carefully away so that neighbors might not notice the doctor who makes house calls on paupers every morning, then at the corner does a racing shift and turns on shivering wheels to get back to the hospital for the CPC, where he and the other staff will eat sandwiches and look at slides and try to puzzle why a man dropped dead in his hospital room. He makes plans for Dolores. They are dangerous plans, and he knows they're right.

The conference room is full when Silver carries in his tray—black coffee, a slice of sweating bologna on pulpy white bread. Around them, on the composition-board walls, are black-and-white photos of dead doctors. At one end of the long table is a screen, at the other end a slide projector. Eleven of them, six doctors who chose to come, technicians, nurses, radiologists, and two pathologists, are waiting for the junior doctor on the case, Don Beverly, to try to guess why his patient died.

Donald Beverly, two years out of Upstate Med in Syracuse, looking unshaven at twelve-fifteen, needing sleep and a haircut, staring through dirty glasses, young enough to at least be embarrassed by this death, reads to them from notes scribbled in a looping round hand—his letters will diminish as he ages in the practice, Silver thinks—which cover only the middle third of each lined looseleaf page in the sheaf he grips: "This patient was a sixty-two-year-old male Caucasian with a recent history of breathlessness, dizziness, and inability to sleep." Beverly looks up, past Silver, at the wall. "He had to sit up in the middle of the night because he thought he was choking. I guess he was." He looks down, then looks up again. "He used to fall asleep sitting up for a few hours." Then, from the notes: "Ah, on admission, patient was examined and found to be a well-developed, conscious, coherent, cooperative male who was in acute respiratory distress. Blood pressure on admission of 130/52, pulse 120 per minute, respiration 32 per minute, temperature 100.2. Head, eyes, ears, nose, throat: Bilateral arcus senilis. Pupils round, equal, and reactive. Extraocular movements intact. Ears, nose, throat, and mouth were negative except for some cyanosis of the lips. It was difficult to appreciate heart tones because of the noisy respirations. The lungs showed wheezing all over with some rales of the left mid-lung field. I found no edema. There were good pedal pulses, and the neurological examination was negative. A cardiogram showed some T-wave inversion not present in a cardiogram taken a year ago. There were no known allergies. The patient denied any hemoptysis. You can see from the CBC, blood gasses, and serum electrolytes that we found little of use. His sputum showed no acid-fast bacilli. On April 18 the patient woke up complaining of being dizzy and of heart pounding, but no actual shortness of breath. The heart pounding slowed down momentarily with carotid massage. Blood pressure went down to 90/60. On April 19, he was still febrile and in respiratory distress. On April 20, his PO_2 was still in the 42 to 45 range. On April 23, the patient developed a 3-plus leg edema, more shortness of breath—the output wasn't good even with Lasix. On April 26, a review of the chest films showed possible left upper lung collapse and bilateral effusion. Broncoscopy, pleural tap, and biopsy were contemplated. He was transferred to ICU. Medications were aminophylline and digoxin. Patient expired on the same day. The X rays—Kess, could we, would you show them the films, Kess?"

Kessler, the assistant radiologist, lights up the X-ray display, which is alongside the slide screen. There are four panels on the display, and when tall, stooped Kessler, wearing his radiation monitor like a badge, throws the switch, they brighten from left to right, one at a time, long translucent ghost shapes. Silver studies their changes: the heart border blurs over the weeks, there are slight interstitial changes, a veil-like density which Kessler points to with pride as the left side of the patient's body disappears into a mist. In the final film, the left upper lobe of the lung has collapsed, and Kessler knows that the man is nearly dead.

And then he is dead, and Don Beverly reads to them from the medical literature he's researched, his voice anxious, as if he has something at stake in telling them all the possible known causes for the death of this stranger. They hear the odds on this and that, and then they speculate, and the stranger is gone and they are talking about reasons and bodies while they eat cool clam chowder or grapefruit sections or bologna slices with rigid, slightly brown-green borders. What the doctors are doing is re-educating themselves, Silver too, while on the walls thirty-one dead physicians stare at them. They discuss "the patient" and "this patient," they ask whether he smoked, and under what atmospheric conditions he worked, and how he lived during his retirement, and what he ate. Silver chews his lunch. The death of anyone so old, so far from being five and proud of riding a bike without training wheels, someone who does not wear Sears, Roebuck blue jeans and Dexter work shoes and Dallas Cowboy sweatshirts, becomes no more than data for him, and he works with interest like the others. Daddy'll be right back.

Then it is the turn of Elden, the senior physician on the case, handsome in his middle age, with a great tanned beak and a four-hundred-dollar suit, long curling black and gray hair just receding. He stands and says, "Ladies and gentlemen, this is a complicated set of circumstances, but I think my sense of cause here is as likely as any. I'm inclined toward a fulminating bacterial infection—it's low down in the casebooks, but it happens this gradually, with sudden deterioration and lung collapse. The pernicious thing is, for me, if you can spot it, you can treat with ampicillin and Chloromycetin. At least that's the procedure of choice at Flower-Fifth, where they have records on six cases like this in four years, can you believe it? I talked to Hossenfleck about this on the phone. They didn't catch *one* of them. Anyway, I'll go for the fulminating bacterial, plus myocarditis. My second choice? TB. I think this guy might have worked in the clothing mills when he was younger."

Behind Eli Silver, Artemo Boraz, the pathologist, hunchbacked and chuckling, his milky-brown Filipino face lost in chins, whispers, "Eli, this is medical bullshit, you will see. I wrote up a case like this in California in 1956. Wait till I show the slides."

Beverly shakes his head. Kessler, the radiologist, says, "I'll pin my hat on pulmonary alveolar proteinosis."

Beverly shakes his head harder and then asks, "How does that explain the leg edema? He couldn't even get socks on when he was chilly, near the end. I don't get that."

Boraz stands, smiling, and his assistant, a Filipino woman, turns off the room lights and the screen brightens, the slide show begins. The dead man's organ sections jump at them in lovely purple and pink lab stains; the whole organs themselves, lung, liver, heart, all are brown and green and pulpy-looking: garbage in a poor person's house. And there, in the illuminated cells which now belong to no one, are pneumonia, carcinoma, metastasis, periocarditis, the signatures, in the final slide, of infarcts on the stranger's meat. Silver sees total death first heard of as a fever—a man sitting up at night to breathe enough to sleep. Elden makes it clear that he couldn't have been expected to know that a metastatic carcinoma of the lung had grown beneath the surface, finally invading the heart, hiding from him. Beverly, his junior on the case, agrees. Kessler turns the X rays off; they flicker out in reverse order, one at a time. The room lights go on, the low roaring of the slide projector diminishes, Elden calls, "Thank you, gentlemen. And ladies!"

In the corridor, at one-fifteen, already late for clinic hours in the annex to his house, Silver walks beside Boraz and listens to him tell the joke, one more time, about what you get when you cross a rooster with a jar of peanut butter. Silver has already forced the smile up by the time Boraz, breathlessly chuckling, says, "A cock that sticks to the roof of your mouth!"

Silver drives to his home and adjacent clinic. The waiting room is full, Silver knows, as he lets himself into his little office with its pediatrics texts on the wall behind his desk, the light squares on the opposite wall where family pictures hung, and his diplomas, which he's taken down, too. The daily stack of mail is waiting, and Silver is thinking abstractly about intracardiac extension of bronchogenic carcinoma as he reads through a surgical supply catalogue offering him special deals on syringes and ampicillin trihydrate, a brochure on pediatric decongestants, an orthopedist's announcement that he's in practice in Utica, New York, the new *Journal* of the AMA, another hustle for Valium, a flier on bluegrass pollen, a bulletin from the Department of Agriculture on low-calorie infant formulas, a letter from the Linus Pauling Institute, one from the

American Heart Association, receipts from a local pharmacy to which Silver's office had phoned in prescriptions for Phenobarbitol elixir and Librium; there is "New Information," "The New Edition of a Classic," "The Safest, Most Comfortable Eye Protection for Babies during Phototherapy," "The Most Widely Used Stool Softener," "Flexible Dosage to Meet the Intensity of Anxiety," and he is up from his desk, finding no letters from anyone who wants to talk with him about his life.

In the anteroom to his office, a small lab equipped with autoclave, culture incubator, sink, and starter samples, he loads the pockets of his long blue lab coat with tongue depressors, agar plate for culture collections, medicated discs for culture tests, swabs, otoscope, and stethoscope and, going to the first of his four examination rooms, waving to Billie, his nurse, and Maxine, in the office, he charges into room 1 and begins.

Silver is doing rounds, and even as he forces himself to go slowly, to concentrate, to put his hands on the children—feel for heat, for leg pulses, abdominal hardness, shotty nodes—he is watching himself work too quickly, too automatically, and at the same time he is noticing what he normally doesn't: the ringing of telephones, the high tin music of the TV in the waiting room, the crying of the children outside, low disgruntled tones of impatient parents, loud false laughter of a drug salesman being shown to his office to wait for half an afternoon. He still, however, sniffs the sweet hair of a four-year-old boy who needs a polio vaccine booster, he still tells the mother of a six-months infant that her baby gains weight and is perfect: "You're doing a *perfect* job." He doesn't stop, he moves from room to room, carrying charts, handing them back to Billie or Maxine, answering calls from the hospital, but mostly moving —prying a throat culture from a red-faced gagging baby, stamping a TB tine test onto a ten-year-old's stringy arm, cautioning the mother of an eight-year-old boy not to worry about bed-wetting—"How many fifty-year-olds do you know who wet their beds?" The boy, his face set and crimson, doesn't smile.

According to his patients, he has been on vacation. They think he is back after some weeks away. Silver doesn't know if they're right. He sees a mongoloid child cared for by his grandmother. She does it, she says, "because it's a little too much for Jeff's mother. But Jeffie's kinda special to me. You know?" Silver takes a culture from the boy, who is green-pale and thin, with a great long-nosed face and perpetually moving fingers with half-inch nails. When the grandmother dresses him, while he sits on the examination table, Jeff's arm goes along her shoulder in total confidence. Silver looks at the chart he no longer needs. He is getting tired early today.

He tells the mother of an infant that it's normal for a child so young to breathe so rapidly. She frowns in disbelief, then tells him she's waited an hour. Silver says, "Isn't it a bitch? But you've got a *gorgeous* baby there, you know that?" He feels his face fail to move. A bright, excited blind boy, nine years old, chattering because he fears a penicillin shot, rolls his eyes and says, "You must use a lot of clean sheets for examining your patients, I suspect." Silver slows down and pushes his belly toward the boy and hugs him in, and for half a minute he stands still.

A pale blond girl is there because of her chronic constipation. Her mother shows Silver a chart of bowel movements and keens, "She's doing so *well*, Dr. Silver, isn't she?" A three-year-old redheaded girl with unusual brown eyes, rushed in by her redheaded, brown-eyed mother, gasping and terrified, soon begins to breathe normally with some adrenaline pumped in her. Silver tells the mother about sudden allergic reactions, they rehearse the child's day, until Silver hears the mother say that she was spraying laundry with an aerosol detergent while the child sat nearby on the floor. Silver shouts, "You used that shit while your baby was there? You know what you got? You got a chemical bronchitis here! Jesus!" And then he remembers to look at the mother, and then he sees her wet eyes and red skin, and then he hugs the child and mother together, and they decide not to use aerosol sprays. He is vulnerable again, very slightly out of control, when he sees a huge, happy infant accompanied by her blind mother and short squat father who smells of manure but whose clothes are hard-washed and pressed. The father changes the diapers, the heavy mother sits in a plastic chair and grins because she knows that they all are all right. When Silver has finished the routine examination, and has gone on to clean an abscess on the hand of an eleven-year-old boy who howls while Silver cuts away pus and lets the wound drain, then has cultured for staph and given a starter of antibiotics, Eli Silver is, at three-forty-five, with twenty patients waiting, too close to the end of what he can offer.

He goes toward his office, then remembers the waiting drug salesman, turns and goes to one of the rooms to examine a bruised shin for sub-periosteal bleeding, which he finds. He cleans impetigo scabs, one by one, from the body of a six-year-old boy. The mother, reeking as if of very old urine, yells at the boy: "You shut your mouth while the doctor's working on you, Lawrence!"—and Silver cannot talk to her. He writes "No charge" on her chart because he knows she never will pay. He walks out without having said a word; he suspects he will see her other four children tomorrow, and will clean their impetigo, too. The hallway smells of the mother, and Maxine is spraying bathroom freshener into the air, her thin red lips compressed, her dyed yellow hair hair bouncing to her anger.

He gives allergy shots, weighs babies, writes prescriptions, he counsels teenage girls on menstruation, and mothers on genetically linked insanity, he takes the blood pressure of a colleague's eighty-year-old mother because he owes a favor, accepts samples from the drug salesman, answers phone calls, talks to

Maxine and Billie, removes six sutures, then does every other case again in only slightly different ways, and it is half-past six when he sits in his kitchen with his jacket and bow tie on the back of his chair, drinking from a tumbler filled with ice and Irish whiskey, rubbing the back of his neck, claiming to ignore the other twelve rooms, which are dark and which, in the usual way, are coming closer now.

He has moved the drinks tray in from the living room as he has consolidated most of the household, and he lives only in several rooms, because then he needn't risk feeling with naked toes the rest of his life, the nap of history, and so with very few motions he has another drink and is beginning to despise what he will make of his night. He suspects that tragic emotion is so like melodrama, so close to cheap thrills, that Eli Silver no longer can be trusted. Holding his drink, he fries a small frozen steak, eats black and bloody meat in a sauce of peanut oil, washes the dishes and his face at the same sink, and leaves the house to do his evening rounds.

The hospital Emergency Room is quiet in half light, four people sit on folding chairs in the hallway outside the X-ray room, no one is summoned on the intercom. The night nurse in Pediatrics gives him lab reports, he looks through a glass wall at the sleeping girl whose possible concussion is refuted now by the echo-encephalograph report and by the eye exam, he tells the brown-skinned boy that he will go home in the morning, he looks at the new CBC of the girl who vomits every three weeks and decides that blood sugar isn't her problem, he *is* dealing with minds, and then, as if he hadn't sat for an hour in his house, he suddenly stops. In a folding chair near the chart desk, beside a small fish tank in which bubbles come from the helmet of a little metal deep-sea diver, his long legs together, his arms folded in his lap, he sits in the entire stillness of someone who has forgotten for days or even weeks to rest.

The night nurse sits before the charts, the brown-skinned boy watches television—gunshots, wheels, a shrill bubbling shriek—the fish-tank aerator chirs and pumps, and before the crooked *a* of William's drawing, Eli Silver sleeps in a safe place. He nearly sleeps. He drifts on the surface of his sleep and sometimes drops, then rises to drop again, thinking of fast cars —not thinking: seeing them, listening to them—and watching children limp in green parks, seeing blood in the ears of broken boys on roadsides, seeing children with amphibians' appendages caused by the dumping of Vietnam War defoliants into rivers near their homes, reading articles on crib death caused by honey, bearing botulism, fed to infants, seeing the eyes of children drift because of tumors in the retina, watching children weep for headaches made by fatal amoebae in the sinuses, hearing mothers tell how daughters are raped by fathers every night. And that is not all: he sees long unpolluted rivers, where picnics are possible; he hears a parent describing an infant's first word—it is always a happy one, never complaint—and he says congratulations with the same bored pleasure of his office routine. He shifts in the chair, opens his eyes, closes them again, tells his wife he will soon get out of bed to help with breakfast, and then, because waking is easy, he does it, and is injured by the night and place and time of his life that he wakes to. Without speaking to the night nurse, he leaves.

Silver thinks of taking barbiturates with him. He decides not to. At the doors to the Emergency Room, he thinks of them again, stands on the green tile floor near cast saw and heart tray and oxygen tank, permitting the ER nurse to look up from her paperback novel and stare at him. It is as if, in the half light and silence of the hospital at night, there were an atmosphere, interior sky, which has dropped to his shoulders; his head and neck poke over the air that the others breathe, and he considers the life below. He thinks of calling down to the duty nurse, who looks at him, "What do you think I should—" But he cannot supply a verb: *do? be? say? want? need? mourn?* But if he says *mourn,* he must also ask her *whom:* himself? his buried child? Gwen, his absent wife? Dolores, whom he cannot save but maybe, barely, assist? There are too many questions up there, above the air, and he feels himself hyperventilating, he tells himself what he should ask: *Can I have the keys to the drug cabinet, please?* He wonders about helping himself from Pediatrics, but wants, he supposes, somebody else to know—he doesn't trust this sadness—that he isn't self-sufficient any more: there are patients to one day protect from him if he starts, tonight, to carry home drugs. "Son of a bitch," he hears himself whisper down to the nurse, "I've still got the instincts of a doctor."

He sees only the bright purple cover of her book, the shimmer of light on her eyeglasses, when she says, "Excuse me, Doctor?"

"Okay," he says, "I was saying good night."

"Good night, Doctor."

"Okay. Good night."

That is when the outside doors, twenty feet away from him, swing in. The bright lights of the ambulance pavilion pour onto the shiny green floor, but there is no ambulance outside, there is an old white dirty gull-wing Volvo, and there is a woman walking in on the light. She is tall and broad-shouldered, long-armed, her nearly honey-blond hair is cut short, she wears sandals and white slacks, a long-sleeved patterned blouse which has been ironed. Silver is out of the sky now, studying, he looks for damage. The duty nurse stands. They see no blood, no crooked limb, the woman is alert and answers the nurse's questions. Silver walks closer and finds, from three or four feet away, a silver-gray stain on the right side of the woman's neck; the stain is shaped like a cone, narrow end pointing toward her throbbing carotid, wide end vanishing under her ear.

He says, "I'll see this woman. You don't have to call anyone. All right? Would you like to talk to me, miss?"

She nods, leaves an insurance card with the nurse, and follows him into the examination room. He motions toward the table and she slowly slides onto it, holding her feet stiffly in place once she is up. She looks at the small X-ray machine hanging from the ceiling, the deadened operating lamp, the plaster-cast dust which has adhered to high surfaces, the boxes and bundles of labeled apparatus, the canes and crutches which hang on the walls. Her underlip is slightly thick, the upper one thin, the nose nearly fleshy, the neck strong and broad. She is built like an athlete, a swimmer. Her hands are wide, the fingers long, the arm and thigh muscles look developed and tough. A light film of sweat is on the golden hair above her lip and on her cheeks. Silver takes his jacket off and washes his hands, soaks surgical sponge in hydrogen peroxide, and slowly approaches her, begins to delicately wash the stain on her neck.

He sees the tiny granulations, but they are as superficial as he suspected, and there is only enough abrasion to make her wince. He stands alongside her leg, leaning against it intentionally, gradually letting his weight push at her so that she must feel it and, as he expected, respond. She leans toward him, and when he has cleaned her, when he has chucked the sponge to the floor, he extends his left arm in front of her, waits for her to stiffen, then puts his right hand behind her, holds the back of her neck, helps her drop her forehead onto his shoulder and start to weep.

She stifles it, sniffs, and lets it go again, and cries hard. Rather than leave her, he says, "Wipe your nose on my sleeve." She gasps a kind of laughter, rubs her face on him, nods, pulls her head back. He steps away.

"All right?" he says.

She nods. Her skin is blotched, her eyes as red as if the blood poured in from the brain. She knows what she looks like, because she points at her eyes, says, "Oh, my," and then cries terribly, her face curling—the lips frowning, the cheeks fighting to control them—like a child's.

Silver steps back again, reaches for a tissue, hands it to her, and after she has blown her nose, a loud brash honk, a child's, and once she is breathing more slowly, he says, "A handgun?"

She lets all her breath out and pallor takes over. "It was a pistol," she says. "It isn't mine. It's a hunting pistol one of the students had confiscated by the proctor. I swiped it out of his office."

"He stores them loaded?"

She shrugs.

"You didn't want to kill yourself," Silver says. "No one can miss by that much except on purpose. You barely got powder crystals under the tissue."

She closes her eyes, flushing again. "I *thought* I really did. I believed I did."

"Well, you didn't."

"Well, I did."

"Did think so."

"Yes."

"But now you know you didn't."

"Yes."

"So you know how dumb it would be to do anything with guns again, or—"

"Or pills, or ropes, or razors, or knives, or cars, or anything."

"Yeah, Jesus, watch how you drive, will you? That's the *easiest* way."

"It is?"

"Never mind. Listen: you didn't want to do it. You don't. I think you should understand—what's your name?"

"Doctor, I think *you* should understand. I know you won't believe it. Don't laugh: I'm the psychological counselor at the college. I *help* people. I'm supposed to. I'm supposed to be able to. I'm a fucking *joke*. I'm a *fucking* joke, is more like it. Excuse me. My name is Elizabeth. My name is Elizabeth Bean."

"Lizzie Bean."

She smiles. "Yeah, it gets to that. Lizzie Bean."

"My name is Eli Silver."

When they shake hands, Silver feels that hers is cold. "Dr. Silver," she says, "thank you very much. I'm sorry about the hysterics."

"Nah," he says, "that's why you came here, right? To have them with strangers?"

She almost smiles, tightens her mouth, again like a child being brave, then she controls the tears, or almost does: a perfect round clear tear moves from each eye down to her mouth. They do not make her lovely; she grows ugly and blotched again. This time she uses her own sleeves.

"Do you have to report me to the police? You know, gunshot wounds?"

"Just like TV, right? Listen, if I report this, the sheriff'll laugh at me—not you, you understand. At me. And it's none of his business. Would you take your clothes off, please, and put a gown on? I'll call the nurse."

"I won't say you raped me. Couldn't this be private?"

Silver doesn't say that a woman who can shoot herself, or nearly try to, can also cry rape. He summons the nurse, and Lizzie Bean takes her clothes off, refuses the gown, stands naked on the floor, although Silver would have told her to leave her panties and brassiere on, and he checks her blood pressure, pupil dilation, heart and lungs. He tells her to dress, the nurse is dismissed after she hands him the chart she has prepared, and Silver writes, in the area labeled *Preliminary Findings:* "A responsive cooperative pregnant Caucasian female complaining of sudden bleeding. Patient was told to consult GYN of her choice and to restrict activity until such time. A cursory examination shows vital functions are within normal limits."

Silver shows the chart to Lizzie Bean. He says, "The bleeding is a lie, but it's plausible. Your insurance company won't pay for this, you'll have to fork over twenty-nine bucks for the ER fee, and I'll bill you separately, except this one's on me. But you are pregnant, right?"

"Is that a guess?" she says, her back to him, her hands on buttons. And now that her clothes are on, he sees the slightest pot belly, small breasts with little nipples, heavy collarbone, straight muscled back. She says, "Did you guess, or can people really tell already?"

"I can maybe tell a little, and I got the idea from what you said about *fucking* joke. And the thing with the gun."

"I'm not crazy."

"And you won't do anything like it again."

"No."

"And you're pregnant."

"And not married. And won't be."

"Abortions are legal in New York State."

"I can't do that."

"You're a Catholic?"

"I'm a coward. I keep seeing those pictures, the soft little eyelids on it. The thumb in its mouth. I can't do it."

"So you're stuck. Biology's a bitch, isn't it?"

She keeps her back to him.

"And you thought you'd tell someone with your stolen gun."

"Men can't get pregnant, Doctor. I've got a baby in the oven. Please don't be smug with me."

"I'm not smug," Silver says. "I'm sorry, I'm trying to act like a doctor."

"You're probably a very good doctor," she says. "You're a nice man. Thank you."

"I'm a baby doctor. I take care of babies."

She turns around and looks at him. Her eyes are large and reddened. Lizzie Bean is not a beautiful woman, he thinks. He thinks to himself how beautiful she is. He reaches out to fasten the top button of her blouse.

"Would you take care of my baby?" she says.

Silver tells her, "Better than my own."

3 | The Clear Expressions

It was still hot on the third floor of his classroom building, although September was cool that morning, and Sorenson sweated as he walked from his shared office to his first class of the day. A tall pear-shaped man in a bright-green polyester leisure suit nodded to him in the hall, and said, running his words together, "You get a big enrollment? Werner, Chet Werner, linguistics."

Phil wiped his wet hand on his khakis and held it out. It was hard and chopped and ugly with scabs and flaps of cut flesh. Werner held his coffee mug up in one hand, his textbook in the other, shrugged, smiled, and moved on. "Phil Sorenson," Phil said.

"Right," Werner called behind him.

Students talked loudly and bounced from room to room, a bell high up on the wall rang loud and long, and the hall emptied. In his room, in front of eight brown-skinned students, all male, and two huge white boys with the wide necks and overdeveloped shoulders of football linemen, Sorenson cleared his throat, rubbed his hands on his pants, set his legs, smiled, said softly, "I thought they only rang bells like that in high school."

No one smiled or laughed.

"Okay," Phil said. "You're here because you can't write. You can make the letters, some of you. Some of you can even make words." He waited for smiles, received none, went ahead, talking faster, wondering how much time he'd used up, how much he had left to fill. "But you've got problems with clear expression. That's all they want here, and they asked me to give you an idea of how to do it. By the end of the term, you'll be— *maybe* you'll be able, probably, really, if you just listen to me and work hard, I can show you: clear expression, is all, which is what we're after."

A fat coffee-colored boy with long, unwashed hair and a T-shirt that said STONES shifted in his chair and raised his hand. "Man, we don't know your name, you know?"

"Sorenson. What's yours?"

"Diaz. I'm a freshman, I don' know what I'm *doin'* here, man."

"You're all freshmen, right? You're all new, you have trouble writing, some of you have to spend afternoons at practice, some of you talk Spanish most of the time—"

"Some of us," called a tall thin blue-black kid from the far seat of the last row, "got the racials, you know?"

"What's the racials?"

"We here because we black or Chicano and maybe we do a 4.5 on the forty and catch some footballs on the way, but we mostly black, which is why they like us comin' here. You know —"

"You pissed off already?" Sorenson said.

The kid grinned back, adjusting the collar of his pink and green body shirt. "Man, I ain't pissed off. I got out of my en-*vi*-roh-men. You know what I seen here for three days? Nothin' but white folks and cows, is what."

"That," Sorenson said, "is clear expression."

"If that's what that is," the kid said, "you can get the clear expressions out of *me* any time you do but ask."

He assigned them textbooks they wouldn't read, told them about essays they'd be unable to write, gave them his office hours, and suggested that they all go home. The chairs scraped, notebooks with the college seal flapped shut, and Phil waited for someone to ask to be advised. No one asked, and he walked down the hall and to the department office, where Werner was drinking coffee and telling the short middle-aged secretary that his seniors were unmotivated. He lifted his chin at Phil, who went out again, calling "Hi!"

In his office, at an oak desk in a far corner, Phil put letterhead in a drawer, wrote "How far have you come from home?" on a legal pad to remind himself of the assignment due in two days, thought about walking into the English office to see his chairman, thought of driving the truck back home, and left. As he walked down the stairs, his chairman walked up: Mead Weeks, short and slight and breathless, pale and shaved clean, dressed in a suit and vest of darkest gray with a tiny thread of red running through it, carrying his blue-black shiny necktie in a small hand, touching with the other the bluish pouches under his eyes. His hair was dyed bright blond and reached his eyebrows in the front, his collar at the back and sides. His breath rumbled as if it stirred fluid in his lungs.

"Are you settled in, Phil?"

"Sure am, Mead."

"And how are your, oh, special charges, could we say?"

"Scared. Illiterate. Okay kids, I guess. I think they need about two years' worth of work, but I'll do what I can, Mead."

"That's why we brought you on board, Phil."

"I'm on my way back to the house now, Mead, we're still settling in."

"That's fine, Phil."

"So, I'll see you later, Mead."

"That's fine, Phil. Have a pleasant day."

" 'Bye, Mead."

" 'Bye, Phil."

"Bye-bye."

" 'Bye."

On the way home, Phil remembered the preliminary forms he'd left in his desk—the application to be interviewed before being listed by county agents, so they could wait eight months, ten, a year, before a child might be available for adoption. He heard himself telling Annie how he'd meant to fill out the forms and bring them home. Then he heard himself admitting that he'd left them there, among the grammar books and brochures for new faculty and mimeographed injunctions against personal phone calls, because it seemed as good a place as any to bury the idea of begging for babies. He heard again how he might simply say *forgot*. He saw her sitting on the porch of the New Hampshire house, her white nightgown bright in a dark bug-swarmed evening, rocking so slowly as to seem still, saying nothing more about their baby bleeding onto the hardwood floor again. He stopped the truck on the two-lane out of town, shifted, turned against traffic, waving at the car he'd cut off, and drove back to the office for the forms.

And that night, with a coarse wind signaling new weather, with unsubtly brilliant stars in the usual undecipherable patterns lying low around their hill, they sat in rockers on the porch and drank to the small advance that Phil had drawn on his pay. Annie sipped Dry Sack over ice from a long pilsner glass and Phil drank cognac from a squat thick tumbler.

Annie said, "They didn't ask any questions about race."

"They will. They probably do it in the interview, so they can't get caught. They'll be sly."

Making her voice burble in her throat, Annie said, "Mrs. Sorenson, is your ancestry—no, they . . . how would they do it? They'll *do* it."

"They'll say, 'Do you have any racial preferences?' or something. Something like that."

"No, they can't do that." She made her voice drop into the tones of a Professional Woman: "Is you is, or is you isn't, *Caucasian?*"

"No," Phil said, "they don't really care. What they have is, they have about ten thousand little black kids they can't place. When they talk about race, they'll talk about the *kids*. They'll be glad to take your word for it that you're from the master race. What they'll do is get you to say you want anything that moves without too many wheels."

For about a minute, while the wind pawed at the high grass and sang below them in the pines near the swamp, Annie sat still in her rocker, and then she began to move again, like a little boat stirred at its mooring. Her glass clinked and Phil poured more for each of them. His bare feet were planted on the paint-slicked porch, and he bent stiffly. The wind shifted, a smell like water from a dirty fish tank came up, and then the wind moved to bring in only the smell of the sky. Annie's pink and gray mobile drifted, and the figures spun.

"What was that?" Annie said. "That smell?"

"The marsh, probably."

"That's ugly."

"It's okay."

"But ugly."

"Just old."

"And rotten."

"Just old and rotten."

"We're old and rotten."

"Absolutely not," Phil said. "No philosophical speculations or black ruminations."

"That's what we'll tell them," Annie said. "You got any of those black ruminations we could adopt?"

"To be legal, we have to tell them we'll take Chicano ruminations, too."

"That would—I think it would be called Hispanic ruminations. And your basic Native American ruminations, too."

"What about albino ruminations?"

"That would be *Other*," she said. *"Other* ruminations."

"I think we better drink a little bit more."

They did that, then rocked in the wind until Annie said, "There's a thing there about age. You have to tell them when you were born. That's fair."

"Fair enough," Phil said. "What they don't want is old people getting little kids. You know, you get a couple of people in iron lungs, it's really tough walking the baby."

"Yeah, but they'd save money on toys, if the kid liked machinery. And they'd always *be* there, wouldn't they?"

"We're not too old," Phil said.

"Except, I thought you said we *were* too old."

"No," Phil said, "that was before you told me you wanted this a lot."

"You have a way with the truth," Annie said.

"Any truth you want, you get."

"Atta boy."

"Thank you."

"Asshole."

"Absolutely. *Asshole* is a noun, right? I have to make sure I keep sharp for the class."

"You think you'll survive it? That zoo they put you in?"

"They're okay kids," Phil said. "They're imported. They're in the wrong place, and they're pretty sure it's the wrong place, and they're scared. I'll give them all C's and B's, and they'll move on to help me chalk up my quota of pedagogical success and then flunk out."

"We could adopt them," Annie said.

"We could adopt them and move their parents into the shed, maybe set tents up on the lawn: Father and Mother Sorenson's Home for Transient Beings. You want to try some of this brandy?" He poured more. "It has a certain ethyl alcohol je ne voo voo."

"No, thank you," she said, pouring sherry while chewing an ice cube.

"What?"

"I was eating ice."

"Well, why not?"

"You think I should go back to teaching?"

He smiled and nodded, said, "Damn fucking right." Then: "No, you can't, or—you have to decide about that. They don't *care* about working mothers, they're supposed to say. Except they will, and if you tell them you'll be home all the time—"

"In my iron lung."

"—it'll probably be better, you know, sound better to the caseworker or whatever they call it. That's a thing to decide about."

"I haven't worked for a long time."

"We haven't had a baby for a long time."

She drank and clacked her teeth on the rim of the glass. "You think I really know what I'm doing, Phil?"

"Yes."

"That's what I was afraid of." She drank more and said, "I really want to walk into a nursery in a hospital and see about seventy-five little babies, every goddamn color from purple to red, and walk around and touch them and end up saying, 'Give me that baby. Give me *that* one.' And come out with him— it'll be a boy, I'm willing to bet you. And carry him out and hand him over to you and watch you try to figure out how to hold him."

She was crying. Phil rocked himself forward and stumbled around the porch, holding the cognac bottle by its long neck, saying, as he passed and slowly circled her in the darkness, "Come on. Come on."

She said, "What in hell are you doing?"

"Acting distraught."

"Oh."

"It's hard to tell, isn't it?"

"So when do we finish filling out the forms?"

"Tomorrow. Tomorrow morning. Tomorrow night."

He came to rest behind her chair. Putting the bottle down softly on the porch, he leaned over her and cupped her breasts, resting his face on her hair. He held her with his fingertips on the nipples and then squeezed handfuls in, pulling harder, then slid his hand into the top of her coarse cotton shirt, cupping the breasts up hard, kissing the side of her neck. She leaned to kiss a forearm, then pulled one hand up with both of hers and, with her eyes closed, slid each of his fingers, slowly, one at a time, into her mouth.

"Come here," she said.

And when he stood before her, his eyes closed too, she opened his trousers and held his penis with both hands, kissing the head lightly.

"Don't come," she whispered, and took him in.

He whispered, moaned, "You are *always* telling me what to do."

She nipped with her teeth, then pulled at his buttocks, drew him in further, and then started to laugh.

"What are you *doing?*" he said.

She drew back again, kissed his penis, said, "Having fun, stupid."

"Oh."

"And getting a mouthful."

"Have more."

His knees hit the arms of the rocker, he held it and reared his head as she licked and licked and then opened her mouth wider and slid it over him. Then he held her head, and they rocked together, shuddered in place; she drank the night's last drink. Now he was kneeling beside the chair, and she was standing to pull her shirt off and slide down her jeans and underpants, and was above him, pulling his head toward her groin. He leaned back, stood, then moved her until she sat on the top porch step. He kissed the inside of each thigh. He gently pushed her legs apart, wider, and she slumped, spread further, leaned her arms behind her to hold where she could see him, kneeling at the bottom step, burrowing his head, kissing, probing, as her legs spread even wider, then snapped together around his head, and she gasped, then called a wild noise and bucked so that her rising body lifted his head, and they held that way, before dropping to be separate again.

After a while, pawing his hair, she said, "You want to fuck around tonight?"

"No," he said, "I'm too tired. I have a headache."

"Pansy," she said.

He kissed her thigh, then bit it. She yelped, and he said, "Are you ready?"

She pushed his head back. "You're too old to do it again."

"Give me a minute. Twenty seconds."

She stood and walked in naked except for her tennis shoes. "I'm counting," she said.

He stood too, gathered bottles and glasses, poked with his foot to herd her clothing until it was settled near the door, then put the bottles down, the glasses too, and went into the house, away from New Hampshire.

Annie dressed like the college girls on the morning she drove Phil to his classroom building, then took the truck downhill toward the library. She wore jeans and work shoes and a cotton plaid shirt, and she walked several times in several directions once she was inside, making purposeful studies, until she felt that she looked as if she ought to be in the library. Then, with her spiral notebook banging against her leg, she went to the catalogue room and began her investigations. She got the floor wrong, first, and became lost in English novels. In case anyone was watching, she looked at a book about Thomas Hardy's training in architecture. She found the stairwell on the other side of the stacks and went down to the basement, where she drifted among biographies. She found *The Book of Dates*, turned the wrong corner, was boxed in by half-empty steel shelves and a wire-mesh gate behind which were books with no titles, a metal-shaded light on the ceiling swinging as if a wind had just blown, and then she turned another corner and walked into a small room in which were three salmon-colored cushioned chairs. A very short, very thin boy with gold-rimmed glasses was gathered around a joint. Looking up at her, talking over his smoke, he said, "Consider it the aesthetic equivalent of a coffee break. Right?" Annie smiled, stopped herself from bowing, forced herself not to back away, turned around, walked slowly, felt middle-aged. "Hey," the boy called, "it's better than the moral equivalent of war."

She crossed the aisle, turning lights on as she went. Some switches illuminated the row of stacks she was next to, some lit up a row ahead or to the left. Some switches were already up, and she turned lights off without wanting to. The basement floor remained half lit, but it flickered around her as she went, running her hands along the spines of books, becoming sad. Near a small gray metal desk, at a window that was barred and that looked into a cement wall, under a light someone else had turned on, she found *The Book of Names*.

She sat with it, opened her notebook, smoothed the pages with the edge of her hand, clicked her pen, examined the point, cleared her throat very softly. She sat straight, her feet planted flat, and, because she had told Phil that their adopted child would be a boy, she looked first at *Abraham*. In the book, she wrote his name. She turned some pages, stopped, wrote *Blair*. Then *Blaise, Cormac, Glenville*. She turned pages, shrugged, and wrote *Aretha*, heard small careful steps at the mouth of the alley of shelves, smelled spice and sweat, listened to the steps stop. *Bettina:* why not another woman in the house? She heard the steps again as she was writing *Dorothy*. She closed her notebook, closed *The Book of Names*, went to the shelves to hold a book in her hand as if she was examining it, looked from under her brows to watch the dusk-lit corridor, and saw the boy, his toke out of sight, standing to study her.

"Greetings," he said.

"I'm busy."

"That's no problem," he said. "I'm into activity."

"Did you want a book here, young man?"

"What? You call me *young man?*"

He walked down the alley of shelves, his skin changing from gray-pale to cheesy orange as he came into the light. He was dressed like her, but in smaller sizes, and his complexion was delicately marred with an acne that looked painted on.

"I'm"—she heard this, then heard herself telling it to Phil, then saw him wanting to crush small boys and all professors— "I'm a faculty wife, young man."

"*Young man?*"

Annie backed to the desk, put the camouflage book on top of *The Book of Names*, seized her notebook so that when she struck with it the spiral edges would catch him in the larynx.

"Listen," the boy said, stopping, "I'm into age, too. Understand? It's all okay, lady. Listen: I'm a faculty *kid.*"

Annie sat on the edge of the desk. The boy stayed where he was. "What's your name?" she snapped.

"Mead Weeks II."

"What?"

"You know, the Second? Roman two? *Not* junior. What's yours?"

"Never mind. I don't like Mead."

"No," he said, "that's cool. I don't like *Weeks.*"

"Back up."

"Back up?"

"Back up."

"Back up," he said. "You got it."

When he had moved to the mouth of the alley, Annie walked quickly toward him, holding the notebook at right angles to her chest, slid past him, and strode toward the stairs. "Go the other way," he called. "Make a sharp right: you're going to the men's room."

Annie drove up the hill toward Phil's building, and in the parking lot beneath his office window she leaned on the horn and counted to ten, then released it and drove home. On the way, passing sumac turned brilliant red, thinking that she ought to really look at it hard before everything turned brown for the rest of the year, she decided to strip the paper from the kitchen walls. She leaned again, hard, on the horn, and pulled into their drive in the center of the sound.

"Morning sickness," she said, before she went in.

She took the sheets from their queen-sized mattress and several others from a closet upstairs. She draped the sheets over the stove and counters, then shoved an aluminum six-foot stepladder at a wall, put a plastic bucket of soapy hot water on its tool rest, rolled up her college-girl sleeves, dipped a nearly bristleless scrub brush into the water, and soaked four feet of wall, from tongue-and-groove siding, five feet up, to the ceiling. Then, with a long-handled wedge-fronted razor knife, she began to peel. The paper on top was brown fleurs-de-lis on a cream background. As she drove that away, in short chops, in long curling swathes, she uncovered a thick embossed white paper suitable for bathrooms of the fifties. Under that was a hand-painted cabbage-rose pattern, and under that the unevenly plastered wall, so old that horsehair, mixed in for consistency and insulation, came away with seventy years' worth of paper. Sometimes the stripping knife stuck in the softened wall, and then chunks of plaster fell away, leaving craters. She didn't stop. Generations of work were bathed and sliced and torn, the wet paper clung to her legs and shoulders, hung from the rungs of the ladder and the edge of the steaming pail. When the water cooled, she got hotter water, and when her arm tired from pushing upward, she clawed down with her fingernails.

There was a stink in the kitchen after an hour, a boiled smell of horse glue and old walls. Annie moved the ladder, shifted sheets, hauled water, drove the scraper up, pulled down layers of paper. The water ran onto the tongue-and-groove siding below her and made it glisten; it pooled on the polished hardwood kitchen floor and slowly dried, leaving plaster dust and paper fragments in dirty knots. As the off-white walls, rounded in places from old leaks, indented elsewhere from too much plasterer's pressure, began to dominate the cream-colored paper and embossed paper and cabbage-rose paper, the kitchen stepped forward. Sitting on the top of the ladder, Annie saw the table, which had sat in three kitchens, the chairs, which Phil and she had taken apart and reglued, the wrought-iron chandelier they'd taken from an abandoned carriage house in Vermont and wired, the framed pressed mountain flowers they'd collected in Scotland, a yellow can of Revelation tobacco which Phil had found in a New Hampshire barn.

Then she saw Phil holding his hand, pressing it between his legs as the lawnmower howled and he did too, and the blood jumped from the stump of his thumb and stained the lawn in New Hampshire. She saw him days later, on his hands and knees, still taking little blue pills for the pain, his eyes enormous and young, looking through the partly cut grass for his finger. She saw her doctor's face, and the lips of the nurse, but couldn't remember which nurse, the one in the first hospital or the second, she tried to display the events on the buckled plaster kitchen walls, like slides in an art class, then decided not to think about teaching classes or making pictures, or babies either, and looking at the walls, her right hand as weak as it always grew when she thought of Phil and the lawnmower, she threw the stripper across the room at the sink and called him things because he wasn't home.

Abraham, Aretha. She remembered that he couldn't be home unless she went for him in the truck. She looked at the walls half undone, the frayed feathered layers of drying paper. She wondered if his students stared at his hand—or his colleagues, keeping their distance from the shaggy, sweaty grammar jock. Washing her hands, opening her blouse two more buttons, leaving the wreckage of her archaeology, she went to the truck to bring him back. She drove in second gear so she could look at the sumac, forgetting to look.

In his office, Phil ignored the late September snow to talk with Alonzo I. R. Demby, called I.R., primarily because he refused to answer to Alonzo, but also because he was an alumnus who had starred six years before at linebacker and was the color of milk chocolate: it pleased the white teachers in the department to sound either black or unbiased when they drawled out, "Hey, I.R.," over coffee mugs. I.R.'s desk faced their shared office's door, and he liked to sit staring into the hall, commenting on the coeds—"If she would just sit on my face, Phil, just a little, I'd give her a *bitch* of an Afro-American experience."

Now I.R. had swiveled to face him, asking, "So what do you think of our little camp for the overprivileged?"

"Nice," Phil said, "nice."

"*Nice?*"

"One of my students called it nothing but white folks and cows."

"That's more like it. Except for the local expert on Afro-American Experience. You know I teach that? Splendid. You know what my dissertation is on? Guess."

"Judging from the department—Ezra Pound."

"Close. Try W. C. Williams. The guys with initials stick together. It's called ethnic identity. So I'm teaching the Afro-Trendy Experience. Guess why."

"Pink palms."

I.R. laughed, showing big white teeth, wrinkling his long thin nose. A tall red-haired coed came to the door and I.R. swiveled in his chair as if he'd seen her in a mirror. "Hel-*lo,*" he said, and Phil went back to the journal, written in Maine in a battered boathouse in their field over the bay, then left to mildew and curl, carried to New York, dug out of sheafs of manuscripts and letters and, in new black ink, written again with the left-handed scribble he'd learned, saying back at him: Annie is sketching again, she's made a drawing of the road that goes down to the swamp. She says she hates the swamp, but she watches it a lot. When we have drinks on the porch, she stares at it, though you can't really see much unless there's a full moon. We're doing another house again. Even though neither of us thinks we're going to be here awfully long. Habit, I suppose. You come to some place and you claim it. We do that by rebuilding. We manufacture where we live. Though I wonder if we'll want to leave again. We both think about things like getting old and having money to live on. And neither of us said anything about it out loud, but we're worried. Because if we do adopt a kid, then we have to change. We have to put money away and always buy things. It's going to be very different soon. I can feel it. The early snow doesn't help—he had just added this, and was staring not at the page but at the stump of his thumb when the kid named Turner walked past I.R.'s desk with the city limp-and-swagger Phil loved to watch, stood alongside Phil's desk, made a half bow, and lifted his fist partway to his face, then brought it down.

Phil looked at him closely: very long slender legs, tight waist, broad shoulders, long athlete's muscles in the biceps and forearms, the blue-black skin full of power. "You don't play football," Phil said.

"Oh, yes, I do," Turner said. "Don't you but come to practice and watch me, you see the NFL's premier wide receiver coming up, and soon."

"Yeah," Phil said, "but you did Golden Gloves in New York, right? Or the Police Athletic League? You copy the Olympics things, where they bow at the crowd and kiss their fist to the judges. What weight?"

"They don't do no boxing team here. I go light."

"Yeah. Hold your arms out." Turner did, and Phil stood, lifted his, and nodded. "Your arms are as long as mine and I carry maybe eighty pounds more than you. And you're a wide receiver, so you're fast. Can you *move*, though? I don't mean can you swing your can like Ali when he plays around. Can you move your legs? Can you— When's your first class?"

Turner stared at Phil, his eyes large and happy in the long dark face. "You gonna be my coach? You one of them born coach-types?"

"One of *those.*"

"Yeah. Okay: one of those."

"*Those* do the action, *them* receive it. Like a quarterback throwing you a slant-in: he's a *those*, you're a *them.*"

"That's cool. We gonna box?"

"No," Phil said, "I'm going to train you."

"You are? Who say but you?"

"Who says."

"White-folks English. I talk black."

"Bull *shee*-it," I.R. called over his shoulder. "You talk *talk.*"

"I don' believe that," Turner said.

"Maybe you will," I.R. said.

"Yeah," Turner said. "Three-fifteen."

"You bring gloves with you?"

"They got some in the gym, for playing around. They a little heavy, but we can use 'em."

"They *are* a little heavy," Phil said.

Turner told him, "Look, Mr. Sorenson, you do me one *those* and *them* a day while you winning my hearts and minds, and then we see. Can you dig that kind of white-folks magic?" He was grinning. "On account of we can't rush this ed-u-cational number lest I find out how you doing your teacher type of thing on my frizzy head."

"Hay-id," Phil corrected.

"Yazzuh," Turner said. "Mistuh *Suh.*"

"Couple of assholes," I.R. said. The coed smiled, but blushed. "It's okay," I.R. told her, "it's how we won in Southeast Asia, too."

So that day, Phil came home red and sweating, drank two cans of beer over ice, skipped his afternoon run, and sat in a rocker on the lawn, smiling at ill-typed and worse-written themes, scrawling in margins *Ref?* and then crossing it out to say *What does this word point to?*, writing *I don't get it* or *Use a dictionary!* or, once in a while, *Nice.* The sun began to drop, and the surface of the swamp glowed red, eddying in the wind that had brought them snow and had promptly taken it away. He wore a heavy red Woolrich shirt with the collar up and huddled happily in it, making scribbles that wouldn't help, his arms a little heavy, his knees sore from going five rounds with a kid from New York who knew how to fight.

Annie slammed the door behind him and he jumped. A crow in their shedding maple flapped slowly up, and two squirrels froze upright as she came to give him a sip of her coffee. She stood beside him, looking down the hill. Her eyes were dazed and tired, and they reserved most of their energy for looking in, which meant to him that she'd been painting or drawing, which meant he ought to keep shut. He did, stole another sip of coffee by pulling her arm to his face, then scrawled *Another fragment?* in a margin, rolled the papers into a club, and gently swatted her with it.

"I sent the application in," she said.

Phil said, "Here we go."

"Here we go."

After a while, Phil said, "Where?"

"Pork chops."

"What?"

"Why don't you make a fire and do some marinated pork chops and we'll drink a little wine, and then I'd like it if you could hook up the TV set so I can watch something where everybody cries except the doctors, who know it'll be all right, and then it is."

The football season opened with a game at Bucknell. The Friday before the game, the campus began to empty at eleven in the morning, and by early afternoon, classes were thinned out as the campus migrated to attend the game. A sign over the chapel doors said BEAT BUCKNELL. "Such a clever turn of phrase," Chet Werner said, after talking to a class of three linguistics fans. I.R. was absent from his classes because he had gone to Pennsylvania on Thursday night to drink beer with an assistant coach. Mead Weeks, paler than usual, shuttled from his office to the secretary's desk to a classroom to the Bailey municipal building, where he was negotiating the future of his son, who had been arrested for setting fire to a straw man hung from a two-by-four propped in the ground in front of the Deke house; when the police came to rescue him from the brothers, who were separating his right shoulder and breaking his nose, he had explained that his purpose was to wage an unremitting war on ritual. Phil had explained to his class that "Jew" and "Negro" took capital letters, had received assent to the rule, and had sent them away. In the English office, not drinking coffee because he'd forgotten to provide a mug, he stood at a long, white-painted counter which ran the length of the room and supported mailboxes. He read through a stack of interoffice memos he'd ignored for a week, and said hello to the tall handsome man who taught Dryden, Swift, and Pope, the fat surly man—he made the best jokes about the students and the college—who taught Coleridge, the bearded man with flared nostrils and six different corduroy sport coats who taught contemporary literature and wrote articles—there were offprints left on the counter: "The Book Review as Cultural Artifact" —and then the pale busy woman who taught Joyce and Eliot, and several others, all of whom said "Hello" in one variation or another, and to each of whom, with varying tones because he couldn't think of varying words, Phil said, too loudly, "Hello," in return.

Annie was raking leaves from randomly selected patches of lawn. On a basin of wide stones which Phil had collected, she was burning the leaves slowly, watching the gray smoke blur up and disappear. The swamp seemed motionless, etched, with its bare deciduous trees and red and yellow weed, pointed dead marsh stalks, on the ocher fields and cloudless sky. She sang as she raked, whistled between her teeth as she stood to watch the smoke or look back at the stone house, which nearly was ready for winter. After a while, she wetted the fire with the hose so that it smoldered more slowly, then sprayed the battered green truck, and, with one of Phil's undershirts from the line, polished its pitted paint. She heard herself singing, "That's why

I'm in love with you, pret-ty *ba*—" and stood to listen, refusing at first to believe that the top of her mind could announce itself with such distressing banal clarity.

Turner did wind sprints in Lewisburg, Pa., churning up gravel in the Bucknell parking lot, until his coach, stepping down from the team bus, told him to stop trying to frighten the parked cars with his breakaway speed. Werner, pursing his lips, told Mann Oliver, the chubby Romantics teacher, that reading no longer seemed essential to a degree in English. Oliver answered that since it hadn't been at Chapel Hill, when Oliver had done his undergraduate work, there was no reason to expect it here. L'Ordinet, flared nostrils and corduroy, leaving the office, instructed them both, and Mrs. DeAngelo, the secretary, that clear expression, imparted and received, was a moral obligation in the age of enormity. Werner whistled and changed the subject to the autumn seeding of lawns, saying he thought it immoral—L'Ordinet was out of the office by then —to permit dogs to leave yellow patches of urine burn on lawns. Oliver laughed a gurgling chainsmoker's cough, said, "Indeed." Primatis, the woman who taught Joyce, asked Phil how he and his wife liked living in the country. Phil smiled and said, "Fine, fine." Mead Weeks returned to the office, loosening his tie, pushing his hair back out of his collar. Annie soaked the small patch of wallpaper left over the sink, beneath the cupboards, and began to strip it. Rolls of Morris paper, shipped from New York, beyond their means, were stacked on the kitchen counter. Leicester, the eighteenth-century man, held his saucer in a large red hand, rocked on his toes, smoothed at his graying sideburns, and mentioned school tax re-evaluations. Phil bit at the fringes of his mustache. Turner limped his perfect health to the Bucknell student union, in quest of a snack and a woman.

A neatly typed memorandum from E. Bean, the campus psychologist, suggested to Phil that one of his freshmen, Diaz, was shown by pre-admission tests to be reading dysfunctional. Bean wondered if Phil would care to confer. Phil crumpled the letter and tossed it over the corner of a filing cabinet and into the wastebasket beside Mrs. DeAngelo, who, without looking up, signaled with her fingers that he'd scored two points.

The teachers stood silently as the bell rang, signifying the start of a two-twenty class, then they went out, and then Chairman Mead Weeks, knotting his tie, followed them. Phil read a memo from a dean, advising new faculty that attendance at the president's chapel talk, "What *Are*, After All, the Liberal Arts?", was expected and advised. He crumpled it, tossed it, missed the basket, and went to pick the memo up. Kneeling before the wastepaper basket, throwing in the letter from the dean, Phil retrieved E. Bean's memorandum. "This kid will be desperate in the not too distant future," E. Bean had written. "Shouldn't we do something to *help?*" He read those sentences again, more slowly, cocked his head like the woodchuck standing at the edge of the drive outside the kitchen window, beyond which Annie was putting up the tobacco-colored Morris paper.

"What'd you say?" asked Mrs. DeAngelo.

Turner in Lewisburg smiled all his teeth at the woman in the blazer who was drinking coffee and reading a chemistry text, interrupted her with, "Hello, *momma!*"

Werner told a classroom of five students that expression was a science, not an art.

Oliver said that romanticism was *not* a collection of poems beginning with "I."

L'Ordinet said that Dreiser was not a realist at all, but a moralist, and so was Hemingway.

Leicester said that Dryden wasn't boring, really, once you knew at whom his finger pointed in *Absalom and Achitophel.*

Primatis said that *Dubliners* was not only a book of stories but something more like a novel.

Annie, papering, sang all the songs from *Oklahoma!*, then turned the radio on, turned it off when the two-thirty newscaster said that cancer among the young was increasing in the upstate New York area, according to statistics gathered from local hospitals.

Phil told Mrs. DeAngelo, "I really have to read these memos more carefully, don't I?"

Mrs. DeAngelo, turning to type up Mead Weeks's agenda for the department meeting, said, "My ass."

4 | Alluvial Light

Waking is easy, but not when it begins with a small high drilling sound in the center of the brain which repeats, enlarging like a pupil slowly opening wider and wider to stare, becoming music with a resonating electric bass and gunfire rim shots, and that is what Eli Silver feels and then hears; he is on his way from sleep in his bedroom, which is almost a hotel's, but he hasn't wakened yet, he knows as his head aches that he is on sleep's horizon, remembering.

He remembers a night when waking was far too easy, after the death of a child and the flight of a wife, and he dressed at 2 a.m. in moccasins and dungarees, the day's dirty shirt, and drove the Hawk in low gear on the narrow unpaved roads across Route 12, high in the hills which bordered on the state-owned forests of dense evergreen and old thick maple and ash, bright birch. It was a night of full moon and sudden winds, leaves blew across the road, and through his open window he heard them; when he took his foot off the gas, the leaves were like animals, scuttling. The sky was dark lavender silk, and it reached the ground. Things called to each other, or simply away from themselves, and he was cold. Going north in the engine's low murmur, the rattle of dead leaves, he followed a long dip in the road to a part of the forest away from snowmobile trails and hunters' reserves, to where there was only the bright tan road, a T-junction, forest pressing close.

He saw parallel incisions in the soft surface of the road, and then he heard the music, the beating of electric instruments, the blurred *Ba-by, Ba-by* of a woman singing love. He followed in a smooth arc where the skid marks went, and then he had to stop because a boy in drenched and darkened clothes stood shivering in the road, arrested in the long stride of a panicked run. He moved around to Silver's side of the car and said, "Can you help me? Help me!"

The boy pointed, and Silver looked across the road and down about thirty yards, to where the brush was broken, frosty-looking in moonlight where thick stalks had been cracked to expose the white wet wood inside. Through the brush, for the first time, Silver saw the incandescence of lighted water. He turned the motor off and heard the river pour. Then he shut his lights off and followed the boy, running, saying nothing, sliding down a short bank to see the long sedan nose-down in the water, its lights still shining under the surface. Alluvial mud and weeds eddied around the front of the car in the bright water, and the car's radio still played, *Ba-by, Ba-by,* and the boy, shaking so hard and so pumped with adrenalin that his voice gobbled like a bird song, said, "She got thrown out. She's over there."

Silver saw the yellow and white full skirt drifting in the eddies at the rear right wheel. He splashed in, slipping on the stones, to come closer to her legs, pinned beneath the wheel when the car settled upon her, tearing her stockings, letting the skirt wash up in the current "to expose her buttocks in bright blue panties." Her hair poured forward in the flow of the river, and so did her arms, her face was down, her head bobbed as the water cuffed her. The boy said, "I can't get her up."

Silver said, "When?"

"I don't know, a while ago, a minute, I don't know, can you *help* me?"

Silver said, "No." But he stooped at the rear bumper and shoved, in slow bursts of strength, in steady rhythms, and the boy pulled at her dress, saying "Ah," again and again, repelled by her, afraid to touch her flesh.

And the car did slide, an inch, a smooth little bit, and she pushed forward into her boyfriend's knees—he cried the nightmare "Ah! Ah!"—and then Silver, standing again where he'd slipped to his hands and knees on the rocks and river slime, pulled her partway onto the bank and, crawling over her, began to breathe into her mouth.

Her lips were cold, she tasted of vomit and spiced meat and salty snacks. Silver closed his eyes, saw long white writhing river things crawl up her throat, made himself not gag, and, pinching her nose, pushing at her chest, breathed down into her lungs.

When he stopped and looked away, shaking his head, the boy punched him, missed his face, banged at his sternum, knocked him backward, and began to wail. The radio was doing a series of commercials—beer, new Fords, aluminum siding—when Silver found his feet and pulled the boy away to the Hawk. As they drove south again, toward the state police barracks on Route 12, both shivering, the boy said, "My fuckin' battery's gonna be shot by the time we get back. You carry jump cables? In case my battery goes?"

Now he rises in the bedroom of his house, remembering. He dresses in the trousers he will wear when the day begins, forces himself not to think yet of the business of this day's rounds, and thinks instead of women. He is without lust, without energy, and without the women he considers. Elizabeth Bean, hysterical in her slow quiet way—her panic like rust instead of

| 75

fire, but oxidizing all the same, consuming her. She is a woman who needs, but doesn't know what; nor does he know, though he wants to, and thinks he will, or can. And Gwen Silver, thirty-eight, tall as Elizabeth, but with a high round ass that juts and slowly sways no matter how she tries to contain the tempo of her walk. Gwen has large, thick-nippled breasts—he is without energy, but he speculates on lust: all he can envision is his own penis, red and standing up. He cannot see himself with Gwen or any woman, and he is relieved. Gwen in her large horn-rimmed glasses, in a gray English pullover and white canvas slacks, in a tailored sand-colored suit, in an airplane flying to LaGuardia and then home, to Second City, Texas, and her loud father with his dun-colored, whiskey-veined face, Gwen in a car, and Gwen in blood on the highway, and the little boy lying curled as if in sleep, and soon not breathing. Daddy'll be right back. He says, *"Women!"* He moves—the bathroom, the steps, the slightly unkempt kitchen and the coffee pot—to keep ahead of his thoughts. He tells himself: Elizabeth Bean, counselor and counseled, but sees Gwen Silver at an airport, unwilling to tell him goodbye.

Silver drinks a pot of strong coffee and toasts a frozen bagel, which he smears with strawberry jam: he is being good to himself, he is an excellent doctor, and he knows what babies like—full mouths, warm smells, the service of generous hands —so he gives himself something of what he requires.

Blue jays complain outside, starlings from the eaves of the garage attack the larger birds, garbage trucks whine in neighboring streets, a door slams, the day has legitimately started, and Silver goes upstairs for tie and light tweed jacket, shoes and socks, clean shirt, and then he is outside and in the Hawk, his teeth pressed hard together, squealing the Michelins outside his driveway, racing to the hospital as if suddenly a life—but only his—depends on his being there at once.

Ada hands him tablets and water, tells him that Mrs. Podolak of the social-services administration wants to talk with him sometime during the morning. Ada reports on the almost empty infants' ward, mentions that the new resident in Osteo has bought his second new car in a week, says she'd like to do something new for Halloween, which isn't far off, and they begin to do the charts.

Neither of them mentions Dolores until he has ordered a second CBC on the small boy whose widowed father thinks his child had a convulsion while the father was at work, has examined a toddler with enlarged lymph nodes in the armpits and groin, and has found what he thinks to be pneumonia in the daughter of an executive at the shoe factory.

Dolores sleeps, or lies, in a coma, or dies; her fever rises but no one cares about the numbers because she is the weight of a five-year-old, looks—in the nearly raw-bone thinness of her arms and legs, the hollow blackened eyes, protruding cheek-bone—like a death-camp victim. The mound on her face has risen, her temple is disappearing, and her ear, the cancer is eating her head. When Silver told her father, Walt, that it was time for her to go to the hospital, he put his small face on Silver's shirt—he had been waiting for this ease, Silver knew—and coughed deep cries up from his chest. Silver checks the flow of her IV, then goes to the door and shuts it. He carries the plastic IV bag to the sink, empties it, fills it with half-normal saline solution from the bottle he has hidden in her closet, and then he replaces the bag on her bedside rack. Another day of diminishing nutriments; he counts back to when he stopped the normal treatment and found the nerve to do what he does. He bites the inside of his lower lip at the word *treatment*—dispensing death by drugged starvation. He administers a massive shot of methadone, into the IV tube, checks the flow again, pushes Dolores's hair, the little that is left, and goes out. He doesn't tell Ada goodbye.

Downstairs, in the office used by the head of the teenage

Candy Striper volunteers, and by visiting local officials on part-time errands, he finds Mrs. Podolak. She is enormous, tall and fat, puffy, a woman of many chins and stomachs, small rounded nose, the bright-blue eyes of a child. She smokes an unfiltered cigarette and wanly waves to him, as if to communicate that the exhaustion she finds on his face is precisely hers too. She holds up papers when he is seated, his legs straight out and crossed at the ankle to relieve the pressure on his aching knee. The way she holds the papers is to squeeze them, wrinkling them with her fist and wetting them with her sweating hands.

"Eli," she says, in a voice that is lower than his, "we got a couple in the county—they live north of here, near some little —oh, right, outside of Bailey. He teaches something at the college. They want us to let them adopt a child."

Silver nods. "Good," he says. "Got any babies left?"

"What, since the politicians in Albany said it's just *wonderful* to murder babies in the womb?"

"You haven't got any babies left, Yvonne."

"Well, we got a foundling with polio, maybe they like the clankety-clank of little braces in the house. We got some older kids in the home in Chenango, if they like kids who set fire to things and run away. We got—this one's on special, all year— we got a little girl bastard who's half Chinese and half, I don't know, palomino. That's what we got."

"So you have to tell them no."

"Old folks, Eli. They're almost as old as you."

"They're senile, Yvonne. Dear God. So they're too old, you've got how many? A hundred? You've got plenty of couples who are younger, and no little babies, so you tell them no. Or ask them to take what you've got."

Yvonne Podolak lights another cigarette, Eli hears the smoke drawn down, waits for it to hiss away, but she makes no other sound until she says, "I interviewed them."

"Yvonne, you're getting soft. Don't get human on us, we depend on you to keep saying no."

"Thank you, Eli. You're *such* a son of a bitch."

"I try," he says modestly.

"She's a nice kid, nice woman. She looks very young. He's one of those big hippie-looking guys left over from when everybody looked like a hairy moose. But he talks very soft, he's smart. He builds things with his hands. And she—she's tense, because she wants it so much. But she's a nice kid. She knew all these facts and figures on adoption. They want to get a kid so much, especially her. What I'm saying is, whoever these people adopt will be, I think I'm right about this, whoever it is will be lucky. I mean, they're some kid's *chance.* Maybe. If I'm right."

"Good," Silver says. "That's what we need. But with no babies—"

Yvonne Podolak nods, puts her cigarette out. "But I'm moving them up on the list. Not to the top, it wouldn't be fair. But up a little bit, ahead of some of those creeps out of caves who we get. I mean, you never know when a baby's going to show up. It could happen. And if you could check them out?"

"*Me?*"

"To make sure I'm right about them?"

"Why me?"

"Because you take care of kids. You know a lot of parents, you know more parents than anybody else around here, and you're a sucker for taking care of kids, and you do things for people when they ask you to."

Silver rubs his sore knee and holds his hand out for the papers. "Maybe," he says.

"These are confidential. Even to you. For now. Okay?"

She writes on a clean sheet of paper *Philip and Anne Sorenson, R.D. 1, Bailey, off Shawler's Brook Road,* adds a telephone number, places it, already wrinkled and moist, in his hand. "Maybe," he says.

"That's right," Mrs. Podolak says.

In his mailbox, on the way out, he finds the rheumatology

report, which confirms a diagnosis by Boraz. Silver didn't believe it when Boraz first guessed that Silver suffered from gout. Short of aspiration of fluid from the joint when it grows swollen, painful to move, hot to the touch, the conclusion is as certain as possible: Silver, very long and very lean, who sometimes forgets to eat, has gout, the sickness of syphilitic fat men who dine on partridge and deer, drink ruby port, and live in two-hundred-year-old cartoons. When he leaves the hospital, he limps.

Back at his office, the afternoon is itchy with bickering voices: Billie, his nurse, complains that the rolls of paper sheet for the examination tables are a week overdue; Maxine gives him a typed list of patients who haven't paid for six months, and she mutters about welfare clients in Cadillacs; a child's arm swells up immediately after her allergy shot, she begins to wheeze, Silver spikes her with Benadryl to stop the reaction, and her mother complains; two weeping parents carry in a half-shocked child with a broken arm, and Silver bellows with rage that they should have gone to the hospital ER; a tired father, waiting for his infant to be given a DPT booster, argues that the injured child was tended out of turn; Silver tells him to find another doctor, and Billie takes the father into Silver's office for coffee and some calming down.

"This isn't practicing medicine," Silver snarls at Maxine.

Billie, coming from his office, chants, "Oh, yes, it is, Doctor." And Maxine nods.

Then there is croup; there is diarrhea; there are mouth lesions from Coxsackie A virus, a mother paying her bill with loaves of fresh-baked bread, a baby vomiting, an infant's arm that is covered with flea bites, a boy who writhes with chicken pox, a little girl with red vulva from masturbation, a six-year-old boy with signs of lead poisoning, an older hyperactive boy who crawls in circles, jumps from the table, pushes at chairs. Silver gives starters of decongestant, of erythromycin, of ampicillin. He takes throat cultures, peers down ears and up nostrils, looks at blinking eyes. His hands are on hardened stomachs, jumping pulses of the foot, distended muscles of the groin, swelled throats. He hears lungs that burble and hearts that roar, he hears the TV soap operas—pregnant teenaged girls, then crippled surgeons, then women who cannot talk with their sons—and then he talks with untelevised parents of pregnant girls, with women whose children are swallowing their mothers' lives, and his knee wants, during the late afternoon, to lock and drag.

The noise at the waiting-room door presses hard and then slackens, the TV set is off, he incubates the last two cultures of the day and sits in his office while Billie leaves, and then Maxine; he slumps in his chair and swivels slowly in small arcs, turning toward nothing in particular, waiting for the day to go away.

He does what other doctors do, and what he rarely does— telephones the pediatrics ward, talks with the night nurse from seven until seven-fifteen, gives orders which he'll sign for in the morning, hopes that her judgments are right, tells her to call him at home because he won't be into the ward—pressing consultations, he says—and then he asks her to transfer his call to Records, where, after a search by a grouchy orderly, he is given E. Bean's telephone number. Pressing consultation, he says, but the orderly has hung up the phone.

Lizzie Bean answers on the second ring, her voice is a little more breathless than he remembers, and it is defensive, falls away rather than rises, crouches against bad news.

"Oh," she says, "Dr. Silver."

"Right. Right. The guy at the—"

"Yes, I remember. You were very nice to me."

"You feeling all right?"

"Sure, a little bit pregnant, a little bit dumb, fine, fine. How are you?"

"Fine, thank you. I just wondered how you were."

"Fine."

They wait, and then Silver, blushing, says, "Would you like to have a drink some time?"

"Medicinal purposes only," Lizzie says.

"What?"

"It's an old joke, from a movie, I think. You know."

"Oh. That's right."

"Are you sad, Doctor?"

"Tonight."

"What?"

"Would you please drive over to my house and have a drink —I can't leave, I'm on call. Well, I could leave your number with the hospital and come over there, but I thought maybe you'd like to come here. And then if you needed anything, you know, any medicines or anything you needed, that you wanted me to get for you, then they'd *be* here."

"Medicines?"

He breathes out and hears the harshness she must hear, the static of his helplessness. He says, "Well."

"What's your address?" she says.

So Elizabeth Bean drives twenty miles of defiled county road —Blue Bird Restaurant, its rounded vertical neon sign and twittering Disney-bird wings a souvenir of 1940; a billboard, peeling like Anne Sorenson's wallpaper, that shows half a flag and the motto, FLY IT PROUDLY; long mobile homes weighing a ton and propped on eight small cinderblocks, unlighted except for the radioactive color of television sets; the towns three streets long with slanted hotel bars and stalwart churches and

Agway stores; the high power lines that blur the radio music for minutes—and she passes the hospital, the doctors' large Victorian houses, supermarkets, YMCA, three Catholic churches, to turn up Eli Silver's driveway, and finds him on his side steps, tall and neatly dressed; and yet, because they both are in something less than control, he looks disheveled, he seems somehow scared.

He leads her into the kitchen, where the trails of his sponge still evaporate from the table. There is an ornate bucket of ice on the counter near the stove, and bottles of whiskey, wine. He offers, she guesses, and when they settle on something he has, Campari-soda, and when he's poured himself an Irish over ice, and when they're sitting opposite one another, saying, "Well," and "There," Silver stands too suddenly and fetches from the tall refrigerator a plate of crackers and cheese.

Sitting again, Silver looks at her in jeans and a plum-colored sweater, says, "You look fine."

"It shows," she says, "just not a lot. I don't know why. I was never *little.*"

"You'll wake up tomorrow morning, and pop, there it'll be."

"You think so?"

Silver nods, drinks a long sip.

"Did you ever go to Italy, Dr. Silver?"

"Couldn't you—really, you should call me Eli. Isn't this a date?"

Without coloring or pausing, she nods, says, "Eli. That's nice. Did you?"

"Excuse me?"

"Italy?"

"Oh. Oh, yes, I did. I was there last—a while ago, a little while ago, I just came back a little while ago. I went to Venice."

"Oh, God. I loved it. That's where I learned about Campari-and-soda. All those little whatchamacallits near the canal, you just sit down and drink all day and watch the tourists and pretend you aren't one."

Silver nods, thinking that she isn't beautiful, and that he doesn't remember the pleasure of watching people walk near the canal.

"And Siena," she says. "It was so *brown.*"

Silver nods again, says, "Is that where the color comes from, that we used to use in the crayons in school? Burnt Siena?"

They both laugh over crayons, Crayola crayons, in boxes of 16 and 32 and 64, and Lizzie tells him that now you can buy 128, and he says that he knows, one of his patients showed him.

"How's the practice?" she says.

"Good. Okay. A little boring, sometimes. You know. How's yours?"

Lizzie pushes at her short hair and drinks, ducks her head forward into a recollection, shakes her head. "A lot of black and brown kids who belong in cities or places where there are other black and brown people—very difficult adjustment for them. I keep telling them it's what they have to do. *Compete.* Forget the politics, get better than their classmates, beat them out of jobs, law school, that kind of thing. They don't believe me."

"No."

"And there was this girl, woman. Shit, she was a girl, she was nineteen, knocked up and what the hell, she wanted me to get her a leave from her classes so she could go to Tucson and have her abortion. 'I need a week off,' she says. Cool, calm, all crotch and dumb courage. I wanted to take a crochet hook to her."

"Knitting needle."

"Ah."

"It's the instrument of choice, I think."

"Yes." Lizzie Bean holds her glass out for more Campari, so Silver finishes his whiskey and makes them another drink.

"There we go," Silver says, desperate at his wordlessness, but Lizzie Bean is being skilled, professional, she permits them their silences, and she smiles when he peeks from around his glass.

"Eli," she says, "can you make love when you're pregnant?"

Silver squeezes his own leg and thinks of shouting, but he nods and quietly says, "Yes. I can tell you a little about it. Got something cooking?"

Lizzie shakes her head quite casually. "I was only wondering," she says.

"The guy, the father is still around?"

"Not around me," she says.

And Silver, in music dreadful to his ears, says, "Good."

Lizzie looks at him, then she studies her Campari and drinks some. She says, "You're not what I'd call a helpless male, you're very competent. You might think of these things, but I doubt it, and you're probably too busy—lettuce spinner, striped asbestos glove and matching apron, Creuset pots, the meat thermometer."

"The— You saw those already?"

"I don't only get hysterical and shoot guns over my shoulder."

"No."

"So who's the woman? Are you divorced?"

"I forgot about the lettuce spinner," he says.

Lizzie holds her glass out, and Silver makes refills.

When he's seated again, this time leaning on the table with his elbows, Lizzie says, "The woman?"

"A wife."

"Is this a furtive meeting, Eli?"

"She's in Second City, Texas. She went there."

"You're separated."

"We sure ain't together."

Slowly, walking slippery stones, Lizzie says, "I'm sorry. Are you?"

Showing all his teeth, whinnying a labored laugh, Eli says,

"I'm not sorry, I'm forty-three. That's a joke, that's a dumb joke. Lizzie, I don't know."

"That's fair," she says, "that's understandable. And what about the kid, the child?"

"Oh."

"When I asked you if you'd take care of my—oh, brother: my baby—my baby. You said, better than your own. Are there any children?"

"There was a son. We had a son. He died." Silver takes her half-filled glass, and his empty one, and stands to make more drinks.

"Oh, boy," Lizzie whispers. "I'm so sorry. I'm so sorry. This, it's just, this was as tough on me as it was on you, this ridiculous evening you nearly planned, and I didn't know what to say, and then I was being cool; it was like ice skating, you have to keep moving. I got heady and I thought I was doing okay. Eli, I'm so sorry."

Standing behind her to place the Campari on the table, Silver leans over and kisses her high on the cheek. She leans back, and he kisses her lower on the cheek, and then the neck. She turns and he kisses her mouth.

She says, "Sit." He leans down, and this time she kisses him softly, so that their lips part slowly, they are friends. "Sit down on the other side of the table, please."

He does, and he smiles a great stupid grin, leans back in his chair full-weight for the first time that night since she's come—they are waiting now, and there isn't much rush—and Lizzie tells him stories about minds, and Silver tells stories about flesh.

And then she stops talking, she doesn't smile, she looks at him hard. "How can you laugh at all, after what you said? About your child? I'm sorry, but: *but.*"

"I have been dreaming about him. I have been *talking* to him. I keep him pinned up on the inside of my skull like a fucking *Christmas* card. What the hell kind of question is that? I fucking *killed* him, Mizz Elizabeth Bean, psychology-thing counselor, Annie Get Your Gun, skilled interrogator of the bereaved. I fucking killed him."

"Oh, look, Eli—"

"Yessiree, boy. You can do it. You could stop breathing here and I could do the wrong thing just the same as I could do the right thing. Any place, anybody could do it—in the fucking OR, they could do it. You slip with the cutter, you stitch your best stopwatch inside, you misread a blood count, you look at two people in the road near a wrecked car, you're a little bit in the bag, not more than other times, and you get scared out of your *pee,* so who needs you more? You gonna know? Fuck that, lady: you *guess.* You believe this? *Guess.* It's all you can do. So you take care of the wrong one, goodbye, sorry, over and out, and they say, later on, in the ER, they say, 'Oh, he wouldn't of made it, anyway, Eli,' things like that, 'You couldn't of helped.' You hear it? Sure. And they're probably right. Maybe they're right. You know what? *So what* is what. Because he's dead. Don't look at me. Don't look at me. I apologize. Don't look at me."

Silver is not thinking. Or he is thinking that it isn't fair that he's come apart now, instead of with Gwen, who needed him to do it when she was home, who begged him to talk, who waited to weep with him instead of in another bed and in another room. He hears a man vomiting tears and noises and then hears him hold them back with his teeth, she is holding him, someone is holding him, someone is hugging his head as if it were a person separate from the long body, which hugs its chest with its own arms.

The arms and then the chest follow where the head is led, the separate pieces fall to separate places—on the cold linoleum floor, onto naked softer arms and tight breasts, onto hard short pubic hair and thighs, into her, into Lizzie Bean, who isn't Gwen, into Lizzie Bean and at a fetus made with someone else, but it is Lizzie Bean, and he knows it and he punishes, he drives her at the floor because she isn't only his, because a baby will survive the pounding and be born not his, because his son lies on a county road, brain drowning in blood, and Eli Silver tends a wife merely broken, not dead, and then he is— it happens near the end, it happens—he is living in the wet forked body of a woman who is here and not in his mind. Struggling now to breathe and not stop, he knows that later he will know this.

Lizzie and Eli, touring the Farmers Museum at Cooperstown on a cold Wednesday afternoon, hold hands through their gloves. The giant barn of a building, displaying a six-foot fowling piece, and a Conestoga wagon, and rugs as made by forefathers, and a pioneer's kitchen, is more bitterly chilled than the brown and tan hills around Cooperstown. Their breath is smoke in the dull light, and their voices hang around them like their breath. They walk through two floors of history, pausing without agreement—they bump into each other—at axes and cornhusk brooms. They are alone in the museum, making the wooden floors creak.

Then outside, in the direction of the restored colonial print shop, they stand at the huge Cardiff Giant, planted in the fields of New York State to be dug up and displayed, a long stone hoax about missing evolutionary links. He lies in disgrace behind a mesh screen in a sort of manger. "How could anyone have been fooled by him?" Lizzie says.

"They wanted to be. Everybody wants the secret."

"What secret?"

"Any secret."

As they walk on the frozen short grass to the restored colonial inn where postcards and cocoa are sold, near the fence behind which exhibited oxen wheel slowly in their wooden yoke, Lizzie says, "We should have stayed home."

"No," Eli says, "we're being friends. We're being cultural. We're exploring each other."

"You're often undersexed, did you know that?"

"I sometimes forget to wear my body. Yes."

"You should sometimes forget to wear your mind."

That night, they are in the Silver living room. The sofa and wing chairs are covered with mail and magazines, medical protocols and supermarket fliers—it looks as if no one has lived in the house for months; the litter is the temporary sort that vacations create, as neighbors hoard junk for the owners' return. Lizzie and Eli sit on the dark-tan rug and drink from a bottle of Bâtarde Montrachet. Eli says, "No."

"Okay."

"I'm not trying to keep anything away from you."

"You are," Lizzie says. "You're allowed to. I just wondered about the details of it. I thought you might want to tell me."

"Isn't this beautiful wine? And if I don't tell you all the little terrible parts, I'm not sharing? I'm a selfish lover?"

"You're a generous lover, Eli. And you don't have to tell me anything."

"Except I'm not doing it right if I keep it to myself. Lizzie, it isn't some wonderful thing I'm saving the last bite of."

"I am not picking a fight. Finding fault. Are you?"

"You think I'm being grouchy?"

"Oh, no. I think you're private and crazy. *Your* problem is you can't *stay* crazy. Then you'd be rid of it."

"What in hell is that supposed to mean, Liz?"

"Trust me. I'm an expert. I even know you, some. The only way you'll end up glad is if you run around naked and foam at the mouth and you get somebody to lock you up and pump you full of happy juice for the rest of your life. Believe me. And I love you, incidentally."

"Incidentally, thank you. Whatever I should say. I'm somewhat embarrassed."

"By me?"

"The love-you business. I'm not used to being loved."

"That's so ugly, that kind of humility. You're used to it, Doc. You just miss not having it all the time."

Eli pours more wine for them, stalling. Then he says, "Do you *like* me?"

"Probably."

"But you do love me."

"I think so, yes."

"You're a glutton for punishment, aren't you?"

"I'm somewhat accident-prone. Do you love me?"

"This *is* embarrassing. I'll tell you what happened."

"No, thank you. I have to go home."

"Lizzie, are you mad at me?"

"You're so out of practice, you know that? You do your wooing with tongue depressors and Band-Aids. You're a hundred and fifty years old. But I'm giving you a little time. I'm generous, see. I'm desperate. I'm dumb."

"Yes, I love you."

"Thank you, Dr. Cardiff Giant."

It is another Wednesday afternoon, and Silver has stolen Lizzie from her office. She wears a tented maroon dress and a parka shell, high boots, and when she walks from his car, carrying his small rucksack while he carries the canvas bag of tools, the wind pushes her clothes against her and she looks like a woman carrying a child.

They are off the secondary road near Oneida called Bear's Pass, at the edge of an empty field which is gently mounded and empty of buildings and trees; a distant black forest helps shape the field, which is vast and rippling in October winds, and they—the swelling woman, the high man—are small against the tan-green, low-cropped grass. Lizzie watches him as he studies the ground ahead of them; when she is away from him, Silver watches her. She doesn't speak, because she's learning about his hours spent away from her; he means this afternoon as a gift, he knows her silence is work—that she means to learn how to take what he can give.

Where the small hill rises, where the winds are harsher, where the sky seems thinner and cold, he drops the tool bag and walks on cleared ground among low wooden pegs which are tagged with colored plastic labels. Heavy string runs among the stakes to make a trapezoid, almost a capital T. Near the wide end, strings are closer together, dividing the shape into square yards, each one staked in the center. Silver, in work boots, falls to his knees, but with control, and with a garden trowel he begins to slowly dig, sometimes sifting the dirt through a framed piece of screening, occasionally picking up lumps which he rubs on his flannel shirt, then setting them aside.

Fifteen minutes later, twenty minutes later, he says, "Cooking fire," putting a larger lump behind him. He digs and sifts very slowly, the winds continue, Lizzie shivers, sitting with her knees together on a folded canvas sheet from the knapsack, and Silver says, "Water pot, the edge is fluted. Nothing special." In forty minutes, he has entered notes in a pad and has moved to another square, where he digs for twenty minutes more, saying nothing, finding nothing, writing in his notebook, moving on.

When he stands to stretch, she stands too, walks to him, her

hands in the parka pockets, and leans against his arm. He hugs
her and then looks surprised at what he's done. Lizzie nods as
if agreeing with the near-alarm on his long face. But she says
only, "Most doctors play golf on Wednesday afternoons. Or—
what do they do around here?—they go to Rotary lunches."

"They see their mistresses," Silver says.

"But in motels, right? Or apartments. Not Iroquois long-
houses."

Silver hugs her again, then moves away. "I've been saving
the garbage as a treat. Anyway, a treat for me. Want to see it?"

He is away again, and she follows him, down the other side
of the slope, at the sharpest descent, where a shape of stones,
recently placed, marks the dig he starts to work at. In the
center of the crooked stone circle, on his knees, he digs roughly
at first, with a small folding shovel, and then, eight inches
down, he begins again, with a curiously awkward but delicate
motion of the wrist, to dig with the trowel, sometimes sifting,
looking for the ancient garbage of Indians.

A narrow bone comb, a pitted bear's tooth, a piece of junk
that Silver insists is a drill, a shattered stone, the edge of which
is shaped, he says, for pounding other stones into useful de-
signs, and an arrow point, long and thick, used for bringing
deer down: he finds these, and shards of water vessels, pebbles,
thin dark worms, dead root strings. And he is at a long distance
and with himself, and Lizzie, growing colder, dutifully sits and
shifts and shakes as the winds come on, bringing low dirty
clouds and darker skies.

"I'm bored," she calls, at last.

Silver looks back at her and says, "I didn't forget you, Liz."

"Yes, you did."

He rocks back onto his hams and nods his head: "A little bit,
maybe, for a minute."

"I want to go home and get warm. Can a woman this far
gone make love?"

"I believe we can work at it."

"Listen," she calls against the gray wind, "I can get some kicks from the basic perversions, too."

"I believe there are some of your basic perversions available to us."

They stand together now, and Silver draws the ground sheet around her shoulders like a shawl. "Can we get hit by lightning out here?" The clouds are lower, black now.

"Nah," he says. "I don't think so."

"No," she says, "I'd like some *assurance.*"

Silver, packing fragments and relics in the bag, standing to hug her again, says, "Then maybe we should run like hell."

He writes last entries in his notebook, picks up the rucksack and tool bag, and they walk through the first of the cold rain. Then, as the sky blinks orange-white, as thunder at the other end of the distant forest groans to begin, but falters, they run for the car, she wiggling awkwardly, an old lady in a shawl, he borne down by tools and bones and broken pots.

Friday night, at the end of the calendar sheet that hangs on the brick wall of the kitchen, and Silver, sitting at his table, alone, looking at a tall brown bag from the supermarket, bangs the ice of his empty glass against his lips. He puts more Jameson in the tumbler and sees Dolores, whom he visited that morning. Then he sees the day without her, rife with pus-filled sinuses and ECHO virus and something new, he hasn't incubated enough smears to know it, but something running through the community which gives little kids twenty-four hours of high fever and vomiting, bright sick eyes, and lymph nodes big as lima beans. He has emptied his shelves of Sudafed and V-Cillin K, guessing, he thinks he's right, but he guessed, that 250 mg doses of the V-Cillin K would get it. He's given three prescriptions for phenobarbital, to drop the fevers of infants who spiked, and whose brains can be scrambled like eggs by temperatures that run too high for too long. He had a child in convulsions and doesn't know why; he thinks to phone the hospital and thinks, too, of a neurological consult, because it could have been *grand mal,* with the pale-blue eyes rolling up and lids fluttering fast, the knees giving way, then extending like wood, the head banging on the floor, tongue sliding back and forth in saliva froth. He worked from one-fifteen to six, closing early, and glad, because his knee has ached all day, all week, despite the allopurinol he takes in 300 mg doses every morning to block his uric acid's flow into the bloodstream, where it crystallizes at the sore joints and where the grains fray at the articular surfaces of the femur, turning the knee red, making it feel broken. But he closed early for the neighborhood children, not for himself, and he tears the side of the grocery bag down, letting the plastic packets of spuri-ously colored candy spill, yellow and orange corn and Three Musketeers and black and orange leering little corn-syrup pumpkins: their irregular swollen faces make him think, despite his efforts not to, of Dolores, who swells while shrinking, one side of her face bulging out as if to receive what diminishes on the other side.

He did it again. He poured her nutriments into the sink and fed her saline solution, furtively, exactly like the thief he had become, doping her and robbing her, helping her to die. He says, inside, *Now murderer: not thief any more, murderer.* The words make no difference, though, because this is his prescrip-tion, his therapy, what he leaves off the charts but what he knows to do: kill her. Dolores was dying, now she dies more, she is closer to death, his only available gift, and it grows harder to think of her in the present tense. The present tense is always more dangerous. Dolores *was* dying this morning at the hospital when Silver fed her drugs and solution and helped her body start to stop.

So: not that Gwen now lives in Second City, Texas; not that Eli Silver, Practice Restricted to Children and Unwed Mothers, draws his Friday practice to an early close—but *lived* and *drew, waddled* and *blushed,* or *stopped for Halloween.*

The doorbell rings again: the doorbell *rang,* he realizes, and he calls out "Absolutely!" tears at plastic, dumps the candy into a huge Mexican salad bowl, carries it to the front door, where little monsters wait. When they have chanted their threats and giggled at the tall staring man and his smiles, he makes himself another drink and sits in the foyer on the flagstone floor, his back against the side of the stairway, drinking Jameson, waiting for the bell, standing, when he opens the door, with his weight shifted to the sounder knee, making bogeyman faces to chattering witches and trolls, demons and Spidermen, hunchbacks, space creatures, vampires pale with face powder, scarred harridans and bucktoothed Hulks, and most call, Trick or Treat, and some stand silent in the fright they feel because some of the children know that ghosts are walking through trees and out of street-light stanchions and up from the ooze of sewers to catch their souls or perforate their eyes or suck their breath over black tongues. They are all children—the parents stand embarrassed down the steps, away—and some he has treated from birth. They are also fear-creatures, deformed and crippled and colored vaguely wrong; and they are frightening because scared, or because of their almost recognizable faces, or because he doesn't know them all, because these strangers in artificial blood and faked friendly threat are nearly children toward whose care he must—sometimes forcing himself—labor.

He has drunk too much. He knows this not because he sees ghosts on Halloween, when his job is to feed kids candy, but because he sees the bottle of Jameson on the flagstone floor, and whiskey in his tumbler, and no fresh ice. He works nonetheless, carrying apples and bubble gum when the sweets are gone, offering bribes to goblins driven down from the hills by sallow parents from far away who will impound what is useful, apples for sauce and pies, cookies for brown-bag school lunches, the profits of haunting.

It occurs to him that he would enjoy shouting. He drinks more whiskey, and Dolores is dying, *was* dying, *was* quite close to dead, and the boy—Silver works at science and resents the intimate autumn ghosts—was dead in minutes on Route 12 while his wife, she went to Second City, Texas, thrashed in pain and the certainty that everything was wrong. Daddy'll be right back. The doorbell rings less, and he has drunk more, and it is late, maybe too late for children, it is possible that he has sat too long on the stones inside his door, uselessly waiting, but the doorbell has rung, he heard it ring, it rang, and so he opened the door, with nothing in his hand but a stick of grape-flavored gum and a small golden apple, all that was left, his eyes rolled up and fluttering, his teeth bared, his tongue gurgling monster noises, saying with twisted lips—he was defending himself—"Take your choice before I *haunt* you."

Lizzie said, "I'm not a kid, Eli."

Opening his eyes, rocking, almost letting it go, Eli, caught in the monster voice, said, "Will you please come into my house?"

5 | Natural Causes

I.R. Demby, as Phil said, "Maybe, but why?" was turning at his desk to tell Turner, "No."

Turner, a long, dark tube of muscle in his black trousers and green turtleneck, said, "You guys will have to get the de-part-mental act together on this, you know? One say Yes and one say No, but the poor student caught in the *midst* of you is the person takes the test."

I.R. wasn't smiling. He said, "You know—you *knew* we have mid-terms in October and November, and being as it's Wednesday, the fifth of November, and everybody on the floor is getting tests, and you're part of the everybody in question, you will have to do it. Suffer the same as the white folks, friend."

Phil said, "Probably, he's right."

Turner said, "Man, I get out on that *field*, I hustle my *ass* for them coaches—"

"Those," I.R. said.

"Oh, sure, *those*," Turner said. "But I can't get no more *time* for the books which I need to do all right on the examination, sir."

"Don't sound like a turkey, turkey," I.R. said.

"I'm the teacher of the course, right?"

I.R. told Phil, "Don't cave in to him."

Phil said, "But I am the teacher of the course."

Turner said, "That's why I axed."

Phil said, "Don't use cabin-nigger talk with *either* of us, Turner, all right? Mr. Demby doesn't want you to act like a professional shoeshine boy, and I don't want you to talk like one, and I don't like the way you smile when you come wangling."

"Wangling?" Turner said.

"You look like Louis Armstrong playing for a room full of crackers," Phil said, "and I don't want to feel like a cracker."

"That must be up to you," Turner said solemnly.

"Make him do it, Phil."

"I.R., I was leading up to it."

"I never do listen to Louis Armstrong," Turner said.

"Because you don't care about good music," I.R. said. "Because you listen to assholes with electric guitars. You're going to improve yourself, or I'm going to help fire your ass *out* of here."

"Excepting, he's the teacher," Turner said.

"And I'm the enemy," I.R. told him, swiveling his chair so that his back was to Turner and Phil.

"Take the test," Phil said.

"Okay," Turner said, "excepting I will fail."

And Mead Weeks, appearing at the office door, said, "You can learn success from failing, son."

I.R. put his face in his hands.

Turner did a Boy Scout about-face and, holding his back rigid, his hands at his sides, barked, "Thank you, *sirs.*" He marched hard on his heels past I.R.'s desk, past Weeks—" 'Scuse me, *sir!*"—and away.

Phil, in the silence that followed, looked at Weeks and finally said, "He's a boxer. Fast hands."

I.R. shook his head, still with his hands attached to it.

Weeks said, "I presume you're encouraging that skill to help him write faster."

And then Weeks went around the corner and down the hall, and I.R. said, over his shoulder and through his palms, "You *may* be in the wrong business. Or the wrong place."

"Both," Phil said.

"Why not?"

Leaning to his desk, looking at the wall and then at the notebook which he'd covered with his arm while talking, Phil wrote: Insulation done. Chimney cleaned. Storm windows repaired and up. Some firewood sawed, some split and stacked. Annie working on a picture, I'm sure of it. Getting ready for winter again, but better this time. No word on adoption except from her. I think I hope nothing happens. She wants it, me too —because she does. But I know I really hope nothing happens. It would be too big for us.

When L'Ordinet, in black corduroy suit, black shirt, wide tan tie, came in, Phil looked up, closed the notebook, leaned back in the wooden swivel chair, and tried to smile a kind of welcome. I.R. said, "Ho-*ho*, how's the function of criticism at the present time?"

Talking quickly, his nostrils wide and his eyes under blue-tinted, wire-framed glasses most serious, L'Ordinet said, "Don't be a pagan, I.R." He smiled with tartared teeth.

Demby said, "Don't be a Christian. No: don't be a critic."

"I can dig that," L'Ordinet said.

I.R. looked at Phil and said, "We all be brothers, 'cause we getting *day*-oun, you dig it, Phil? Hoo-*whee!* And goodbye."

I.R. Demby left, carrying his coffee mug.

L'Ordinet said, "Phil, do you understand him? I love him, but he's a little crazy. He's very sensitive."

"Poetry," Phil said. "He reads too much poetry. His nerves are affected."

L'Ordinet said, "One of the things—I wanted to talk to you about this. One of the things I do is, I spend Saturday mornings in the reading room, down at the library. I catch up on the usual magazines, and sometimes I read the little journals, the quarterlies, lit. mags, you know. And I saw these poems, this was a long time ago, but I checked up on it this weekend, I was wondering: are you the Philip Sorenson that used to publish poems? I'm thinking of *Carleton Miscellany* and it was that little one in New York—*Chelsea*? Was that you? Because there was an absolutely beautiful thing about napalm in the Plain of Jars, it captured the *entire* war—"

"No."

"It wasn't? It said you lived in New Hampshire, this Sorenson, anyway, and I know you used to live in New Hampshire, am I right? So I figured it was you."

"No. I don't write poems."

"Oh. I thought it was you."

"I don't write poetry, no."

"Oh. Hey, maybe we could have a drink some time, and talk."

Maybe only because he had said it to Turner, but maybe for the book of stuttered history he pressed his arm upon, Phil said, "No. I don't think so."

"Excuse me?"

"I don't write poems and I don't drink spirits. I'm sorry. I abstain."

When Lizzie Bean returned from the ladies' room of the Bailey Inn, Eli had ordered a Bloody Mary for each, and was looking at the notepaper that said *off Shawler's Brook*

Road. He smiled as she sat. "You look like a pregnant person," he said.

"God, I feel like one. I feel like a pregnant elephant, the way they look at me in the office. The dean, there's this dean I work under"—she looked at him and smiled—"only in the bureaucratic sense, dumbo. And he would *love* to fire me. I'm setting a bad example for the female students, you see."

"I doubt it," Eli said. "*They* never get so flustered they forget to use something."

"Rarely."

"That was an uncalled-for comment, wasn't it? I'm sorry. I apologize."

"I know you do. I know you do."

"So you think he'll can you?"

"He can't. He hates it that women fuck when they want to, but he can't find a law to claim I broke by getting knocked up."

"How about moral turpitude? Isn't that the way they fire people?"

"That's the way they fire drunk professors and men who screw coeds by bribing them with grades."

"They should fire the coeds, too."

"And arrest women for being raped? I don't think you want to have this conversation with me, Eli."

Elderly men in sport coats and ties drank martinis, students in cable-knit sweaters drank beer, and a tall slender black kid named Turner, drinking something dark with a cherry in it, prodded the burning logs in the fireplace with a long foot. A mural over the fireplace showed white men shooting Indians, and Turner saluted them all with his glass.

Eli and Lizzie ate steak sandwiches and Turner had another drink, the local businessmen hunched over smoke and murmured about land, looking up with some distress when one of the students shouted, "I can't fucking *believe* it!" The early afternoon passed, more vodka and tomato juice, more students in and out, more beer, the businessmen leaving, two tall women in elegant dresses and leather coats who talked to each other in urgent whispers, Turner finally pouring his second drink into the fire and leaving alone, drawing looks with his long limp-and-stride, and Eli Silver saying, "I wonder if this is a good time for you to tell me about the baby's father."

"What?"

"The father? The man—"

"A mistake."

"And you don't want to talk about him."

"Everybody makes mistakes, Eli."

"I'm wondering about the outcome, here. The baby. What you would tell some kid in a counseling session: the consequences."

"Every mistake has consequences."

"I'm aware of that. Thank you."

"Easy, love," she said. "We're trying to talk evasively about *me.*"

"Wholly," he said. "Second apology."

"Ditto, taken as read, forget the whole thing, but no more drinks for me. And what shall we talk about before I go back to work and you go digging?"

"I won't dig today. It froze again last night, and it'll snow later."

"What are you doing today?"

"I'm wondering about the baby. What will you do when it's born?"

She put her fingers on her chest and said, "Feed it? Do we have to call it *it?*"

"The baby."

"*It's* easier. And I don't know. I have to think about that."

"Oh, you've been thinking about it."

"By *it,* you mean what I'm going to do."

"Yes."

"Are you willing to advise me?"

"Yes."

"Are we still lovers?"

"Yes."

"And we love each other?"

"Of course we do."

"I don't mean it that way. I mean *love.*"

Eli said, "I think we should just go ahead with it."

"Have you noticed how many *its* we're dealing with today?"

"I'm not sure what to say about it—I mean, I don't know, and I want us to be together and let's see. Is that all right, Liz?"

"I don't think we have a right to insist on anything else, to tell you the truth. And it isn't that shaky. And let's just go."

"By which you mean—"

"Let's go *on,* is what I'm saying. Do I have to say that?"

"No, but it's nice to hear. I enjoy it."

"So do I. Except, I want to know what you were leading me into with all that talk about the baby, after it's born."

"Liz, your life'll change."

"You suspected that, too?"

"What I'm saying is, do you want to live with a baby?"

She sat back and her shoulders went down. Then, leaning forward, her eyes looking dark and damaged, she said, "No."

And Silver was a doctor again, he was taking care of babies. "I thought you'd say that. I'll be talking about it soon. I think I know what we'll do, if you want."

"Don't rush into it," Lizzie said, "telling me about some terrific plans you're hatching. I understand I'm only marginally involved. Come *on!*"

"I will."

"Don't act like a goddamn executive, Eli. Don't act like some kind of—*man.*"

"I'm acting like a doctor."

"Well, don't do that, either."

"Liz, it's the best I can do."

Kids reading grammar books and falling asleep, then waking. The sounds in the dormitory: loud music, mostly bass; the slamming of doors, the flushing of toilets; young men and women calling in fury that the phone call is for someone else; the slamming of books. And then, sleepy black kids reading, "We might happen to read a story for pleasure, but when we discuss it, or try to, we find—" And Canada geese calling in the black skies. Owls invisible in the forests above the college, near the quarries used for campus building stones. The roads half a mile outside Bailey were unlighted, and only the high beams of the Hawk showed the brush and bare trees between farms and trailers and occasional passing pickups. Eli Silver was braking the car near a stand of evergreens that the wind whipped. He stood at the hot radiator grill, and in the wind and the brightness of his headlights, he urinated a high thin stream, after which he spat, shaking his head, wiping his mouth—his grandfather's peasant cure for nightmares, which his father had taught him and which he had taught the boy with Gwen's face and his own long body, and which didn't always take. He had told the boy, "Really. It really works, I remember from when I was a kid just like you. You wee-wee, you spit the dream out, you flush it, and it's gone. You'll see." Leading him blind with sleep through the lighted hallway, giving him his magic for safety in the dark mind.

When he turned onto Shawler's Brook Road, he was driving slowly enough to look out the window at the swamp fringed with low bushes and stands of spruce, stripped maple, the slowly moving phosphorescent surface. Up the hill and set back from the road, the old stone house looked like a good place to be. He shifted lower and went faster than he meant to, as if to force himself out of the door and onto the wooden porch with its rockers and swinging mobile and a stiff pile of old newspapers, two sizes of Wellingtons near the door. When he knocked, and when she opened the door, he said, "Thank you."

"Did you want something?"

The heat of a Franklin stove came at him, and then the cushioned thump of a big man's stockinged feet. He knew that he was inside someone else's life again, and he thought of driving quickly on the county road toward home. "My name is Eli Silver, I'm a doctor."

"Oh," she said, keeping the door mostly closed, smiling in her safety. "Nobody here is sick. Last I *heard,* anyway. You're a medical doctor, not a Ph.D.?"

"Medical doctor," Silver said.

"Thank God you're not a Ph.D."

"I'm a baby doctor," he said, "a pediatrician. I might have some news."

"About babies?"

"You're Mrs. Sorenson?"

"Oh, my God," she said. "This isn't a mistake. I mean, you came here for *us.* "

A large scarred hand drew the door back, and the big blond bearded man stood aside, surrendering his house, and Silver slowly walked in, started happening to them.

They sat in the kitchen, half of the walls tongue-in-groove board, the upper halves a dark and sinuous pattern of wallpaper, the room dark except for the orchidaceous yellow light from the Franklin stove at the far wall, where apple wood hissed as its sap boiled. Phil leaned out of a small low wooden chair, Annie stood near the pile of split firewood, and Eli sat at the far side of the kitchen table. They all drank tea without sugar or milk, as if someone were ill. Nobody smoked, and nobody spoke; Phil watched Annie stand in place, acting calm; Eli looked at the fire.

Then Phil said, "Ten o'clock—"

"Nine-thirty-five," Annie said.

"No," Eli said, "they don't make surprise calls to check on you. They'll telephone you and set up a second interview at the regional office, sometimes at this office they use in the hospital. Mrs. Podolak does it—well, her secretary calls, usually, but she does the interview. It's all right, they understand a good deal about people's dignity. You've met her. It could still happen, in six months or a year, a year and a half. And then—I'm sure you'd do all right. Then you'd have to wait maybe a couple of years."

"Unless we picked an older kid?" Annie said.

Her tone was combative, and Phil shuffled his feet and lifted an arm as if to calm her. But Eli only said, "Oh, they'd love it if you could give one of those children a good home. But it's so damned hard. But I didn't come here to catch you by surprise, I don't think. I really don't. And I didn't come to foist off unwanted kids on you. Yes, I did. No: not unwanted. I know a child. I know a *mother*, the child is on its way. She can't take care of it. She isn't in a position to raise a child. She is a lovely, educated, healthy woman who simply couldn't raise a child. She's a patient of mine."

"I thought you were a baby doctor," Annie said.

"Well, she's carrying a baby." Eli smiled, and Phil did too, sat back. "It would be a private adoption."

Annie said, "One of those black-market deals? I read about one. They flew this baby in from Arkansas, and these parents, this couple, went down to the airport and picked her up—it was a girl baby, they picked her up like an air-freight package. They paid ten thousand dollars for this *package*. Some lawyer in New York had this airport thing going—"

Phil said, "I'm sure this is something else."

"This is something else," Eli said. "It would be a straight, legal, honorable, exciting private adoption. You should do it with a lawyer, I can help you find one you trust. You meet me, or anybody else I designate whom you trust, say it's at the lawyer's office. You see, you mustn't see the mother and she mustn't see you."

"That's right," Annie said. "It would have to be a secret."

"It would be a secret," Eli said. "And the lawyer would file papers for you with the county—family court, they call it here. Sometimes it's called surrogate's court. The mother, someplace else now—the mother doesn't see you. I have to say she's in the area, really close. Maybe too close. But I know that won't be a problem. I can guarantee it won't. This would be a private adoption, and we can do it any way we like. I can see to that. The mother signs some release forms, and you sign some forms at the lawyer's and he files them for you. After a little while, the judge interviews you, you hold the baby on your lap and the judge looks both of you over, and then *he* signs something, and that's the magic."

Phil and Annie looked over as if Eli had farted or started to weep, because his body was in the tone of his voice, throat narrowed, sinuses leaked, blood jumped into his face and thickened his voice. "The judge says something like *I grant this*, something along those lines, and in a few weeks, sometimes it can happen sooner, you get a photocopy of a birth certificate—your baby's name and birth date, and under *Parents*, it says you. It's birth, it's a kind of birth, it really is. And that's it. And when your baby is old enough to understand, as soon as it knows what the words mean, or can even start to *think* about them, you tell the kid it's adopted and that you said, 'Give me *that* one, *that's* the one I love.' Because with a little luck, you know, it really works that way. It does."

Silver's face was red, his hands were trembling as he forced them around his mug of tea.

Annie was saying, "Why us?" and "How come you

came here *now?*" and "What else do we have to do?" and "Did—" and she was stuttering, most of what she said was noise, and the words didn't fall entirely in the room.

Phil was the one who wept. He rocked on his chair so that it tilted dangerously backward, his long legs pushed hard at the stained-dark floor planks, and his eyes—they were small and blue, pouched beneath with blue-black rings of worry and fatigue—were wet and running. He pawed with the back of a large hand at one eye, sniffed deep, let the chair settle to the floor.

Annie sat, her legs wide, on the low stack of split apple. It settled beneath her, but she balanced herself and looked at Eli, not Phil; she looked away from Phil when she said, "There must be—strings? There must be something imperfect about all of this."

"Just us," Eli said, very low. He looked up and blinked rapidly, as if in brighter light. "The woman, the mother, is very healthy. The law is the law, the procedure is pretty much what I said. And you want a baby to adopt. You want a baby, period. And I'm just helping out."

Phil pinched the end of his nose and cleared his throat, said softly, "Why?"

"Why am I doing it? Like this?"

"No," Phil said.

"Why am I doing it at all?"

Phil said, "That. And then, why us?"

"Mrs. Podolak liked you in the first interview. The second one would usually be to make certain, that's her own rule, not a county rule. But she liked you, she decided to break her own rule. She asked me to arrange this privately, in fact. That's one thing. The other thing is, I happened to be—no: I meant to be here, just a little earlier. And I should have called. It just worked out this way, more or less. I think she's right." Eli waved his hand at the fire, at the room, at them.

"And I'm helping the mother, I want her baby to have a good life."

"We'd try and do that," Phil said.

Eli said, "Yes, I think so."

Annie said, "Disposable diapers, right?"

"They're more sanitary," Silver said. "And you don't risk allergic reactions to certain soaps. You don't worry about getting the wash water hot enough to kill off bacteria. Yes. Unless you think you'd enjoy washing diapers. Some mothers like that."

"I don't even know how to pin them *on*," Annie said. She was smiling and sitting straight.

Eli sipped at his cold tea, Phil reached for his mug, which was on the floor, then let it stay. Annie sat tall, as if the logs she rode were moving straight but fast. Eli rinsed his mouth, the staleness of the long day, with the sour, acidic tea.

"This is *hap*pening this way," Phil said.

And then a silence, and then Annie: "Doctor."

"Silver. Eli Silver."

"Dr. Silver, it's a Caucasian baby?"

"The mother's white."

"And the father is too," she said for him.

Silver paused, then tried to camouflage his sudden apprehension of ignorance, of work done clumsily, of pure mistake, by drinking more tea and flushing it through his teeth before noisily swallowing. "Yup," he said. "Yes, sir."

"I don't care if he isn't," Phil said.

"Well, you might," Silver said.

Phil shrugged his shoulders, bit the ends of his mustache, rubbed the whiskers at his jaw. Silver studied the stump of Phil's thumb.

Annie said, "How long do we wait?"

"Because it's tough, around here, raising a black child. It could be tough."

"Not if we love him," Phil said.

"You know it's a him?" Annie said. "So do I."

Phil said, "I'd love a girl. Or a boy. Or half of each. Both."

Annie said, "How long would it be?"

"It happens fast," Eli said. But he wasn't listening to himself; he was seeing, as if for the first time that night, the sweatshirt Annie wore: faded and black, a yellow and white bottle tilted across the chest, the words curving over it and under it, faded too, but legible: SOUTHERN COMFORT.

Phil watched him stare, then turned to look at her, too. Annie said, again, "And the father—"

But Eli, looking, said, "So here we all are."

Turner read the exam again, opened his bluebook, opened his fountain pen, scratched on the page, shook the pen, capped it. "Anybody got a pen?" he said.

Phil flipped a ballpoint pen from a local Texaco station across the room and Turner caught it. He looked at Phil and shook his head, then bent to the bluebook again. He wrote slowly, consulting the mimeographed question sheet, wrote some more, perhaps a short paragraph's worth, then stopped. He picked up the question sheet and slowly, carefully, smoothing the folds, shaped it into an eleven-inch paper airplane and sailed it across the room. It hit the blackboard, where Phil had scrawled TIME, and it fell onto the chalk ledge.

One of the students, not looking up, said, "Air disaster."

"Everybody died," another said.

The Puerto Rican kid laughed out loud and looked around the room, saying, "I got to go on automatic pilot myself."

And someone in the back cried, "My *brains* was on board. What do I do *now?*"

Phil stood and walked across the first row of desk chairs,

collecting bluebooks while pens still wrote on them. The kids watched, Phil said nothing, walked the second row, kneeing chairs out of his way, to collect more bluebooks. He took Turner's without commenting, then wove his way to the back, where most of the class sat, as if distance meant safety.

At the front of the drafty room, its windows frosted from body heat and breath, Phil dropped the bundle of booklets into a dark-green metal wastebasket. "I can't ask you to write about H. G. Wells and independent clauses when we've all just witnessed such an unnerving event. Take off."

And when the room was empty, the hallway filled with hoots and banging feet, then echoes of ringing metal stair risers, Phil said to Turner, still sitting in his chair, "Come here."

Turner stood a few feet from him, his arms hanging loosely at his sides. Phil turned his left side toward Turner, dropped his right hand and made a fist, raised his left, started edging in, dragging his right foot. Turner said, "You kidding me? You *that* angry?"

"No," Phil said, tapping Turner on the cheek with the open fingers of his left hand, "I'm not mad." Turner went into a stance and started moving his head, feinting, ducking back. Phil caught him again, hit Turner's head with an open right lead, dropped back into his stance, and poked him again with a sloppy left.

Turner didn't smile, his eyes were frightened, his rage—at the test, at his failure, at Phil for forcing questions, at the craziness he endured—was in his tears, which the loose slaps could not have caused. "It ain't fair, Mr. Sorenson, you know it ain't fair. We not *allowed* to hit the teachers."

Phil moved in, as if to come up from underneath, then hugged Turner, pulled him to his chest and squeezed him steadily and firmly, but with no hurt intended, and Turner stayed where he was.

"Don't say ain't," Phil said. "And don't hit. I was teasing you. I'm sorry. But listen." He released Turner, wiped at

Turner's tears with his ruined hand, then stopped and stepped farther back. "I embarrassed you, and I shouldn't have—I'll learn more about that. But listen: you read the books I tell you to read. You *study* when you have to. I don't want you wasted here. Work out with me this afternoon, and you get to hit me if you can. Maybe you can, all right? And then I'm reschedul-ing the test, and everybody's taking it, and you are, too. You remember what Mr. Demby said?"

Turner shrugged. His face was a mask.

"Then remember what *I* said. You do it all, and when you get out of here, and I mean you to stay for four years and hack it, then you *decide,* you get to *vote* on your life. I'm sorry I scared you."

"I wasn't scared," Turner said. "I wasn't but deciding how long to wait before I put you down."

"Okay," Phil said. "You meeting me in the gym?"

"I probably might end up there," Turner said. "But you come on like a neo-colonialist, you know that?"

"*That's* a word," Phil said.

"Oh, I know the words," Turner said.

Eli buzzed for Ada and told her to send for the father, Walt. "And a priest," he called after her. "He'll want a priest."

"Priests we got," Ada called back.

It had gone on too long for him to weep, but he rubbed his eyes as if he'd wept nevertheless. He looked at her tiny fingers and bone-wrists, they were curved as if she were an infant in sleep. The pink lids were locked, the mouth slightly open. He turned her face on the pillow so that she lay on top of the tumor, so that her father wouldn't look at what had eaten her while Silver had forced her to starve—had *helped* her, he said to himself, being fair. Had *killed* her, he told himself. Another victim for Dr. Doom, he crowed. In his nighttime mind he pranced across a stage like a rock singer in tight pants, riding his microphone, yawping and bleating and whining nearly in tune: Dr. Doom. Another. Metastasis of the pediatrician, crazy cells, and water salty enough to season a hard-cooked egg, yes, ma'am, and a letter from the cardinal's actual *secretary*, promising prayers, and lovely Pope John on the jigsaw board, everything fits together, folks, when you ride the friendly skies of biochemical wonderment to Second City, Texas

where the babies bloom

and the oil rigs boom

in the hospital room

with Dr. Doom. He pulled the stethoscope apart and whipped the pieces past the bed at the closet. Then he went to the closet, removed the hidden bottle of solution, and carried it to the sink, was pouring when Ada returned.

"Can I do something, Eli?"

"No," he said, "I'm just cleaning up. Thank you."

"Is this something you want me to know about?"

He handed the bottle to Ada. "We don't need this," he said.

"Should I know about this?"

He leaned against the sink as if to sit. "Sure," he said. "What would you like to know?"

Ada dropped the bottle into the garbage pail. She shook her head and smiled. "I wouldn't know where to begin," she said.

"No," he said, "I wouldn't either. Start with your birthday. When's your birthday?"

"August. Why?"

"Happy birthday."

"Same to you, Eli."

"Thank you very much. Did you tell Walt?"

"He knew when he heard who it was. He's coming, he'll be here soon."

"Happy birthday to Walt, too."

"All right."

"Happy birthday to me, don't forget me."

"I said it already, Eli."

"Yes, you did. Did I thank you?"

"Uh-huh. Why don't we go someplace else now?"

"Can't take it, huh?"

"You know how women get about these things."

"Oh, boy. Ada, this one was tough. This one was a goddamn *bastard.*"

"You did all right," she said. "You did it all. Nothing was enough, and you knew it six months ago, and maybe we could go back and look at some charts and write some orders."

"The old hard-bitten nurse routine, huh? Very good. Very boring and very tiresome and very unspontaneous and very true. I think you need a vacation, but you're right. You're right."

"Let's go back to the station and do charts, Eli."

"Let's not treat me like I'm hysterical, how's that one?"

"Eli, did you hear the one about the bishop and the choir boy?"

"You gonna tell me something filthy, Ada?"

"Perversion is in the eye of the beholder."

"And the mouth. And the nose."

"In this particular case, in the armpit."

"*Arm*pit perversion! I love it already. You hear this one during Mass, you old harridan?"

"Did you say ass?"

"Ada, why not: the ass too."

"That's why I liked working with doctors, all these years. They're a better class of individual." They went into the hall and Ada pulled the door shut behind them. "But only if you stay healthy," she said.

Barbara, Bedelia, Jeptha, Jonathan, Sophronia, and Jerome, Sloane, Burke, Reynolds, and Annie was thinking, perhaps they'd call it Boy for a while, or Girl, but that was too much like their friends coming through Vermont and New Hampshire during the sixties—thin people in fringed clothes that smelled of smoke, driving rusted vans and dented VW camper-buses, eyes wide with amphetamines, gabbling for hours while eating thick sandwiches and drinking beer, smiling at naked children named Sunflower and Harmony, talking about good teaching gigs and communes, calling a mill race a visual high, disappearing into Kalamazoo and Albuquerque and Woodstock, not coming back, sending cryptic postcards—HERE WE ARE, MAYBE—and then the long silence. Mitering molding for the downstairs bathroom, Annie said, "We'll use the squarest names we can think of. Being lucky is square."

Nobody answered her because Phil was outside, shoveling heavy wet snow from their drive. She smelled the coffee that warmed on the stove, the high spice of burning apple wood, the stuffy heat of old radiators, the freshness of sawed softwood. She nailed the molding at the base of the bathroom wall, making the rhythm of her hammering a regular household music, and she sang the syllables of old-fashioned names, keeping time.

Mead Weeks II and his father, one in a sling and the other stooped as if injured, looked at the snowblower that wouldn't start. The father shivered, the boy smiled, and they stood in the drifts of their driveway, squinting into the granules of ice that blew in the wind. Mead Weeks II said, "These machines are a drug on the market." At *drug*, the father turned to stare at his son. Turner, in sweatsuit and watch cap and heavy boots, jogged past the house, one of six on University Drive with a sunken living room. Mead Weeks II saluted with his unslung fist, and Turner shook his head, smiling, running on. Chairman Mead Weeks looked after him.

L'Ordinet, wearing a corduroy sport coat over his white Irish turtleneck and a Princeton scarf draped over his shoulders, carrying a green canvas book bag, entered the library's Saturday hush. In the reading room, he folded his scarf and blew on his fingers, selected some small magazines, and, sitting near the unlighted fireplace, turned on a bridge lamp and looked at poems. When he found something about courage and death, he copied lines in his notebook. Often, he looked up, inspecting the women who passed and letting himself be seen to inspect.

And Eli Silver conducted his Saturday clinic, which was mainly for allergy shots, but at which he also saw children taken suddenly ill. In room 2, an eight-year-old boy lay stripped to the waist, face down, his back scratched with the twenty scrapes of a test for local allergies. Billie weighed an infant who hadn't eaten enough for three days. The hospital telephoned with a patient's X-ray results. Silver took serum from his small refrigerator, measured out syringe loads, and bruised the muscles of children, keeping them from sinus infections caused by allergy. The boy who was being tested had dripped an infection and, two weeks later, after the mildest of sore throats, had slowly stopped eating and had gone gray-pale. He had begun to limp on the stairs and to drag his knees when walking to school. The strep, invading the muscle joints, hadn't yet damaged the heart. But the streptococci were waiting in the cardiac tissue, and Silver wanted to prevent another infection, and the noise he would then hear in the stethoscope, the husky whistle of a damaged valve. So the boy lay with his face on his arms and tears in his eyes while Silver scratched his back and poured in allergens to see what was in the air that hurt him.

But he didn't stay in room 2, and he didn't stay in the corridor, laughing loudly and teasing the children out of their pain. He went to his office and phoned Lizzie Bean in Bailey, saying hello, answering questions and asking some, and then, closing his eyes, saying, "I need to know about the father, Liz."

"Are we talking about my baby?"

"Yes, ma'am."

"Eli, *why?*"

"Your baby is going to be adopted."

"It is?"

"I think so, yes."

She waited, he kept his eyes closed. Then she said, with a cold calm, "But I didn't *know* you were my father, Eli. And that it was 1875, and I was twelve years old, and people were deciding these things for me."

"Honey, we talked about it."

"Around it, we talked all the way around it half a dozen times, but you see, nobody *asked* me."

"I said—"

"You said did I think I wanted to live with a baby."

"And you said no."

"You did *not* ask me if I would put my baby up for adoption."

"But you have to, right? I mean, you feel like you have to. You knew this was going to happen, Liz."

"That isn't it."

"Sure it is. What?"

"This is my life, and the baby's. *My* baby's. I have to decide about it. Everything. My sweet Jesus, Eli, I can't believe it. I can't believe *you.* I thought we were lovers."

And he said, "You and the other guy were lovers. That's why you have a baby you don't know what to do with—what you should do. And I'm trying to help you, Liz."

She waited again, then in a low voice—fury, or defeat—she said, "I believe there's a word for what you're on your way to doing here, Eli."

"Oh, yeah. There must be one."

"Iatrogenics, they call it. Am I right? Iatrogenic medicine."

Eli Silver leaned back in his chair, as if the muscles of his chest and shoulders had been slowly cut. "I wouldn't call it that, Liz. Oh, please. Look—"

"Which if I am not mistaken means when a doctor treats somebody for something, and he knows he's making a new problem, he does it anyway. The doctor becomes the disease."

"I know about that."

"Oh, yes. I'm sorry, Eli. I really am. But you're doing it to me. You don't *think* so."

"Honey, I'm trying to *help!*" He heard his shout and swiveled his chair around to face the bookshelves, so that his voice wouldn't carry out the open door and into the corridor of children and their bored parents, waiting for Saturday to start. *Renal Disorders in Infants,* he read. *Handbook of Infant Formulas. Etiology of the Shock Syndrome.* He said, much lower, "I really am."

"I know you are. I know you are."

"What shall I do, Liz?"

"You should have talked to me about it more. See, I'm *not* a patient. You aren't my doctor."

"That's how we started it, though."

"Yes. Your facts are right, you're correct. I think you're right about the baby, even. Probably. Probably, we'll do it, what you said. I'll think about it, and you—no, I'll call you. I'll think about it, and we'll talk. I want to ask you some questions first. Then I'll think about it, and I'll tell you what I decide. Probably you're right. And then we'll do it like a doctor and her patient, except the patient will tell you what happens before you make any more decisions."

"That's fine, Liz. And then?"

"Then? Then, like you said, Eli: doctor and patient."

"But *then?*"

"Oh, that," she said. *"Che sarà."*

"Excuse me?"

"Italian, chum. It means—I'm saying this is about what happens next, and I will let you know. I don't like you any more right now, Eli. Goodbye, Eli, all right?"

Annie leaned against the bathroom wall and whistled, thinking, *Elizabeth, Elvira, Evan, Ernest,* and when Phil slammed the door shut and let firewood clatter to the kitchen floor, she called, "We have to make out wills now. And change the medical insurance. We have to buy stuff."

Stacking the split wood, Phil held a chunk in his five-fingered hand and, with the other, made an incomplete fist and knocked on the wood three times.

"Phil?"

6 | In a Different Vein

On St. Valentine's Day, all the snow melted from the streets in Bailey, leaving only black-spotted ice mounds four and five feet high on front lawns, shoved there by the plows. The skies brightened, the dirty mounds began to melt, undergraduates wore only woolen shirts and down-filled vests, the gutters ran with water and roofs began to leak. Then the skies hardened and dropped, a slimy rain fell, with it the temperature, and the ice mounds rigidified in new and tortured shapes. The streets grew slick with half-hardened ice, which melted at first and then froze solid into gray-white ruts. The streets and sidewalks shone in the evening, under street lights, and the morning looked only slightly less dark than the night. Old people stayed inside for fear of slipping, school was closed because the buses couldn't steer on the slithery hill roads, and, though everyone was home, Bailey in the morning was deserted-looking, quiet, an aftermath.

But by ten in the morning, high-school kids were flopping sleds in the middle of the street, Turner had climbed with the aid of two dining-room forks to the top of a hill near the quarry so he could slide down, hooting, on a large round dinner tray, and Phil and Annie had made love and gone back to sleep. Mead Weeks, having walked to work using a shepherd's stick purchased on sabbatical in Wales, was writing a memorandum. Eli Silver had skidded to work, twenty miles away from Bailey, and was reading the chart of a fifteen-year-old boy whose hands and face had been burned when a wood stove in a trailer had set the plastic wall panels on fire. Elizabeth Bean was talking to herself in her office while she reviewed the files of freshmen on academic probation. Ambulance traffic to the hospital was heavy, other traffic slight. I. R. Demby, his Pontiac having slid tail-first into a bank of ice off Route 12, was thumbing his way to work, shivering. L'Ordinet, keeping his weight on the heels of his insulated Sorels, giving in to temperature by wearing a heavy coat, the kind worn by businessmen over suits, was walking the streets of Bailey.

Tall and broad-shouldered, looking lean of hip even in his coat, aiming his way with the long flared nose, L'Ordinet, serious in metal-framed glasses, was composing. He was saying something to himself about radical moralities, which needed differentiation from situation ethics. Situation ethics needed looking up, but what he said about radical moral needs had to be different from anything said before; he was composing, and he was having difficulty—not with something soluble, like a threatening arcane phrase, but with Elizabeth Bean.

And no matter where he wandered, he was on his way to her, and he lost track—the writings of Anne Frank, of Father Bonhoeffer—until he repeated to himself nothing more than *radical, radical,* looking at stalled cars and their tires, saying, finally, *radial,* and quickening his careful steps toward school, thinking at last of nothing to say.

L'Ordinet's name was Horace, but he called himself H. L'Ordinet in articles, and signed himself H in his letters. He had a comment about the film *M* which he sometimes offered when people talked about the use of *H.* He also had traumatic bursitis of the shoulder, because he had torn a bursal sac in college, lifting a fat nursing student through the top of a Volkswagen convertible. The calcium deposits grated as his arm swung, and in such wet weather, with the cold so deep, he walked with a wounded tightness to keep the ligament from scraping.

He took the tinted glasses off and rubbed them with his fingers as he entered Elizabeth Bean's office, walking past a snow-drenched, frowning, finger-snapping Turner, who waited in the hall. The office was a small room decorated with posters from museums in New York, Rome, and Florence, and with taped-on clippings about student unrest. The desk was stacked with computer printouts and memos in black or purple ink. On top of one stack was a coffee mug that said ENOUGH! Rocks from different beaches, all the same dove-gray, were on the windowsills and a coffee table, among the bright ferny plants. Lizzie Bean was on a small shabby sofa, frayed green tweed, reading a booklet entitled *The AAUP and the Rights of Students.*

L'Ordinet shut her door and opened his coat, adjusted the glasses on his nose, and said, "We need some conversation, Liz." His voice ranged high, his breath came quickly; it always did, he sounded excited about everything. "Would you talk to me?"

Lizzie sat awkwardly, her legs slightly spread and extended to accommodate the bulk of her pregnancy. "Sure," she said, "it's been some time."

"I thought what you told me—what do you mean, it's been some time? We talked to each other this week, the beginning of this week, right? No, last week. Well, we *talked.* I want to talk about what we talked about. Babies. Abortion. *Adoption,* for godsakes."

"Relax, Horace."

"Does it make you feel good to use that name? It's an aggressive thing to do. And when you tell me to relax, it implies you're calm and I'm not, which is also an aggressive act."

Lizzie put the booklet on the sofa and clasped her hands around herself. She said, "Shall we get a referee?"

L'Ordinet walked to the far corner of the office, where a high bookshelf ended, near a dirty window that looked down the ice-covered hill toward Bailey's main street, Route 12, which turned north and went to the Adirondack Mountains with some dismal stops on the way. Leaning his shoulders into the corner, wincing as the weight went onto the injured bursa, L'Ordinet shook his head. "We should be able to talk sometimes," he said.

"That's what I was thinking several months ago."

"I panicked," he said. "I was panicking."

"So was I."

"You're pretty goddamned calm now, it seems."

"That's because I made some decisions."

"Sure," he said. "You decided to keep our baby. Then you decided to get rid of it."

"*Your* language," Lizzie said. "I guess you're welcome to it. But you left out the other decision. It was the one that came first: I decided I didn't need you. And the baby's *mine.*"

"Not unless you're the Virgin Mary," he said, panting a little.

"No, you don't somehow *look* like the Holy Ghost. Our relationship was far from spiritual, Horace."

"The child belongs to us *both.*"

"No. Too late. I didn't see you around four or five months ago. Remember? You signed away your share, you're bought out, this"—she rubbed her stomach as a satisfied child might —"is mine."

"It's like all these women who decide to get abortions. These unilateral decisions—the father never even gets *asked.*"

"Horace," she said, "you *wanted* me to have an abortion. Don't come in here whining about uniwhatchamacallit decisions and the higher codes of conduct. All that moral horseshit. You're out of the picture. You're a hit-and-run driver. And okay. Okay. You made your moves, and I made mine, and I should have known, and you should have known, and we all should have known, and now I'm doing something. I'm not talking, I'm *do*ing. And that's it. That's the decision. I made it. The end."

"And some shit-kicking farmer, some fifty-cent-an-hour pants presser's going to have *my* kid and teach it how to watch car races and drink beer. No, sir."

"No, ma'am, you mean. But I thought you were a democrat, Horace. Remember the family of man? The network of human relationships? The common morality? Your expertise in those matters is extensive, according to several articles by you."

She had been wedging herself forward as she talked, moving to answer the ringing phone. As she stood and leaned forward, L'Ordinet came to the desk and hit the telephone with his fist, kept his fist down. "Leave it," he said. "We have to get to be reasonable, Lizzie. Let it go, let's talk. Please."

"Take your hand off the phone, please."

"You're talking to *me*," he yelled.

"Please let go of the telephone and stop shouting."

He picked the telephone up with both hands and slammed it to the desk. He did it again, wincing, his eyes shut, his face screwed tight. He brought the phone down again, breathing very hard, but it continued to ring.

Lizzie picked up a wooden ruler with a yellow metal edge and brought it down on his wrist, on his knuckles, on his fingers, on his wrist again. Blood came from the very thin cuts and when L'Ordinet saw his rich redness, he squawked—it was a high, thin bird noise—and with his bleeding hand, while the phone still rang, he punched her in the shoulder. She fell backward, onto the arm of her desk chair, off it and backward again, clattering the venetian blinds and holding on to the windowsill. The phone stopped ringing. L'Ordinet came forward, and when he was in front of her, he punched again, in the shoulder again, then again, once more. Lizzie was on her knees now, covering her face. L'Ordinet smacked the side of her head, did it again, and stopped only when Lizzie's head jerked back and knocked a potted plant off the windowsill and onto the yellow nylon rug.

"Don't," L'Ordinet said. "Don't." He was pulling for breath now, and his face and body shook. He rubbed the outraged shoulder, saying, "Don't."

Lizzie stayed the way she was, on her knees, face covered with arms, neck bowed.

"You did this," L'Ordinet said. "Don't blame this on *me*. You did this."

Slowly, Lizzie uncovered her face. It was swollen and red and wet with tears and smeared mucus. She looked up at him, and while he watched, as if he were nailed in place, she slowly seized the flowerpot and drew it back toward her shoulder and, with awkwardness but great strength, planted it in L'Ordinet's crotch. Then she sat back, slumping, while he bent and whispered, coughed. She closed her eyes and took deep breaths. L'Ordinet backed toward the door. When she heard the door lock click, she said, "Your fine, fertile balls."

Lizzie moved her legs, after he was out, and then she pulled herself up on the arm of the desk chair and sat. The telephone rang again and she picked it up, pushed the red Hold button and watched the light blink. She wiped her face with tissues and ordered her desk. The telephone light went out. Turner knocked as he opened the door and said, "Good morning?" His jacket and trousers were wet from the long slide at the quarry, his face was taut with cold, he smiled a public smile. "Good morning? Mizz Bean? Could we do some talking about this personality crisis I been having? I don't but get here and I be on academic *pro*-bation. I can't play ball if that the case. And I can't af*ford* to give that scholarship up, if I want to stay in school and grow up white and well-adjusted. I am having this crisis, see. Can you get me off or something?"

"Mr. Turner," she said, very low, "please get your ass out of my office and come back tomorrow."

"Say *what?*"

"You're the best-adjusted freshman I ever met. Your act is so together you could go on Broadway."

"Lady—"

"Mizz Bean was fine. Goodbye."

"Mizz *Bean*—"

"Later."

"Later?"

"Later."

Turner stared, then smiled a different smile, a tenser one, more full of fun. He nodded and said, "You one hell of a woman, you know?"

Picking up the flecked ruler, dropping it again, Lizzie said, "What in Christ could you possibly know, Mr. Turner? Talk about my womanhood when your testicles descend, all right? And *later.*"

Turner clapped his hands with delight, shook his index finger loosely in the air—You're Number One—and left. Lizzie swiveled in her chair to look at the flowerpot on the rug.

She said, "I am one hell of a woman."

Don Beverly took the call from the ER, and Eli Silver, downstairs after ward rounds, stood in the doorway to watch him work, because he had heard "traffic accident" as

Beverly, unshaven and sleepless, walked past. "Fucking cars," he told Silver and the duty nurse, who was new and anxious.

The ambulance crew was from the New Sherburne volunteer fire department, one man dressed in a business suit, the other in green mechanic's overalls, both eager for emergency, neither particularly trained. They slammed the litter against the partly open pavilion door, and the man on the litter cried out and clutched his thigh, though—Silver saw it at once—it was the tibia that was broken. While Beverly and Silver took over the coffee-colored man, the bridge of whose nose was pale with his pain and whose lip was bitten through and bleeding onto his chin, the nurse took information from the man in overalls.

"He was walking in the road. Probably hitchhiking from Binghamton, they get a lot of them doing that. It's the only way they get to see their families in Utica, a lot of them."

Beverly slowly emptied the air-pressure splint they'd applied while Silver loosened the tourniquet, a length of plastic pipette, and handed the equipment to the volunteer in the steel-gray suit and wide maroon tie. "There he goes," Silver said, pressing with his hand on the pouring vein. Silver said, "OR, Don?"

Beverly, looking into the rolling eyes of I. R. Demby, said, "He's almost out, I get tenderness in the ribs and Christ knows what else happened in there. Let's see if we can tie the bleeder here and then do the rest."

They pushed the litter into the room filled with plaster dust and crutches and saws, and the nurse, dismissing the volunteers, followed them, turning on the operating light and setting up the portable infusion stand. "Five percent?" she said, hanging the bag of glucose in saline.

Silver looked at Beverly, whose call it was. Beverly nodded, and then Silver said, "Find us an anesthesiologist, please."

She said, "Which one, Doctor?"

"We only *got* one in town, the others commute. Call the

reception desk and tell them what we want and say stat, will you do that?" Silver said. His hand and wrist were soaked in venous blood. His trousers were bloody, and blood was on the floor.

As she left, the nurse said, "His name is Demby."

"Hello, Mr. Demby," Beverly said.

Silver held a wad of sponges on the pierced leg. He said, "I can feel pieces floating in there, Don. I think we should open the damn thing up all the way and do it all at the same time."

"And an ortho man—and we only got one of *those*," Beverly called to the nurse. He was at the top of the table on which Elizabeth Bean had sat, sobbing. He turned on the wall valve labeled *Oxygen* and started intubation into Demby's trachea, saying, "There you go, pal."

"Smell it, Don."

"What?"

"Remember the guy in—where was it? Someplace in Pennsylvania?—he didn't know they screwed up in the wall pipes and he put six of them away with too much nitrous oxide and no oxygen in the mix before somebody figured out the builders made a mistake."

"Jesus and *Mary*," Beverly said, removing the tubes, sniffing, shaking his head, then reinserting. "It's okay. What a *mind* you got, Eli."

But Silver, holding the bloody wad down with one hand, was scrubbing the area around it with Betadine, then irrigating the wound with sterile saline. Beverly pumped in the tetanus shot.

The nurse walked in, said, "On the way," looked at the setup, then took sterile packages from a cupboard and a scalpel from the autoclave, handed implements to Silver while Beverly wrapped the cuff of a sphygmomanometer around Demby's arm, which the nurse had exposed. As Silver started to cut, she placed a sterile green sheet over the leg. Beverly pumped for a blood-pressure reading.

"Isn't this fun?" Beverly said.

"I'm in it," Silver said. "You want to do this? I'm supposed to take care of kids."

"You cut nice," Beverly said. "You ever train to be a jock?"

"I didn't think I could stand all the indoor work," Silver said.

"That's a little joke," Beverly told the nurse. But she was working, and so he called out, "We got him at 70 over 20, which is pretty good, considering. Eli, can you spare Miss—"

"Mrs. Wharton."

"Thank you. Could Mrs. Wharton swing the X ray over so we can shoot his gut and see what we got?"

"It's a nick," Eli said, "go ahead."

"We got him at 50 over 15, he's shocky. Would you bring the tube down, dear, and do the flat plate of the abdomen first? The apron's on the bone saw."

She put the black lead apron on and moved the ceiling-mounted X-ray machine over Demby.

"I could close it," Eli said. "But I think we should get at the bone." It gleamed at the puckered incision where Eli sponged. "Don," he said, "should I be using suction on this?"

"Shit," Beverly said. He pumped for blood pressure again, very quickly, and Eli at once took a stethoscope from the wall behind him and moved up on Demby's body to listen to the heart.

"You get a lower one, Don?"

Beverly squeezed the bulb again, nodding.

Eli moved the stethoscope and listened to Demby's lungs, tearing more shirt away as he did. Bending close, closer, nearly lying on Demby as though he might hear better, Eli said, "Don?"

"Son of a bitch," Beverly said.

"He's having an untoward reaction?" Eli said.

"He wants to die," Beverly said. He turned off the nitrous oxide valve and increased the oxygen flow. "The son of a bitch wants to die," Beverly said. He snapped his fingers at Eli and made a squeezing motion.

Eli went to the far wall and took an air bag from the cupboard. He plugged the bag to the intubation apparatus and began to squeeze. Beverly administered Keflin to combat sepsis. Eli said, "Are we doing this right?"

Tench, the ortho man, just arrived, was washing up, watching them. He was extremely small with large hands and big square dark-rimmed glasses. Approaching Demby's legs, not looking at Silver or Beverly, Tench looked at the shattered tibia and whistled, then said, "I might just as well."

"He's reacting untoward, Doctor," the nurse said.

Tench, leaning in, said, "I might just as well, anyway. If he comes through okay, he can walk on it sometime."

"Looking possible," Beverly said.

"He'll do it," Eli said.

"Nice," Tench said, prodding.

Demby's arms jerked and he came up from the slowed metabolism of shock, momentarily emerging from the seethe of his body. He gagged and wheezed, his arms and legs jumped, and he started keening in a high weak voice, then shuddered and his breath hissed out. Beverly pumped for pressure while Eli listened to the heart. He waggled his horizontal hand from side to side. Beverly said, "It's coming up." He pumped again. Silver, listening, waggled his hand. "No, I think it's coming," Beverly said.

Eli said, "Halothane plus O_2 as an alternate?"

Beverly said, "It would be great if we could ask somebody like an anesthesiologist."

"Sheer luxury," Eli said.

"Do him some Pentothal," Tench said.

Eli said, "I don't know. It's too risky. You think?"

Beverly said, "You want to risk it?"

"What the fuck," Tench said. "Nurse, get me an OR, stat,

and a scrub nurse please. This guy's like sand in here. What about it, guys? Do we do it ourselves or is there a gas doctor in the house? Ve need der *gaz.*"

"The Beast of Belsen," Beverly said.

"Shut up," Silver said. "Don't talk like that."

Tench, talking to the leg, said, "Ve haf a vay of dealing mit pipple such as you—"

"No *more!*"

Beverly said, "Let me do this one now, Eli. You bailed me out. You did great, thank you."

"That kind of talk is very disturbing to me. They had doctors in the camps who did things to people."

Tench said, "You want to talk about my Nazi activities, Eli? I'll put a chair over your fuckin' head. I'll take you to fuckin' *court.*"

Beverly said, "Everybody slow down, all right? We're a little tensed up, is all."

Eli, holding the stethoscope at chest height, away from him, as if it were connected to something else, said, "I apologize. I apologize to everybody, I'm sorry."

Tench didn't speak. Beverly said, "I'm doing Thropental before he wakes up, and cross your fingers. Go home, Eli. Okay?"

"I'm sorry."

Tench said, "Stick to kids, you fucker. I lost a grandmother and an uncle in the camps. You fucker. Practice on kids and stay the hell out of my life. Stay out of my *way* from now on. You fucker."

"I wasn't talking about you," Eli said.

Tench said, "Who else did you have in mind, you bastard creep?"

But Silver was out of the room and out of the ER vestibule. He washed up in the public men's room on the first floor, standing with his hands beneath hot water, looking down. The water circling into the drain was the solution he had poured from the bottle he'd hidden in Dolores's room. The blood he saw turn pink was from his son's cracked head. The exile Tench had sentenced him to was Gwen's reservation at the airport, Elizabeth Bean's curt phone calls, his dark house. He lifted his sore knee, flexing it, then he went back toward the pediatrics ward for a couple of nasty words from Ada, and something for his head. He dried his hands by rubbing them on his sport coat as he went upstairs, favoring his gouty knee.

The quarry above the campus was a high half bowl of shadows, and where ice had frozen and run and frozen again among layers of rock there were green reflections of moonlight. Mead Weeks II, dressed in a one-piece snowmobile outfit that made him look like a swollen child in a snowsuit, was flexing his recently unslung arm and building a fire. Wind stayed up in the amphitheater shape of the quarry, so his matches lit and the wet wood, nourished by a can of Sterno he'd shoved under the tepee of twigs, began to burn. His fire gave little light and a lot of smoke; the smoke remained invisible in the darkness, but the flames were reflected on Weeks's eyeglasses. He held his mittened hands over the fire and they steamed. "Man discovers gloves," he said in a reasonable voice. He laid more squaw wood on the fire and then ranged in a wide circle, below the mouth of the quarry, to find more fuel. There wasn't much, so, back near the fire, panting, he took a short-handled trail ax from his father's heavy Norwegian ski pack, last used in Wales on sabbatical, and addressed the nearest pine, seven inches in diameter, its shingled bark frozen into reptile's armor.

Mead Weeks II swung clumsily, mostly with the right arm, since his left shoulder muscle was recently healed and the shoulder and biceps tender, weak. The ax sometimes cut and stuck, but it mostly slapped sideways or at an angle too shallow for the blade to bite. He continued to hammer the tree, though, slowly, regularly, grunting, and even crying out in a high voice. He stopped, once, to gather fragments of wet bark and small white crystallized wood chunks, and he fed them to the slow, guttering fire. Then he went back to banging at the tree.

Suddenly, as if he'd been signaled, Mead Weeks II dropped the ax, scuttled to his father's knapsack, wrestled it, shoved his arm in its throat, and came up with a plastic aspirin bottle. He pried the cover away with his teeth and announced to the Sterno-fed fire and the stones above him, "What we need, in case of emergencies and overexposure to the elements, is the occasional *red*. If you don't eat yo' red, you could find yo'self *dead*." He rolled two triangular orange Dexedrines over the lip of the bottle and into his mouth, swallowed, nodded, said, "De-licious: the survival ration of choice," and rolled another one in, then one more. "Shazam!" he called to the quarry, which sent back no echoes. "Shazam, you-all!"

He walked slowly back to the ax and the pine tree and started to chop. Spicules of ice blew in the air, clouds covered and uncovered the moon—Weeks stopped chopping each time it grew darker, as if his shoulder had been tapped—and the temperature fell. His fire burned out, except for a few sizzling pieces of deadwood that glowed sometimes and sheltered the Sterno from the wind. Soon, by Sterno light alone, he was whacking a pine tree and doing little more than scraping a white wound into it.

"Man cannot live by flammable jelly alone," he announced to the tree. He gathered more splinters and bark and heaped them over the little can, and for a minute there was more light. He went back to the pine, moaning a little now each time he swung the ax, bubbling saliva and mucus. He sang to the tree,

"My father is a bachelor / My mother is bereft / Or surely she'd have felt that way / If she hadn't left / OH! / I am a crazy little boy / Whose strength is quite insane / I brush my teeth with Drano / Just to keep my surface plane—no: *plain.*" He stopped chopping, held the ax beside his leg; considering, he said, "I think plane's okay. It gives you the whole geometry fix, you can go from angles to surfaces, you get the up-and-down of drain cleaner in the pipes, then you do your sideways number with *plane.* Except, you can have a plane that's vertical, too." He sat on his haunches, still holding the ax. "What we need here is a variation of the entire consideration of surfaces that can give us the sense of *axis.* We're lacking the penumbra of axis, running it up and down while running it side to side. They don't teach you *that* in school, and you want to keep a clear head. Survival is predicated on clarity. Though transparency is *not* the issue. What you can see through is not the case. The world, being opaque, is the case." He stood again and walked slowly to the fire, laid the ax handle on it, went back for more chips, carried them to the fire, dropped them over the handle, then lay on his side, propping himself with his healthy arm, watching the fire. "The case of the opaque handle," he said. "I can't remember that song we used to sing around the campfire. But as long as you don't *talk* too much, don't *ever* speed in public, then you're home. Which is, clearly, the opacity of the case. The transparency. Don't speed. Go slow, young man, and burn your big stick. When clear, mix—no, *fold* in the batter. Unless he burned his bat."

L'Ordinet had meant to walk through deep snow, playing his harmonica in the empty woods. His lips had threatened to freeze to the metal of the little silver instrument, and he'd freed himself by drooling on it. And the deep snow was mostly ice. So, with his hands in his pockets, his shoulder aching with the care of his paces, he had strolled uphill with enormous difficulty, wandering, regretting his night, until drawn by a light, no bigger than that of a star, and the chanting of some high voices. From the mouth of the quarry, he saw the boy lying by the little fire, talking to himself in several tones of voice, his leg partly in the fire, his boot or bootlace burning.

L'Ordinet rolled Mead Weeks II away from the fire and brushed his boot with gloved hands. Weeks climbed to his feet by pulling on L'Ordinet's coat, screamed at him with wet-lipped, giant-eyed fury: "Don't fucking think you can sneak up on people and mess with their minds, Professor Ordinaire, you're a butt of sack, you're vin ordinaire, which is French, you're as ordinary as *people*. I'm not unknown to powerful types in the vicinity."

L'Ordinet stepped back, looked at the fire, the collapsed knapsack, the small shrieking boy with singed pants and an arm that flapped like a chicken's wing. "Mead," he said very gently, "Mead, I was trying to help you."

"I have the strength of ten," Weeks instructed.

"It looked like your foot was on fire."

"Yeah, that always happens to me," Weeks said calmly. "Everything goes okay until my foot catches on fire."

L'Ordinet stepped in, sniffed, stepped back. "It isn't booze," he said. "What medication have you been using, Mead?"

"Mead," Weeks said. "A vin ordinaire discusses with a mead the bacchic possibilities of flaming feet. My feet always act up in this weather. I was a frail child, but fortunately I now have the strength of ten."

"What are you *on?*" L'Ordinet moved in again.

"On feet of fire and mind of ice, is what I'm on, Mr. L'Ordinet. May I ask if you continue to bang the lady who—Miss Bean, I believe, the one who shrinks the fears of the fearful and the phalluses of the fortunate?"

L'Ordinet moved in closer, spun Weeks by the shoulder, put a hammerlock on his arm, separating the shoulder muscle again, and, while Weeks warned him of the strength of ten and then started to vomit on his blistered foot, L'Ordinet kicked ice over the fire, stepped on the Sterno can, and, gripping Weeks's arm, pushed him ahead. They walked and slid and shuddered down the hill from the quarry toward University Drive, across the campus, and the home of Mead Weeks I and II.

On a leveler meadow that skirted most of the college buildings, they walked very slowly, their feet sinking through ice crust, pulling up, sinking farther along. High black graceful elms made forked shadows, and willows that were no more than nests of long thick hair whipped in the wind. Car lights, as they approached the road, turned the ice a flickering blue. Mead Weeks II spoke of the First Corinthians in their unceasing war against the Second Corinthians—"But they didn't have a chance, I'm telling you this, although I have every reason to believe I'm suffering incredible pain. See, the Second was a parachute division, they had training in judo and speed reading, that kind of Oriental hand-to-hand kind of loincloth warfare? And they read from right to left, which completely unsettled the First Corinthians, who were all the children of parents. They had to be, to get into the outfit. But of course it weakened their wills and sapped their sap. Which in those days meant everything."

L'Ordinet said only, "We'll take care of you. The one thing even crazy assholes like you can count on is somebody taking care of you. Children always get cared for."

"Yes," Weeks said, in a wholly lucid voice, "but the thing of it is, they get it done by parents. You know what I mean? It's a dilemma."

L'Ordinet stopped and released Weeks's arm. "You're okay."

Weeks said, "I'm okay-er."

"Well, I don't want to have a discussion about parents and children."

"Not with parents and children, you don't."

"You're not crazy," L'Ordinet said.

"Oh, I am. I'm pretty sure I am," Weeks said. "You coming?"

L'Ordinet said, "No. Go home by yourself. You can get home."

"Getting home is never the problem," Weeks said. He was shaking, leaning in within his chest, cuddling the shoulder. L'Ordinet struck off at an angle from him, making for the central part of Bailey. "Thanks for the lift," Weeks called. "Thanks for your advice. Thanks for your guidance. Thanks for your friendship. Thanks for the memory." He walked very slowly, pulling his legs through the ice crust, holding himself. "Hi, Dad," he told the edge of the road that went to University Drive, "guess what happened on the way home from the eggplant cannery?"

L'Ordinet was walking faster now, listening to the crunch of ice and his own breathing, ignoring the shoulder, looking only down at the holes he made in the surface, seeing his feet and tufts of frozen grass that protruded where the wind had scoured the snow and ice away. He realized that he couldn't feel very much below his ankles, that he couldn't hear Weeks's voice, that his ears and cheeks were numb, that he was on his way to Elizabeth Bean's apartment near the shutdown lumberyard, that he was full partner in a cottage industry and didn't want to sell shares.

Eli Silver was finished with his evening rounds early, because only two patients were in the ward. One, a child of four with an infected cut on his jaw, would be released in the morning now that Eli was satisfied the parotid gland was unaffected. The other, also four years old, had been brought to the Emergency Room after having complained of headaches and run a fever. She had vomited, broken out in a rash, and was showing the puckered strawberry tongue, now growing redder, of scarlet fever. A beta hemolytic streptococcus, Silver told himself, and IGE, ESR, CBC, ASTO, CRP, the tests the lab would run. The girl's red lids were like Dolores's, and taking care of babies wasn't fair, his knee felt swollen though it wasn't, and the colchicine he'd dispensed himself would bring relief and diarrhea at the same time. He limped with gout and thought of febrile children. Daddy'll be right back.

In the parking lot, he thought of Lizzie Bean and said, "Enough." Stepping on the clutch made him wince, the pain made him growl it: *"Enough."* He went north instead of south, toward Bailey instead of home, and fast on the still-icy road. He fishtailed on curves, but controlled the car with gears, no brakes, and on the long straightaway between New Sherburne and the outskirts of Bailey, where there were few buildings, and pools of melted snow, refrozen, burned in the bright-blue glow of road lights, he let the car out and did 60, 65, 68, coming to the ROTARY and LIONS and OUR CHURCHES WELCOME YOU signs outside of Bailey, with the Hawk skidding twenty degrees left of the center, blowing his horn to warn the empty road.

He went through Bailey in second gear, wary of the village cop, and when he turned off the main street he went slower, because students were prancing outside bars. Another turn, and he was near the high dark lumberyard whose owner had been brought by ambulance to the hospital, bleeding from the nose and ears after falling from a lumber loft. Across from the yard, in a massive yellow Victorian house, all turrets and cupolas, with a jutting widow's walk, Lizzie Bean lived in three upstairs rooms at the back. Silver walked up her unprotected rough wood staircase, squinting against the wind, still saying to himself, "Enough."

When Lizzie opened the door, she said, "Where's your coat?"

"I forgot it. Where's your bathrobe?"

"Don't you like pajamas?"

Eli stared at the men's red flannel pajamas, the jacket open two buttons at the bottom, the pants baggy and wide, longer than her legs. "It's a charming outfit," he said. "Am I allowed to talk with you?"

The lights were bright in thick glass globes on the ceiling, the record player was loud—he didn't know what music it was —and the rooms were a range of paper mountains, open-mouthed books heaped several volumes high, piles of mimeo paper, creased magazines, legal pads, small pink telephone message slips, clippings from newspapers, Xeroxed sheets. A shot glass of whiskey stood beside a book on the slate-topped coffee table in front of the long sofa covered with a plaid blanket. "I love this place," Eli said, pointing at a bright wall of framed maps and a Hopper reproduction.

"I was having a drink," Lizzie said.

"I'd have one."

"I'm not offering it yet."

"*Yet* is better than nothing," Eli said.

She stood near the coffee table, he stood just inside the door. She held one hand in another, under her breasts. He leaned back on the door.

"But you're right," she said, "we should be talking to each other. I missed you. You're a nice man."

"Though something of a shithead."

"Though that." She went into the kitchen and returned with another shot glass, almost full.

"Did you drink more than that today?" he asked. "We don't know this, but there's a good suspicion, there's some data, I just found out about this—you drink more than a little bit, and you're insulting the fetus."

"I haven't had a drink yet. And look who's talking. And I read that a lot of booze could *help* a pregnant woman. Also, look who's talking about insulting fetuses, huh?"

"I meant in the biological sense. Chemically."

"I know. You just looked so tired, I couldn't resist zapping you a little more." Her eyes jumped red and wet. "I didn't mind doing you a little harm."

"The old chemical insult, huh?"

Lizzie went back to the kitchen and blew her nose loudly. Silver turned the record player off. The needle scratched before the speakers died.

"Be *care*ful, Eli. I built that system. Me and a couple of the students; it's a very delicate system."

"Aren't we all."

"Oh, no. We talk in somber echoing overtones, you can go home, all right? Let's just talk straight tonight, please. I agree to the adoption. It's a good idea. You should have treated me like a person. Preferably, like a lover. I don't want to say any more."

"Are we lovers, Liz? Is that a good thing for us to talk about now?"

"Drink. Have a drink. Do a chemical insult and maybe you would make a fire—I don't want to bend down all that much. Make a fire and then tell me about adoption laws and family court, is that the one? Family court. Tell me about that while I figure out if I should ask you about the parents. Damnit, *I'm* the parent!"

Tearing newspaper and wadding it, stacking the tinder and small logs, Eli said, at the shallow marble-manteled fireplace opposite the sofa, "You're the mother, Liz. Other people get to be the parents. They have all the luck. They get the best. All you get is free." He turned to look at her, still standing near the double kitchen doors in floppy men's pajamas, holding her own hand, and then he turned to light the fire.

"And all I get is, I'm your patient."

Eli nodded at the fire. "That's all I get, too."

"I loved the loving," she said.

He nodded again. "And saving my life?"

"Mutual," she said, "ditto."

He sat with his legs drawn up, handing a bigger log to the fire. His shadow jumped behind him, as if startled by his words—"Is it true? What we're saying? What I mean is, is this what we should say?"—or by the sharp rattle of the door-knob, the sharper steady knock of muffled knuckles on her stairway door.

"I can get it," she said. "We'll keep talking, I'll see who it is."

Eli walked himself around on his haunches and rested his chin on his drawn-up legs, rubbing the sore knee, watching Lizzie waddle in her deerskin moccasins to open the door and let in L'Ordinet, red of face in fogged-up glasses, soaked to the knee, staring right away at Silver on the floor.

Lizzie said, "Horace. This isn't a good time. I mean, go *away*, Horace."

But he closed the door and opened his coat. Lizzie backed toward the center of the room, standing on her own.

"How do you do," L'Ordinet said to Silver. "I'm intruding, obviously."

"It's her house," Silver said.

L'Ordinet pointed at Lizzie and said, in a high angry voice, "It's my *child.*"

"Go away, Horace," Lizzie called.

"You're free to do anything you like," L'Ordinet told her. "You can run four affairs at the same time and do gangbangs —I apologize." He held his hands before him and shook his head. "I'm very very sorry. I'm being a prick about this. I'm sorry. Totally sorry. What I mean is, do what you *want,* Liz."

"Thank you so very much."

"Except give our baby away."

Silver said, "It's none of my business, Horace—"

"I wonder if you'd mind not using my name like that, that isn't really my name."

"—except, where were you when the lights went on?"

"I beg your pardon?"

"She's been alone for a while. I was wondering where you'd been. Being so concerned, as concerned as you seem to be, you know: when she was pretty much on her own."

"Not *she,*" Lizzie said.

Eli said, "That's right. Lizzie. But you know who I mean."

"Whom," L'Ordinet said. "If you don't mind my correcting you, sir. It would be whom."

"Thank you," Silver said.

"I don't believe this," Lizzie said.

Eli went to his knees and climbed to his feet, then walked across the room toward L'Ordinet. "I'm Miss Bean's physician," he said. "My name is Silver."

"Heigh-ho, Silver," L'Ordinet sang, looking up at him.

"I have a patient, I helped treat a patient who's a colleague of yours. We talked about some things when I visited him the other day at the hospital. Miss Bean's name came up and so did yours. He didn't like you. He disliked you a good deal because you taught about delicate matters such as dying, I think it was prisoners tortured in Cambodia, to make your students weep. He said you enjoyed that. I understand that, I really do. Power is delightful, no matter who—*whom?* Correct me. No matter who you do it to. That's wrong. No matter to whom you do it, how's that? But what I would like to say, before you leave, is that Miss Bean is *not* in your classroom or in your life. Excuse me, Lizzie. Animals belong to themselves. Right now, she's performing beast functions. She's giving birth to a smaller animal, and she will do it on her own. All I'm doing is attending. And then she will deal with it on her own."

L'Ordinet's head was down, and Silver's was aimed away from him. Their knees were trembling.

Lizzie backed slowly toward the kitchen, her slippers made hushing sounds on the wood floor.

Still looking down, L'Ordinet, in a wobbly voice, said, "Do you know who I am?"

"I know what you mean," Silver said. "It's almost fair, asking it, and the answer is no. Not really. I'm not thinking about how you feel. And what you feel maybe should matter. But I'm right too. I really am. You're out of it now. You're not allowed to come back in."

"Who *says?*" L'Ordinet begged, looking up at Silver and then out at the kitchen.

"She does. Elizabeth Bean. I do. You did, some time back. You're out."

"Your name is Silver?"

"Dr. Silver. Eli Silver. Silver. Toilethead, idiot, whatever you like, you can call me anything you like. Except, I'm right, you're out now. You can't come back."

"Doctors don't talk like that," L'Ordinet said, buttoning his coat and putting his gloves on.

"I really am a doctor."

"Lovers talk like that." L'Ordinet opened the door and edged a shoulder around it. "What you got was sloppy seconds, Doctor," he said. "I got there first."

Eli kicked at the door and it shut against L'Ordinet's cheekbone, slamming L'Ordinet's head at the jamb. L'Ordinet cried pure sound, deep fright or rage in the last broken syllable, or warning. L'Ordinet pulled his face away, Eli saw the puckering cut and the crushed capillaries where the bruise would be, then fell off balance, one leg up, backward to the floor. L'Ordinet slammed the door behind him, and Silver heard the stairs like closing doors.

I.R. Demby lay on the mattress Phil had stuffed into the back of the Travelall, and Mead Weeks II, wearing a new sling that strapped his forearm to his ribcage for his shoulder's sake, sat next to Phil and rubbed the windshield with newspaper every time the defogger failed. They were slithering from the hospital to Bailey, carrying I.R. home. I.R. was in a leg cast and his ribs were bound, but he was chattering to Phil, who wasn't listening, and to Mead Weeks II, who didn't know what to reply.

Phil was trying to either laugh or be reflective, but he couldn't manage much of either, thinking of Mead Weeks in a dark tweed suit and polished brogans, wide avocado tie, his hair sprayed into place, his eyes pouched more than usual, standing at the door of Phil's office and explaining that since Phil was more of a regular guy, and not one of us fussy intellectual types—"I'm not what you'd call your man of action"—he might be able to communicate with Mead Weeks II: "He's having those emotional afflictions boys of his age often do, he's awfully confused as to goals and modes," take the boy in hand, perhaps teach him some of that boxing Phil had used for communicating with that Negro student, Turner, and, frankly, keep him attuned to healthier activities.

"Healthier than what?" Phil had said.

And Weeks, merely small and stuffy, far from dumb, had said, "Than what he does," nodding Phil into pretended comprehension.

Phil had said, after looking at his covered-up journal—*Bellamy, Bonnie,* Annie's so happy she's tight and stiff as a wood screw—"I don't communicate with Turner by boxing. I just box with him. It's good exercise."

"Whatever you want to call it, Phil. I'd be grateful for your help. Exercise, whatever."

"My help."

"Don't boxers often chop wood to condition themselves?"

"Yes," he said, "some of them. They do."

"Well," Weeks said. "Well. That's fine, then."

So on a dim Saturday morning, having bought Weeks II a container of coffee and a doughnut, having said nothing more than words like "cold" and "ice" and "Sometimes the defroster gives out, it needs to be flushed," Phil was driving Demby home and Weeks to no place special, and he was trying to decide where he'd work next fall, when the college let him go for failing to teach English, to Americans, as a supplementary language. He was thinking of a crib ordered from Sears, and the paper edition of Benjamin Spock on child care, and what they'd do if the baby got sick.

"So this guy comes in—close your ears, Mead, this is official shoptalk—this very tall bald guy with a long face and no smiles in sight," Demby said, "comes in and talks *around* me. He keeps looking at my leg and my chest, talking about fractures of the such-and-such, he even took my blood pressure and asked if I was allergic to things. I said, sure I was: the New York Yankees, fat women, and maybe penicillin. So we're just talking like that. He keeps his hands on me, I don't mean he's queer, it wasn't anything like that. He wasn't a fag. It was like he was *checking*. I have no idea on what.

"He does one of those jumps—you know: you teach there, you know Sarota the school doctor, how's the clinic treating all the flu that's around, and bingo, say, you must know that Miss Bean, the school psychologist."

Phil chewed his mustache ends and forced the truck slowly over the bridge that crossed the Chenango River; the steel bridge was slick, and he kept his hands light on the wheel, his foot away from the brake. Weeks II leaned across him to wipe

Phil's side of the windshield, and Phil moved his arm to brush Weeks out of the way and back to his side of the seat.

"I figured *that's* why he was there," Demby said, "because of her. It was the only thing that made sense. So I said, Oh, sure, a dynamite person, a *hell* of a good lady, fun to drink with, she really cares about the kids, does a good job, and I wait."

" 'You noticed she's pregnant?' he says to me. Seeing as she's a little too large for a phone booth, I tell him that I've noticed, and then he hits me with it—no grease, no preamble: 'Who's the father?' he says."

Mead Weeks II said, "L'Ordinet."

"Thank you, son," Demby said. "A well-informed child. Does your old man know that?"

"He knows everything," Weeks said.

"Including how you would sniff coke from a pile of dogshit if it was the only way for you to turn on?"

The back of Weeks's neck went red, but he calmly nodded, looking at the road, the countryside covered with frozen fog, a nightmare whiteness. "Everything," he said.

"Good man," Demby said.

"Did you tell him that?" Phil asked.

"The doctor?"

"The tall one with the bald head."

"Oh, sure. I mean, he wanted to *know.* Turns out, he was one of the guys kept me alive when I was doing my little allergic-to-breathing routine. Sure. I told him. He nodded very seriously, and then he did a fairly brave little thing. Listen to this: he said, 'You're a black man, and I couldn't care less, all right? I understand it's very boring to listen to white people talk about color.'

"I said that most black guys were soporific on the subject too, what did he want to know? And he said, 'Forgive me, but I need to know—is this professor black or white?'

"Which gave me the laugh of the day. I hurt my rib, giggling. I started to choke, trying not to laugh. I told him, 'White.' Unless he's got Indian blood, Indian and black slave mixed in down the line—that nose, you know? He was a very solemn physician, that guy. All he said was, 'Thank you. I'm grateful.' I tried asking him, 'For *what?*' But he kind of rubbed my shoulder, not gay or anything, and he took off. You understand that?"

"He's a closet racist," Weeks said.

Phil, staring into the rearview mirror after Demby's voice, seeing only the ice-streaked tailgate window and the frosted road, the white bulbous vegetation, streaked black trees, looking through squinted eyes, said, "Shut up, Mead. Shut up for a while, please."

Weeks said, "He sure *sounds* like one."

When Phil turned to look at him, eyes small and jaw lifting, Weeks crossed his legs and looked out his window.

In the silence, Demby groaned a happy fatigue and said, " 'Bye, guys, it's time to dream a little. In black and white."

When no one answered anyone, Weeks began to whistle. After a few bars, Phil reached his right arm out and cuffed the boy hard on the shoulder. "*What?*" Weeks whined.

"What?" Demby mumbled.

Phil flapped his hand at what he saw outside, then patted the boy's arm. "It's all right," he said, "I was thinking."

7 | Deliveries

The wrestlers, unlimited-weight class, were tied up on the mat, exhausted. Sweat dripped, the fat one began to retch—his nose and forehead were mashed into the canvas—and the taller, more muscularly defined boy with the shaved head tried to break the fat boy's bridge. He screamed, "Doe doe doe doe *doe!*" But he couldn't move, the fat one couldn't escape, and then, when the tall one began to turn him, it was the fat one's turn to cry, "Ee*agh!*" and nearly slide out. They both lay flat, suddenly; the fat one's nose bled, and they giggled weakly, congratulating one another on going no place.

A game of four-man, half-court basketball was accelerating at the other end of the gym, short guys playing dirty—elbows in the tall ones' stomachs, asses jutting on the rebounds—while the tall ones pounded heads as they came off the boards. Mead Weeks II watched the ball swish through, not touching the rim, and he called, "Nietzsche would have loved it."

In their corner, under the climbing rope hung from the high ceiling, Turner and Phil shuffled in circles, Phil dragging his right foot in slow pursuit, Turner holding his hands in their heavy gloves at his waist, cocked. He skipped slowly counter-clockwise, then reversed his direction, waiting for a chance to jab. Phil stalked, with his left hand in front of his face, an old-fashioned boxer, while Turner, imitating Ali's imitator, Sugar Ray Leonard, waited for the move. Phil violated the form he'd adopted by throwing a long right-hand lead, which caught Turner on the side of the red leather boxing helmet. Turner, too fast to be hurt, took much of the blow's velocity away by jerking his head as the glove landed, then throwing an off-balance left that Phil took on the collarbone and neck. Phil banged him cheerfully on top of the head, clumsily skipped backward, threw a long left jab, another, a right uppercut, coming in again, that missed, and he took a perfect short-armed combination in the face. He slapped back with a left, and they parted, going slowly in circles again.

"I read your file," he told Turner.

"You can do that?"

"In the name of educating the dopey," Phil said, pawing Turner's jab away, "you can do almost anything."

"I ain't got no privacy, huh?"

"Miss Bean and I were discussing your mind."

"She is one hell of a woman," Turner said. "You can trust her."

"About you?"

"Whatever," Turner said, coming in low, going with his head down to throw fast punches at Phil's gut, landing one good one on the ribs as Phil turned and slid away to suddenly come back fast and hit Turner on the helmet twice.

"That's amateur," Phil said.

"I *am* a amateur."

"*An* amateur," Phil said.

"Well, I be one, whatever you want to call it."

Phil stopped. He pushed a looping right hand away, barked, "Don't charge with your head down unless you were born in

Argentina, and you don't cut over the eyes. Keep your head up, keep your hands up, and talk *right.*" He fell into his crouch again and went after Turner hard, pushing lefts into his face until Turner forgot to dance and circle, then he hit Turner hard in the liver with his right, and waited for Turner to start breathing again.

They shuffled, Turner lifted his hands, Phil smiled to annoy him, and they started boxing. "If I can trust her," Phil said, "then I am prepared to tell you what a shit-faced liar you are. Your old man works for the City of New York and makes sixteen grand a year. Your mother has an A.B. from Queens College. Your brother went to Poly Prep as a jock. And you, jive-mouth, you went to Mount Herman on an *academic* scholarship. You can play Nee-gro all you wants, but you knows how to talk, *yassuh*, you sho' does. Huh?" He moved in and slapped with his left, did it again, then again. "Huh?"

Turner dropped his hands and smiled, looked at the floor, lifted his chin. Phil stopped punching, and Turner hit him hard, in the solar plexus, with a short stiff right that had Turner's shoulder and back behind it. Phil started to cave, grunting, then turned his shoulder and spat onto the canvas mat, and threw Turner back six inches with a left full into the face. Turner took it, came back under it, and hit Phil in the stomach again, skipped around, hit him with a crossing left in the neck and then a right on the cheek, took two jabs in his face, and threw himself backward onto his buttocks, laughing out loud.

"I can fight," he said.

Phil, panting, said, "You can."

"You too," Turner said.

"Me too."

"We can talk sometime," Turner said.

Phil timed his pause, turned to walk to the showers, saying, "Hoopty-doo."

Mead Weeks II watched everybody.

Upstairs, off the corridor that went from the head of the steep steps, Annie repainted the crib. It had come in six pieces from Sears, and she and Phil had assembled it while drinking Spanish wine and listening to the radio. Now she was painting it moss green—"Blue for boys," she'd told Phil, "pink for girls, and green for trolls and orphans"—in very short light careful strokes, not dripping, watching the high-gloss paint begin to dry. The walls were sheetrocked and painted a mustard color, the ceiling was flat white, the floor sanded down to its original wide-planked pine and polyurethaned. "It would take five years' worth of pee to make a dent in it," she'd said. A small secondhand bureau in the corner was the same moss green as the crib.

Annie put her narrow brush across the mouth of the paint can, turned the radio off, wiped her hands on her jeans, and walked the length of the corridor to their bedroom. The bed was unmade, a pair of Phil's pants hung from the top of the closet door, and books, open-mouthed and upside-down, lay on the floor on either side of the bed. She kicked shut the closet door in which their clothes were hanging, and went to a closet in another wall. When she opened the door, she said, "Look out, you guys." Small canvases were stacked, separated by lengths of one-by-two, and several large cardboard portfolios leaned together at the back, on the floor. In dark crayon, dates had been written on them—1972, 1975—and she went for an early portfolio, pulled it out, carried it to the unmade bed, and went searching.

The drawing, in ink on heavy Italian paper, was of an infant's face. The shape was small and very young, the eyes were old and shadowed. It wasn't a lovely drawing, but it was of a baby, drawn by Anne Sorenson, she'd written her name at the bottom, and the date, 1977. She carried the picture down the hall to the baby's room. She held it on a wall and stared. Then she tore the picture in half and carried the pieces back to the bedroom, pushed the halves into the portfolio, tied it, slid it into place in the closet, and went back to paint.

She left the radio off, she worked, and she finished painting the crib. When Phil came home, she picked a quarrel and drove him from the kitchen to the television set. As he turned from channel to channel, watching nothing, looking at the faces and the cars, she carried coffee in for them, stood in the doorway with the cups, changed her mind, went out. He turned the set off, left the dark room to follow her into the bright, stove-heated kitchen.

"Everything is fine," she told him when he entered.

"That's a relief," he said, "because I was imagining—you know how imaginative I get—I was considering you might be upset."

"It's hard, having a baby in your mind. Not using your body. Not having it get you *ready*."

"Well, remember how much fun you had with that twice before."

She looked at his thumb as he drank coffee, staying a distance from her. It rubbed the curve of the cup as if it ached for the warmth.

"This is hard for you, too."

"You noticed, huh?"

"That's right," she said. "You give birth to this one as much as I do."

"I always horn in, don't I."

She spoke across the mouth of the coffee cup, "I am so frightened of this."

In a tremulous burlesque falsetto he screamed, "I'm not! Nope! Not! Not scared! Nope!"

She didn't laugh. He raised his brows and hid by drinking coffee. She did too. And later, in bed, under the down comforter, they hid behind their backs, facing opposite walls. When their bottoms touched, they stayed that way but said nothing; they pressed their buttocks at one another and, like hiding roadside creatures struck by light, held still.

After Elizabeth Bean's fourth week of pregnancy, the fetal heart had begun to beat, concluding a month of tissue differentiation—entoderm, ectoderm, then mesoderm. In the next month, she carried something that went from fish and fowl and even whale—it grew and lost its flippers—and became a human creature weighing little more than a gram. A month after that, its sex was established, blood went from the umbilicus through an actual circulatory system, hemoglobin F was formed, carrying more oxygen than the body would ever carry as an adult's, bile appeared, other digestive juices. The body, now fourteen inches long and weighing one thousand grams, made swimming motions after fourteen weeks; Lizzie felt it move, and then, in its dark ocean, the child began to grasp. Not long afterward, Silver and Lizzie first made love. It seemed that a lot of time had passed, but it had not, before they ceased making love and, for a while, much conversation.

Turner had failed two courses. Phil had failed to teach awfully much to his class, anything to Mead Weeks's son. Weeks had failed to tell Weeks II that love mattered more than amphetamines. Weeks II had failed to help his father learn that a fire in the night is a signal of bright and specific meaning. Demby tutored Turner in his apartment, some nights, and Turner, some nights, failed to return to the dorm. Annie had failed to mount the kitchen molding strips to her satisfaction.

L'Ordinet had failed to place his article on the bleak poetry of Algerian propaganda. Silver had failed to sleep without dreams. The weather had failed to break sharply, and it was a cold early springtime during which the fetus inside Elizabeth Bean notified her it could stretch and flex to the rhythm of their shared blood, it was ready, and Lizzie was ripe.

Silver had spoken with the hospital's OB-GYN man who attended Lizzie, had telephoned a lawyer in Bailey who wanted the child delivered to his office by Silver—not Lizzie—for the sake of confidentiality. His name was Arnold Partse, but according to Ada had been born Arnold Patenstein. "They all change their names when they make money," Ada had said. "They're afraid their parents will hunt them down and ask for a handout." Silver had replied, "Maybe they're afraid of people like you?" To which Ada answered, "How much money do *you* send home?" When Silver had told her his parents were dead, she had said, "I know. But that isn't an excuse, and you know it." And now Lizzie took a week off from work, waiting for the labor pains she'd read about and before which she quailed, as she had before the fists and face and voice of Horace L'Ordinet. And now Silver commuted between his house and the hospital and the offices of Arnold Partse, the apartment of Elizabeth Bean, and the dark country roads. L'Ordinet took long nighttime walks. And Turner insisted on writing a paper for Phil, on Richard Wright. Demby insisted on reading it when Phil graded it B-plus, then tapped his finger on the paper and told Phil, "All this time, and he was in disguise. Isn't he beautiful? For a savage." And Mrs. DeAngelo, the department secretary, endured a hysterectomy, Mead Weeks II wrote to a psychiatrist at Upstate Hospital in Syracuse, Demby published a paper on James Baldwin, Professor Leicester had a short affair with the secretary to the geology department, and Annie tore down the wallpaper in the kitchen because it hadn't set right.

Silver, at home, waiting for the call from Lizzie or the

OB-GYN man's nurse, was drinking tonic water on ice and reading a reprint of a paper on ankyloglossia, because he had taken on a patient, a boy, who suffered from tongue-tie: his tongue was constricted in movement, partially bound to the floor of the mouth by a mucous-membrane band, and was notched at the end from the child's efforts to push it forward over his teeth. The telephone rang and Silver stood up slowly, reminding himself that years of experience made doctors calm. He reached the phone on its second ring, heard a voice, perhaps two voices, and said, "Liz?" The connection broke.

He poured more tonic water and strode the kitchen, reading as he walked, pausing to sip, then walking again. When the telephone rang again, he quietly put the reprint down—"any limitation of the free upward motion of the tongue which directs the tongue thrust only forward will result in excessive growth of the anterior portion of the mandible"—took a quick swallow of tonic water because his lips and gums were dry, and, picking the receiver up, said, "Silver."

"A collect call for anyone from Gwen Silver."

"Excuse me?"

"I have a collect phone call from Second City, Texas, for anyone at that number from a Gwen Silver. Will you accept?"

"Who did she think was here besides me? Never mind—yes, sure. Yes, operator, I'll accept the call." He drank a large swallow too quickly and sputtered, so that he heard only, "Liz."

"*What?*"

"I said who in hell is Liz, Eli?" Gwen's voice was low in her throat, it burred slightly in the connection, which was metallic and which echoed. Other noises worked at the edges of their tones in the wire.

"She's a patient, Gwen. She's having a baby."

"Not yours, I presume."

"Absolutely not mine. Almost not hers. Are you all right?"

"Daddy says to tell you hello."

"Wonderful."

"I thought it was companionly of him."

"Yes, yes, it is. You're right. I'm surprised to hear from you, Gwen."

"After I deserted you and got the hell away from the dirty parts."

"Dirty?"

"Living—" She said nothing then, and he knew she was crying, or trying not to cry, and he waited, closing his eyes and trying to see her father's living room, and seeing, too, an obstetrics nurse dialing his number and hearing the idiot buzz of the busy signal. "Living with it on your own, I intended to say. I'm sorry not to be graceful with you, Eli. I wasn't graceful when it happened, either."

"I'm not sure we need to talk about it any more. Right now, anyway, Gwen. And maybe not for some time."

"Yes, indeed. I think you're right. Now, you just excuse me for the way I'm doing this, will you?"

He nodded, then remembered to say, "Sure, Gwen. No problem."

"Oh, you got problems, child. Do you know why I'm phoning you up? You didn't mind that I did it collect, did you? I'm on one hell of a budget."

"I'd have sent money, Gwen."

"I know, darlin', but I didn't think it proper to take any. You know?"

"I know. I guess I do."

"As to calling like this—calling at all: can you imagine why?"

"You want a divorce."

Then she *was* crying, and he knew it. He heard the short chokings back, a disintegrated "Hang on, darlin'," and the sharp slap of her telephone on something hard. Silver raised the glass and put it down again, licked his lips. She said, "I apologize. I'm distraught."

When he admitted, "So am I," his own eyes filled, and he blinked and cleared his throat as softly as he could.

"I have one of our checkbooks, as you may know."

"You can write anything you want on it, Gwen. What do you need?"

"The price of a plane ticket."

Silver heard his breath on the wires. "One ticket or two?"

"Just one?"

"Fine. Fine, Gwen. Whatever you need."

"I wish to heaven you would ask me where I'm flying to, Eli. This was rehearsed, you see, and I had planned for you to say, 'Where to?' "

"All right."

"Darlin', *say* it, please."

"Where to, Gwen?"

"Home?"

"Here?" Eli said.

"If you can get that Liz moved out in time. If you're of a mind to move her out and move me in. Don't you think I'm showing a great deal of equanimity in talking about someone who's performing unnatural acts in my own bed with my own —"

"Liz is a *patient.*"

"—husband."

"Gwen, I'm surprised."

At which Gwen began to laugh, a high ringing laugh that dropped into her normal throaty register, then climbed again, then dropped and went on. "Oh, my," she said, then interrupted herself with laughter. "Eli, excuse me. Eli, do you know all the things I construed for you to say to me? Can you *imagine?* And you, it was like a temperature you were reading off, or something: 'I'm surprised.' Eli, will you permit me to come home?" Her laughter was gone, its largeness out of her voice and breathing.

"I'm not the one to permit anything, Gwen."

"We're not talking like that, you told me just half a minute ago. Remember? I think it would be of enormous interest to us both—I am hoping so, Eli. I think perhaps it would be interesting and useful. It might even be *nice.*"

Silver said nothing, had nothing to say, had too much to say, months to say, nearly a year to say, and all he did was lick his lips.

Gwen whispered, "Eli."

He had witnessed parents giving permission for possible radical surgery before probably routine exploratories on their children. They had seen only the small unconscious victim on the table, and surgeons busy with procedure—not *their* person —and nurses not knowing their baby's name. They had looked beyond that image into darkness and no control whatever, the hugeness of loss just out of sight but felt nevertheless; and, fearing to say no, they had given their powerless consent. Eli said, "Sure, Gwen. Of course."

In the office copy of Modern Language Association job listings, circled in red, Phil had seen his own job offered. He carried the page home with him, through the muddy back roads, past the swamp that chattered with grackles and ducks and high buzzing insects no one could name. There was blue and orange in the burned-out ocher and faded green at the swamp's edge, but he went past quickly, climbing the hill in first gear because of the deep soft ruts.

In the kitchen, Annie was slashing at wallpaper with a putty knife, softening it with hot water, then stabbing up sloppily to tear away what she'd recently laid down. The radio was off, the kitchen ticked to her slicings, and Phil kept the ad in his coat.

He walked through, she didn't turn from the wall, and in the small living room he took his coat off and threw it past the sofa, aiming for the far wall and hitting it. Back in the kitchen, he said, "That is not necessary."

"Yes, it is," she said.

"We've been fixing houses up for—how many years?"

"Plenty."

"And you've *never* had to repaper so soon. Sweetie?"

"Yes?"

"Will you talk to me, please?"

"I am."

"No, you're not." His finger stabbed downward as the putty knife stabbed up, but she didn't turn to look. "You're just answering me," he said. *"Talk!"*

Annie turned, put her putty knife in the back pocket of her jeans, folded her hands across the front of his flannel shirt, enormous on her, and composed her lips and jaw as if to say she was a good girl and listening.

"Godamnit," he said. She watched his face.

"Look," he said. "You did the molding over, when was it?"

She shrugged and the rolled-up sleeves flopped.

"You repainted the crib and the bureau in the—upstairs. You painted them the same *color,* and you had to do it again. Last night, you told me we should take the wall down between the kitchen and the living room and make the stairs go up in the other direction. We need the room, you said, and that is not the truth, and you know it isn't. Now, look: I love our projects. I love the work we do. I love bringing an old house back, and watching you get turned into butter doing projects, and I like to break down walls and put on roofs for you. For *me.* I like it. I like it for both of us. That's what we do. And that's *fine.* But this is not necessary." He waved his hands at the wallpaper, and she dutifully, stiffly, made her neck turn to direct her face where he pointed. Her expression was that of the girl being bullied, but not scared. He huffed out air and said, softer, "It isn't *nec*essary. It's—what are you so *scared* of? You're hiding in the work. What are you saying with it that you can't say? What are you *do*ing?"

She stood, watching him, and when he had run down, had shaken his head and had tried to smile but had gotten no response, and when he had made fists and banged them against his legs and then had let his fingers fall open, and then had simply stood still, she turned to the wall, took the putty knife from her pocket, squeezed water from a dirty sponge onto the paper in front of her, and went back to work.

"You know," she said. "And don't ask. And you know."

Phil put his hands in his pockets and nodded. Then he barked a kind of laugh, but didn't continue it. He walked toward the wall and stood behind her. He took the sponge from her hand and, reaching high over her, wetted the part of the wall she would need a ladder to scrape. "Of course I do," he said. He took the putty knife from her and, standing on his toes, making a cave with his body, keeping her in it as if she were safe, he gouged at William Morris paper and tore it away. As if she were safe, Annie stayed where she was.

Mead Weeks II, carrying a hand grip—you squeezed it to strengthen the muscles—because his father wanted Phil Sorenson to build him up and set him straight, and because Phil Sorenson spoke with his body, followed Horace L'Ordinet through the evening. They went past the village green, where college and high-school students smoked dope and drank wine until chased by the Bailey patrolman, past the Bailey Inn, where less casual drinking was done and past the movie house, showing *Star Wars* for the third consecutive week. With his hand in his raincoat pocket, and a bright-red Eddie Bauer felt fishing hat on his head, Mead Weeks II strolled in work shoes and squeezed at the hand grip. It didn't squeeze back because he couldn't press the handles together; the open V lay in his pocket, and he gripped it, and tried to make it close, but he couldn't.

L'Ordinet walked around the green, crossed through it, ignoring the students, only a few of whom noticed him, and Weeks II followed. A freshening wind blew, but didn't stir the winter-matted maple leaves on the dark thin grass. L'Ordinet, crossing the street, entered the driveway between Arnold Partse's law office, a high brick colonial house, and the neighboring hardware store. Weeks II, favoring his recently unslung arm, went too, into the dark mouth of the drive, which led to a long, dark alley that ran through the middle of the business block and emerged at Elizabeth Bean's house. Apartments over the alley threw light from their windows, but it never fell to the unpaved alley floor; a yellow haze of light floated over it like spring fog. Weeks II walked on his toes. He stopped when he saw L'Ordinet stop.

When L'Ordinet sneaked through a back yard to stand behind the yellow Victorian boardinghouse, Weeks II lifted the wooden-handled spring above him and said, "Hear, Akela, when the man who follows the man beseeches."

This prayer was followed by a scraping of feet on pebbles, a scuffing of soft earth, and the tinkle of the hand grip striking the ground as L'Ordinet shook Weeks II by the coat, saying, "What are you doing? What are you jolly fucking well doing?"

Weeks II seized his forearm, bent slightly, then pressed the arm to his stomach. "Oh," he said. "Oh. Oh, boy. I think you did it again."

L'Ordinet stepped back, looked at Weeks II, and said, "Nobody separates the same shoulder three times. I didn't even hit you. Cut the shit, kid. I want to know what you're *doing* here."

"It's all right," Weeks said, staring into L'Ordinet's Adam's apple, or through it and out the back of his neck. "It's just tender, don't worry about it."

"Thank you."

"You're very welcome. Should I answer your question?"

"What?"

"What am I doing here?"

L'Ordinet sighed, dropped to an infantryman's one-kneed squat, picked up little rocks and chunked them a few feet. He shook his head. "Sure," he said. "Please. If you don't have any appointments now."

"What am I doing here," Weeks II said, "is I am paying back, with no resentments, understand, the obligation written of by—someone."

"That's good," L'Ordinet said. "Now I understand what you're doing at eight o'clock at night in the only alleyway in Bailey when I happen to be in it."

"Actually, I saw it in a movie," Weeks II said. "Gary Cooper, I think. And Tonto or somebody. Maybe it was the Lone Ranger movies from when I was a kid."

"As opposed to being a grownup," L'Ordinet said.

"When the white man saves the Indian's life, the Indian is obligated to commit his soul to the care of the white man. He owes him a life, if you get my meaning."

"And since you're an Indian," L'Ordinet said.

"Precisely. On the nose."

"Kid, you're crazy. You're a pillhead. You're a fucking pharmaceuticals addict, you know that?"

"I have redeeming virtues," Weeks II said. "I am loyal, and occasionally indomitable. I am known, during selected and urgent situations, to have the strength of ten."

"No," L'Ordinet said. "What you are is, you are insane. You are unstable, you're going to be committed for long-time observation, say fifteen years' worth to begin with. You're a fucking Son of *Sam.*"

"Wasn't he a nut?" Weeks said. "I cannot be insulted if I but try."

"Try. You try, all right," L'Ordinet said. He stood up and looked at Weeks's crippled arm.

Weeks stepped back and held his good arm up. "Don't engage in paranoid fantasies," he said. "Don't be frightened of your friends. The surgeon general has determined that paranoia is harmful to your health."

"Don't you call me crazy, you pistachio nut! You're so loose, you're beginning to *roll.* I want you to go away. Go home. Go away. I'll tell your father."

"Will not."

"I will fucking, *too.*"

"Won't."

"I'm telling you, kid, I *will.*"

"Won't."

L'Ordinet picked up a pebble and threw it. It bounced off Weeks II's raincoat. Weeks II crouched and the next pebble struck his head. "I'll tell him I *killed* you is what I'll tell him," L'Ordinet screamed.

From above them, a voice fell through the cloud of light: "Let him who is without wine raise the first bone."

Weeks straightened, smiled a wide grin, and shouted, "Jump!"

The student in the third-floor apartment, his smile palpable in his voice, intoned, "For it is written, truly, that many are called but often at the wrong number."

"Don't jump!" Weeks II called.

"And the rich man may pass through the sphincter of the camel, while the hump is needled in a coat of many colors."

"Jump!" Weeks called.

"So I say unto you, children of Israel and Bethpage, Long Island, be ye as a child while wetting not the sheets."

"Don't jump!" Weeks called.

L'Ordinet held his hands over his face, then removed them slowly and held them at his sides. He rigidly turned his back and walked away, toward the alley's mouth, away from Elizabeth Bean's apartment. The voice called down, "Build ye a boat, Noah, and put in it an Evinrude of every horsepower, and float ye upon the Sheepshead Bay in Brooklyn until my dove —how-de-*doo!*" The voice above the light crackled laughter, then, "Shmuck!" and the window slammed.

Mead Weeks II, staring up into the unilluminating glow, holding his shoulder, called, "Jump!"

Because, Eli Silver told himself as he lay in bed and didn't sleep, Gwen Silver, when Richard Nixon spoke at a rally in Syracuse, was the woman who stood during his speech to cry at the puppet face and little body, "Do you-all in Washington have plans for freeing the slaves, sir, or aren't they ready to govern their childlike lives?"

Because, after the Caesarian which had split her open, after Silver had waited through four hours of emergency surgery wondering how to live alone, she had said to him in Intensive Care, "Isn't this a bore?"

Because he knew there was always a wadded tissue in the left-hand pocket of her bathrobe.

Because Gwen Silver had lived with him on Cherry Street in Greenwich Village, and Henry Street, and Barrow Street, and in two small overpriced rooms on East Thirty-first Street, where they raced the roaches for dinner each night. Because she had lived with him in Cooperstown, New York, when he did his residency at Mary Imogene Bassett, and she had been the elementary-school teacher with the only winter coat in the district that shed as the weather changed.

Because—he rolled onto his side and stretched his arms and legs out, he didn't want this one, but it came, it often did, in spite of his willing it not to, with faucial diphtheria, with moniliasis, with the edema of kwashiorkor, with newborn pyuria and sweat electrolyte abnormalities—they had raised the exact same healthy child, who now spun under their lives.

Because, too, when he walked from the bed to the little television set and sat before it in the room that could have been in any hotel, watching Jerry Lewis bray and make faces, Silver had to address the darkness of the room: "You bitch. You sentimental bitch."

In the examination room of the nursery, Eli Silver watched a nurse named Marina Yganti roll the high cart with transparent plastic hood toward the table at which he stood, and he insisted that it was nothing more than another baby, it was red and a little puffy, with a grouchy taut face and fists the size of chestnuts.

"The mother says her baby breathes too fast," Marina said, sliding back the plastic shell on top of the cart and lifting the baby from its nest of blankets.

"They always say their babies breathe too fast," he said.

Marina nodded. "She says it has a cold."

Silver raised his eyebrows and winked at Marina, who didn't wink back, because Silver's face made no jokes. He said, "They always say their throats are clogged, too. Or their lungs are collapsing. They've got pneumonia. Instant pneumonia."

"It beats puerperal fever," Marina said.

"Only if you like pneumonia." Silver weighed the infant. "Anyway, puerperal fever used to get more mothers than kids."

"I read that in school, Doctor."

"Sorry," he said, not looking up, and not caring if Marina Yganti was insulted, because he was measuring Lizzie Bean's child, was stretching its limbs, running his hands over every part of its very soft flesh. He was horrified, as he always was at this point of the infant exam, to find that he thought of veal.

Silver listened to the heart, and because children die, he listened twice to the lungs and looked into its mouth and pharynx. He checked each nostril with a catheter. Holding the pelvis with his left hand, he held the flexed legs with his right and pushed. He did it again. "No hip click," he said. Then he lifted the child two inches from the top of the table and dropped it. The arms and legs shot out, collapsed back in. The child embraced itself. And Silver said to Marina, who took it down, "We have a full-term living normal male Caucasian child weighing 7 and 6/16 pounds, twenty-one inches in length, who gives a normal Moro Reflex. This child can be released to routine care in the nursery until the mother is discharged."

Silver stepped back, because one half of his usual job as attending pediatrician was done. Marina replaced the full-term living normal male Caucasian child in the cart, rearranged the blankets as the baby, responding late to its treatment, exposure to a world that wasn't soft, began to wail in short, nagging, monotone cries. The other half of his job began when Silver walked down the hall in his sterile gown and cap to enter Elizabeth Bean's room—it was dark and clean, like a room not occupied yet—to sit in the chair at the foot of her bed and watch her come up from surface drowsing and try to smile.

"Hello," Silver said, "you did a great job. Your baby's great."

Lizzie, her short hair raised by static, her chin and cheek muscles slack, her eyes ringed with fatigue and her face a dirty white, said, low, "Well, I guess everything's great, then."

Silver moved ahead because he didn't know where else to go; he said, "What I usually do now is I tell the mother the best way to breast-feed the child, you know, the easiest posture. Or how to do formulas, which is what I would advise, since the adoptive mother will obviously be using Similac or Enfamil or another prepared formula."

"Obviously."

"And there's stuff about how to wash diapers, or—no, she wants to use disposable diapers, so we don't have to do that."

"We could just get her in here, there's an extra bed. You could tell *her* what you usually tell them now."

"Liz, you're going to be fine. You're tired."

"And when they get tired, women always cry."

"And men bang on their chests and shoot bears, right? Come on, Liz. I'm trying to do this right."

"When will she take it?"

"Him."

"Him. It. Them. You. When?"

"Couple of days? Three, four days? I want to keep an eye on him, it's better to make sure he's absolutely healthy. Let him get strong."

"You're sure you can all wait that long? Because I don't want to hold up the delivery. Am I supposed to *give* it to her personally? You know, hand it over?"

Eli walked to the side of the bed and sat on it. Lizzie winced. He said, "You hurting?"

"Absolutely not. Why should I be?"

"All right, now. Listen." He rubbed at her hair and stroked her slightly moist forehead. She looked very ugly to him, and he didn't like the sweat on his fingertips. He rubbed her hair and head and told her, "Listen."

But he didn't say anything else. Lizzie closed her eyes, then opened them. "Thank you," she said. "I feel like *you* did part of this. Of *him*. You've been incredibly nice to me, and doing the adoption thing is the right thing to do, and I know it is. I want to thank you for being nice and a help, and everything."

"I haven't been nice. I've maybe been helping myself more than you. What I mean is, I'm not that sure I trust myself, darlin'."

"Where'd *that* come from?"

"Excuse me?"

"The 'darlin'.' You don't say that to me."

"I don't?"

"Aren't you the man of surprises."

"Oh," he said, "listen, I'm not just a pretty face, I'm a constant source of amazement."

"Aren't you. Say it again."

"What?"

"Darling—the way you said it."

"Darlin'?"

"Again."

"Darlin'."

"No. It isn't yours. Eli, have you been screwing around recently?"

He kissed her lips—he smelled phlegm and fatigue, he thought of the girl who floated in the lighted river. Standing high and out of reach, he said, "You have no idea how chaste I am."

Lizzie closed her eyes. She said, "I haven't been getting much, either."

Arnold Partse was as small as Mead Weeks, and wore the same suits Weeks did, though he looked as if he enjoyed them. Now, on a morning in March, he rubbed his hands together, making a brown lightweight herringbone jacket flap. His face was lean and long, his head bald with white fuzz brushed across the back, his nose was big and crooked, and his blue eyes were happy. He had a hoarse high voice, and he looked like someone who knew the laws and loved his office— colonial pine furniture in a big pine-paneled room decorated with varnished old maps and scrimshaw and model sailing boats.

"Folks," he said, rubbing his hands. "This is the beginning of getting called a beautiful name. You are parents. Mrs. Sorenson, Anne Sorenson, you're a mother. Right now. Philip Sorenson, you're a father now. Mom and Dad."

Eli stood near the door and held the child, six days old, in a nest of receiving blankets. The baby slept, his face a pale smoothness surrounded by the wrinkles of cloth, of Eli's large spread-fingered hands. Eli looked down at him as if he stared from an enormous distance, and as if he held him at peace with his eyes, and as if he were the father of this child.

Partse watched them all. He looked like a man trying to find something wrong. Then he looked like a man who couldn't, and he smiled, shuffled near his desk, said, "Fine. Fine. Do you want to do it? Are you ready, Mom?"

Annie, in a suede suit with an ironed white blouse and with one hand curled in a tight white fist, nodded. Phil moved back, toward a far corner and a stained highboy, then walked slowly, on his toes, but without resilience, toward Annie, who was moving to Eli Silver, who slowly extended his arms to place the baby in her arms, which assumed the natural curve, and held.

She didn't look at the baby. She looked at Phil. He was crying. "Well, go *ahead*," Phil said.

Annie bent her neck toward the baby. Phil looked at them intently, chewing his mustache, blinking his eyes; he looked away, but then had to turn back to them. Eli and Partse, a couple of bald men who worked in the same profession sometimes—studying laws, living in the odors of their violation— grinned at each other as if they had invented families.

Annie said, "Mike."

8 | Motor Skills

Cleft palate, pellagra, amoebic colitis, missing nipples, cracked spine: in the airport outside of town, as the four-seat commuter from LaGuardia lands, Eli Silver is seeing them all, comforting stunned parents of the twisted newborn, helping the bereaved to order small coffins, cupping the blood of his dead child as if to drink, leaning on a state police car with a handful of blood and a son in the ambulance that wobbles off all lights and sirens, while fire engines cry and his wife, with her broken bone, her flesh sucked white by shock, is taken to the Emergency Room, where they say, "He's gone."

It was late afternoon when Gwen arrived, the sun over the airport was fat and orange and dull behind a filter of violet clouds. And Silver opened his mouth as if the words—*pyloric, cranial, leukocyte*—might drain away like spit, as if the pictures —fine brown hair, small fingers clenched, the waxed eyelids— might drip away onto the blacktop where he stood, waiting, as Gwen came back.

She didn't smile, and Silver didn't speak; they drove like passengers in someone else's car, entered the house like tourists after a long ride, sat at the kitchen table, strangers in a restaurant, until Silver stood and made coffee. "It doesn't feel all *that* different," Gwen said.

"Same house."

"I mean, there you are in a bow tie and a handsome sport jacket, and here's the same old coffee pot and everything."

"Same jacket."

"Eli, darlin', you know what I am saying."

He nodded as the kettle screamed and he poured the boiling water over stale grounds. "You're saying you're home."

"I wish I was. I mean, I *am*. But you have to welcome me, don't you?"

"You mean I'm required to? Or it won't feel right until I do?"

"You do what you want to, darlin'. I'm the one who ran out."

"I'm the one who let him die, and you're right in what you're about to say, we don't need to ever talk about it again, I don't know how we could. Except I want to tell you something: I should have done better and I didn't. Couldn't. Didn't. And you believe that. You did when you went back—when you— Wherever you went. So did I. I do. So it's all right. And nobody owes anybody anything. Do you want it black?"

Gwen nodded, he served her, and they sat to see who drank coffee on the other side of the table. He was very tall and lean and bald, a neat professional man. She was tall, though shorter than he, with a slender body made rounder-looking by heavy breasts and the big glasses with thick lenses that made her face seem full, despite its length and the long nose. Her dark hair was pinned up, her pink clingy shirt under the white corduroy blazer was opened to just above her breasts, and Silver stared there, then made his eyes move.

She said, licking her lips, "You didn't *let* him die."

"I didn't give anyone my permission, no."

"It happened."

"You can't let it go. Just really think that. *Feel* that way about your baby dying on a highway because your husband, the famous baby doctor, screwed up."

"I can't just—I don't know how to think about it, that's why I came home. No. It's a reason. I know there are other things I came for. Other reasons." She leaned forward, her breasts against her forearm. "I wish you could have saved his life, Eli." She whispered it, small tears made dotted lines down each side of her nose, and she said, "I really wish you could have."

Silver, with his eyes squinted, drank the coffee he didn't want and said, "So how's your dad?"

And Gwen, leaning back again at their kitchen table, said, "Could a woman my age have a baby?"

"Would it be by me, or are you just asking for information?"

Gwen sat still, then moved her buttocks in the chair and said, "Daddy's fine. He's going to buy himself a motorcycle, he decided. One of the grain suppliers wants to sell him an old— it's the same name as the car. A German one, BMW. It's some old wonderful model of it or something, all the men chew tobacco and smoke cigarettes and say it's the greatest motorcycle ever built. BMW. It's real quiet, Daddy says. He makes this joke about how the Nazis used it because it was quiet enough for them to sneak up on the Jews. Isn't that tasteless? And him at seventy racing around on a big motorcycle, like he's Marlon Brando. He's got *diabetes*, Eli."

Silver sat and looked at Gwen. She looked back, then down, said, "Daddy's fine."

"Good. He lynch any Catholics lately?"

"Hasn't caught one lately," she said, smiling, looking at her fingers curving over one another on the tabletop.

"We've had a lot of sick kids, lately. There's some kind of ECHO virus going around."

"Isn't there always, this time of year?"

He nodded. "And allergies. All the molds are zapping the kids."

"Good old allergy shots," she said. "They bought us our first freezer, remember?"

"I promised Elden I'd come around tonight. I think he wants to ask me about his granddaughter. She pees her bed all the time, and his son's upset."

"The car salesman's upset? I didn't know he could feel for that long. Or think hard enough to know what was bothering him. I swear, Eli, I think he's a dinosaur—it takes twenty minutes for him to know when he's *shot*."

"They want me to recommend medication. Tofranil. Which I won't do. The side effects are really strange, sometimes. I don't know how good an idea it is."

"Did you tell him I was coming?"

"To his house? No."

"Into town, I mean."

"No."

Her tears came again. She said, "That makes good sense. You couldn't—how could you know if I would stay around long enough not to make a liar out of you?"

"It wasn't that."

"Don't mind it, Eli. You were right. How could you trust me to stay around?"

"It wasn't that, Gwen."

"Well, it doesn't matter. These are confusing times we are living in."

"What?"

"Small talk."

"Oh. Okay. What happened to the Houston Rockets this season?"

"Those kids cannot play team basketball for shit, is what happened. They're all so selfish, aren't they? The *guards*—Eli, I swear, I saw one of their guards decide not to pass off because there was an article that morning about the forwards. They're *so* selfish."

"Did you watch the Superbowl?"

"No. Did you?"

"No."

"Eli, did you fuck other ladies?"

"Did you?"

"I don't like the idea of doing it with women, and you know that. I'm a boringly heterosexual person."

"You know damned good and well what I mean, Gwen."

"I'm not promiscuous."

"You're not exactly a nun, either."

"Do you plan on telling me anything about your sexual life, Eli? I mean, names and dates and details? Because you know what? I think I hate this conversation. I think it's ugly. I don't think you're an ugly person."

"Thank you. I don't think you're an ugly person, either."

"I was hoping you wouldn't. So I think I'd like to propose that we do *not* tell each other this kind of thing. Is that all right?"

"Didn't you just ask me?"

"Oh. Yes, I did, didn't I? Well, that was only on account of I wanted to *know.*"

"That's much clearer."

"I'm trying very hard, darlin', not to pull one of my famous Southwest Texas dithering-lady acts on you. It's just so much easier to hide behind that kind of cackle."

"Gwen, don't you start being honest with me."

"Can't take it, can you?"

"I'd rather fight."

And she said, "Eli, we can't do that with each other any more. We have got to live straight. We have to get some *hope* operating."

"Then I can ask you what you meant about having a baby?"

"Sure you can. Sure. Sure."

"And?"

"If you did, I wouldn't know what to say, however. You see, I kept on thinking, we can't replace him." She stopped talking and looked down again, her fingers fought with each other. Then she looked up and said, "But if we could just find a way to use up some of the love we can't give out now. Instead of letting it sit there and turn rotten."

"You're saying we should have a child?"

"Eli, don't you *love* me?"

Out of the images and the sour stomach and the shortness of breath and the aching knee and the sweat at night, out of the names recited in darkness—*rubella, cleft palate, varicella*—and out of the pit of poisoned words and the blood of children, a stupid wide and unchecked smile emerged to sit on his face and shame him, hiding behind it, helpless to send it away.

"Hello, Eli," she said.

Annie ran barefoot to find Phil standing at the front of the crib, naked except for boxer shorts, while Mike lay wailing on the changing table Annie had painted to match the dresser and crib. Mike wailed because he was wet or because he was cold or because the bottle of formula he required was still in a pan of hot water at the other end of the table. And Phil was caught in the crib. His arm, past the wrist, had been driven through the plywood of the unbarred end. Blood streaked his knuckles, and Annie looked to see if he'd beaten Mike.

Phil guessed, and said, his voice hoarse, "I don't punch kids."

"What'd you *do?*"

"I hit the crib is what I did. I pulled my hand back as hard as I could and I beat the living shit out of the crib because he wouldn't stop *crying.*"

Annie finished changing Mike. She sat down on the rocker they'd moved from the porch—one remained there, and so each rocked above the swamp alone, infrequently—and put the plastic nipple in his mouth. He watched her face carefully, laid two fingers on the bottle, almost touching her own, and swallowed, made a little version of the river sound that cattle make when they chew at cud, *ee-um, ee-um,* and Annie didn't look away from his head, which lay on her knee, or his feet, in white terrycloth pajamas, which lay against her stomach. She held the bottle, and Mike did, and the room was silent except for the swallowing sounds.

After a while, with half the bottle gone and Mike panting as Annie held the bottle away, Phil said, "I think I didn't break anything."

"You broke the crib."

"I'll fix it. I meant my hand."

"Good."

"I wasn't trying to hurt the baby."

"Mike."

"I know his name."

Annie gave him the bottle again, and Mike sighed while he gulped. Annie rubbed his instep, held his foot, said "Yum" to him.

"I ran out, babe."

"Don't call me babe. I'm so pissed off at you—"

"I just ran out. I don't know how to live with anyone else besides us."

She looked up and said, "Start learning."

He bit at his mustache. He said, "Will you help me *out?*"

Annie laughed and bumped Mike, who continued to drink, but who looked surprised. "It's all right, little man," she said. "Not you," she said to Phil. "You stay stuck in there a while, I'll get to you when I'm done with this baby over here."

Phil looked at his swollen streaked hand and flexed the fingers, which protruded. "What is this I see before me," he intoned, trying hard.

Annie watched Mike.

"Babe?" he said.

She put Mike on her shoulder and stood, rubbing his back to burp him. She carried him to where Phil had impaled the crib, and she looked down at his hand. She said, "Sucker punch."

Gwen slept on the sofa in Eli's workroom, and when he brought in coffee on Saturday morning, early, and stood beside her, she was moving slowly in her cocoon of blankets, talking inside clenched jaws and tight lips; her eyelids were fluttering like animal flanks; her arms were moving in the underwater helplessness of dreams. Eli studied the skin of her face, listened to the grinding of her jaws. It is in sleep, he understood, that people who live together for a long time can see the other's face unprepared by even habit. Gwen suddenly lay flatter, the nightmare was gone or interrupted, perhaps by her barest sense of his presence. And he saw her in her death —mouth unflatteringly open, lips crusted and dry except for a glint of drool in the lower right-hand corner, the cheeks and forehead uncomposed. Then she tightened all over and swam again, and her mouth worked. Eli thought that now, it was possible, he was her nightmare—the heat of his flesh, the weight of his waiting, the need in his stare: he was the bad dream. For only seconds she had been alone. And now, her husband the disease, Gwen was febrile again, and fighting.

In his workroom, which was like a small boy's toy room—flints and labeled shards in wooden frames, old arrowheads and new hunting bow, the shotgun given in lieu of fees, the long counter neatly stacked with offprints and clippings and books, the tape recorder and carton of cassettes, the CB radio still in its box that a grateful parent had given for Christmas, a gift-wrapped bottle of Armagnac, the shabby wing chair and shabbier sofa that his wife in seemliness or plain fear had insisted she sleep on—Gwen woke, looked panicky and then relieved, then pleased, then maybe wary, and she said, "How *do* you do?"

She sat up on the sofa, wrapping bedclothes around her, and he sat near her curled feet. They drank coffee together, not speaking. She squinted against the morning light, which shadowed his face. When she squinted again, Eli found her glasses on the floor and handed them to her. She held them and said, "How long have we been doing this?"

"Fifteen years?"

"Pretty damned close to it, I believe. We have an anniversary coming up in July, number sixteen."

"We missed the last one."

"Oh, no. I celebrated at home. I went dining and dancing with a mighty confused cowboy. We had beer with our steak and guitar music with our candlelight, and he insisted on showing me his Southwest apparatus."

Silver looked into his coffee. "That would be directly south, I think."

"I didn't seize the occasion, darlin', if you know what I mean."

"You don't have to tell me that."

"Well, I believe that I *do*. In fact, I would be grateful, Eli, I would appreciate it, if you displayed some interest. Some concern, in point of fact. Some *fury*, for God's sake."

Eli put his coffee mug on the floor and stood, walked the small room with his hands in his pockets. "Did you come home for specific reasons? I mean, did you come home for *some*-thing? Or did you come home because it felt like time to come home? Do you see the difference I'm getting at?"

"No."

"You don't want to."

"That's right."

"Do you know what you want?"

"Yes."

"Will you tell me, please?"

"Surely. I want you to drag me off to bed and for us to feel like it's all right even though I ran off screaming like a crazy person without thinking enough about *you* screaming right here in our house. I would appreciate it if we produced a baby that was healthy enough for us to raise so we could feel like we were living again. *But—*"

Silver was standing at the wall of bookshelves, slapping at bindings, shaking his head.

"*But, god*damn you, will you listen! But I did not come home just to produce a replacement for him. I wouldn't do that. I wouldn't do that. I'm saying *us,* history is something you don't—" She panted, rubbed the skin above the breasts, along her wide shoulder. "What am I trying to say here, Eli?" She laid her head on her hand and squeezed her own face.

Eli pushed with his palm at the gouty knee and said, "You said it. History. You're right. I wish I'd said it to you. It means you're staying here, doesn't it?"

"I do not intend to take off."

"Are you married to me?"

"I always have been. Sometimes I do it better than other times is all. Do you intend to stop asking me questions?"

"Yes."

"Do you intend to start pitching woo at me?"

"No."

"If I ask you why, will it humiliate me?"

"Allergy shots. It's Saturday morning. I have to go. I don't know what to say, anyhow."

"You'll be back, though."

"I will."

"But what I'm wondering about," she said. "You loved me so much. You loved me more than him. Will you tell me how I'm supposed to learn how to forgive you for that?"

Phil was typing, with all nine fingers, at a vita sheet to photocopy and send out to prep schools and high schools and small colleges that might require an athlete of the participle for the autumn to come. Annie, sitting in the kitchen, was looking at books about babies. She read aloud: "One of the most interesting things about a newborn baby is that he is a fairly efficient living machine."

At the kitchen table, tapping slowly, Phil said, "He's a peeing machine, and a pooping machine, and you can count on him to wake up like a fire engine if you just fell asleep."

"I'm reading about motor skills," Annie said.

"He's got a motor, all right. It never winds down."

Annie looked over and said, "He's a person, Phil."

Phil nodded and typed in the lie about being Phi Beta Kappa. He felt her looking, and he said, "Mike's beautiful."

"Except you get so *mad.*"

"I'm not used to it."

"How much time do you think you need?"

Phil typed a few extra years of teaching experience onto the vita and blushed when he thought of being interviewed by men and women of good intention and deep fatigue at the Modern Language Association convention in New York. He struck *e* instead of 3 and pulled the sheet from the platen. "How much time can you give me?"

But the next afternoon, with Mike, he was smiling as he watched the Washington Bullets stalk Golden State. The picture broke up periodically, and the whine of the offending chain saw, from the far edge of the swamp, came up each time the red and blue static fuzzed the image. Mike was on his chest, peering down into his face, then collapsing onto it with his own, as Phil, propped on a cushion, looked over and around the bobbing small head. Mike drooled cool sweet saliva onto Phil's mouth, and when Mike's head dropped, his lips lay against Phil's mustache. Phil leaned back and closed his eyes and nibbled, and Mike made a low burring sound. Then he started to nurse on Phil's lip.

From the corner of his mouth, Phil said, "He's eating me."

"Enjoy it," Annie said. "Pretty soon, he won't even talk to you."

"You leaving me, Mike?" Phil said. "You going away from your old man?"

Mike turned his cheek onto Phil's face and curled a fist in his whiskers.

"I wish I had a camera," Annie said.

Phil said, "Shh."

"Is he asleep?"

"Shh."

"It's time to heat the milk," Annie said. "Stay there with him, I'll do it."

"Shh."

That morning, he had heated the milk. At four o'clock, swallows already fighting outside in the leaking weak light, with Mike's room dark behind drawn curtains, Annie sat on the rocker and held Mike's bottle to his mouth as he lay on her knees. Phil sat on top of the bureau and slowly swung his bare legs. They had been talking about New Hampshire and then the house in Maine where they had lived after two miscarried infants, and Phil was speculating on the new owners of their house above the bay that went out to the Atlantic and the dark-gray waters where seals rose.

"They probably tore out the wood stove and the well and put in central heating and six high-power lines."

Mike cooed in his throat as he drank. "No," Annie said, "they put in the power lines, but they left the well. They painted the box white and they grow flowers in it."

"Geraniums, probably. Big fat red suburban flowers."

"Do you miss it?" she said.

"It was a great house. Except we weren't happy in it."

"We weren't happy anyplace, I don't think."

Phil said, "You mean our whole life was crap until we got Mike?"

"No. And you know it. Except—you know, I used to sleep so late there so many mornings."

"It was cold."

"It was not wanting to get up, always."

"And now you do."

She said, "This is corny. I actually feel glad to get up because I can see him. Isn't that—"

"What?"

"It makes you mad, doesn't it?"

Phil said, "I refuse to whine."

"But?"

"I thought maybe sometimes you didn't mind meeting me, coming around a corner sometimes."

"I didn't mind meeting you, asshole."

"Well, it doesn't sound as if it was all that good."

"You know damned good and well I was—upset."

"Death does that."

"Thank you."

"Well, what about *me*, Annie?"

"You're a father."

"What's that supposed to mean?"

Moving the bottle slowly in Mike's mouth, watching him suck after it, Annie said, "Damned if I know."

"Well, don't be cute, all right?"

"Don't be jealous, all right?"

"*Me?*"

"Yes."

He rubbed his hands together as if they were cold. The chafing of the calluses was coarse in the warm room smelling of lotion and the baby's breath. "Yes," he said.

He complained less as April grew out of the ground, with high tiger lily leaves and last autumn's oak cemented to the earth beneath them. The swamp was in an uproar, it spread to their hill and the budding trees, and on good days, Phil and Annie spread a tarpaulin for Mike to lie on while Phil watched, or crawled above him, and Annie, still afraid of doing everything wrong, read Spock and Gesell and Orlansky, checking on Mike's development. She was sure that he was precocious because he had raised his head two weeks before Sweeny & Vincent had predicted he might. Phil lay on his back, sometimes, and held Mike's yellow rubber hedgehog in his mouth and keened. Annie lay on her back and held Mike, in soft corduroy overalls, above her head, slowly spinning him, gently bringing him down to her chest. Phil taught the second semester of his first semester's failure, and Annie commuted, every three weeks, to Eli Silver's office, where she reported on Mike's reactions to weather and new pulped vegetables. Lizzie Bean returned to work, replied to ads for deans and college counselors, evaded L'Ordinet, and avoided being a patient of Eli Silver. Phil pointed to the sputum stains on the shoulders of his flannel shirts. Mike said, "Ooh!" and Annie noted it on the margin of a newspaper that she lost. Phil received two postcards telling him that his qualifications were not precisely what Macungie College, Macungie, Pa., had in mind, and that the

Milton Academy was of the opinion that its students didn't need preparation in elementary composition.

Turner and Phil boxed less, but continued to meet in the gym, to shuffle and sweat; Turner sounded less like the old Turner, but not yet like someone else. Mead Weeks II took a leave of absence from school, at Miss Bean's sugestion, but sat in Phil's office, occasionally, not speaking, watching Phil write in his journal—*Annie happiest*—for the last time. Demby and Oliver drove to Wampsville to bail out Horace L'Ordinet, who had been arrested for drunken driving, speeding, and reckless endangerment. Mead Weeks issued a memorandum on *Conduct Becoming a Professor*, which Phil brought home, and which he read aloud to Annie.

She started to hoot, that Friday afternoon, as they drank whiskey over ice in the kitchen while Mike, in his playpen, burred and gurgled at clothespins he gummed. She hooted harder and more crazily when Phil, standing to declaim, read, "A professor is a professional."

"And a professional is a professor."

"A hooker's a professional," Phil said.

"That's right! So a teacher's a hooker."

"A hooker's a teacher."

"When does she act like she's becoming a professor?" Annie asked.

"When she takes your money and lies down," Phil said.

"This is becoming dumb," Annie said.

That silenced them, for a few seconds, until Phil said, "What do you call a whore who doesn't work on Sundays?"

Annie said, "I got a little worried about money today."

"There's enough."

"I mean about next year. I'm sorry."

"No. It's a thought."

"It's actually more of a terror," she said.

"I'll get something."

"You probably will. But we'll end up living in Council Bluffs, Arkansas, or someplace."

"Isn't Council Bluffs in Indiana?"

"Ohio."

"No," he said, "no, it's one of those—Dakota?"

"Which Dakota? *Idaho!* That's where it is, Idaho."

"Jesus," Phil said. "I don't want to go to Idaho. Where's Idaho?"

"Near that Mormon place? Utah?"

"It is?"

"I don't *know.* You see why I got worried? We don't even want to go there, and they didn't even ask us, and if they do, then what? We'll never even find it."

Phil said, "We can ask them to send us a map."

"Is there a job in Idaho?"

"I don't even know if there's a school in Idaho," he said.

"Phil, so what are we going to do?"

"I think we should stand on our dignity and refuse."

"Refuse *what?*"

"I don't know. What would you like to refuse?"

"Let's refuse to discuss money."

"Done. It's a subject unbecoming."

"Yeah," she said, "but it's on its way."

"But it will have to wait its turn," Phil said. "There are so many subjects on their way."

"Name six."

"Me," he said, putting his glass down, rising from the table, charging at her.

"No," Silver said into the phone in his kitchen, "I don't celebrate Passover, it's all right. You can call me anytime. It's fine."

"Is she the one?" Gwen whispered, carrying in his jacket and tie.

Silver waved his palm at her and said, "If he runs a temp, you bring him in tomorrow at ten, I give allergy shots but I can look at him—ten on the dot, maybe a minute before. Okay?"

"Bullshit," Gwen whispered, "it's her."

"That's right, love. The vaporizer for hot steam, but keep it down and away from the crib, you don't want a boiled baby. And the pediatric nosedrops, Tyzine, yes. No medication, though, right? Nothing else. Now, it's probably a little sinusitis, nothing more than a cold. But if he has *any* trouble breathing, any difficulty at all, you make a croup tent—just put a sheet, tape a sheet over the top of the crib to catch the steam, and if he changes color, or his lips get blue, anything like that, turn on the shower full blast, sit there with him, keep him sitting up so he doesn't panic, keep him calm. See, if they can't breathe well a little, they panic and they start to cry. Then you get the airway constricted, and it gets worse. Now, if there's any change in color and he spikes a temp, you do what I told you and have your husband—Phil, yes. He calls me right away, and if you can't get me, or if you get scared, you get right the hell down to the Emergency Room. They'll call me. Yes, they'll know whether he needs oxygen. But it probably—that won't happen, love. It's just a little cold, probably. All right? And don't worry. I mean it. I'm here if you need me. Yes."

"If you're not putting her away—"

"Gwen."

"I'm just joking, darlin'. I promised you, I told you I wouldn't ask and I am not asking. Am I?"

"Let's go to the party, Gwen."

"Except, who is she?"

"Gwen, she's one of my mothers. She's the one I found the baby for. That's all."

"As long as you didn't make the baby for her."

"It's a deal. I didn't."

She handed him the tie and watched him make a knot. "How much future do you suppose we might have left, Eli?"

He took the jacket from her and put it on. "Are you serious? Are you that lonely? Am I making you that lonely?"

Gwen turned her back to him and said, "Nope. I'm a brave lady from Second City."

"I'm sorry," he said.

"Sugar," she said, "*that's* the price of admission here."

"I'd love you to be happy, Gwen."

"Thank you, darlin'."

"Gwen."

"No, honestly. Thank you very much. I hope that little baby's healthy as he can be, too."

"Gwen—he'll be fine."

"I hope it doesn't die. I hope nobody dies."

"Die? Nobody's dying, Gwen."

"I hope he lives forever."

"He'll be fine. He will."

"Then what was that about the Emergency Room, Eli? And high fever, and all of that? Is that baby gonna be all right?"

"I promise."

She walked toward the door that led to the hallway. "What would you like to talk about in cheerful tones on our way over?" she said.

9 | Articulations of the Upper Extremity

Bluets, vetch, and joe-pye weed were bright in the state forests above Route 12 where Horace L'Ordinet parked his Chevrolet, its tires deep in black earth. Then he walked. He carried the ax, its handle charred, that Mead Weeks II had left near the quarry above the campus, and on his back was the knapsack that Weeks II had abandoned. The sack was heavy, bulging, and equipment hung from its old leather straps—half-gallon water bottle in a canvas casing, foot-long bush knife in a leather scabbard, a forest-green musette bag, a four-foot, bow-shaped trail saw with a red handle. L'Ordinet was dressed in dark clothing and wore high black rubber boots. The weeds and flowers were purple and blue and yellow; protruding from fallen wet trees, growing from the sides of thick black stumps, were wide soft golden fungi that looked like disease.

He walked in silence, making silence where he went—along a faint track, very narrow, through thick evergreen forest, through small clearings where the afternoon sun was the color of fungus, over a small fast stream where midges pooled in the air, then back into the darkness made by evergreens—and everywhere he walked, clumsily, his ax banging trees, his knapsack ringing, his breath whistling, his voice in the larynx going "Unh," the jays made warning cries and then went quiet, the sparrows and bobwhites held still. A quail hen threw herself, wing dragging, across his path, decoying him from her young; L'Ordinet walked away from her, saying nothing to acknowledge that she'd scared him breathless, open-mouthed.

Where a floor of glacial rock interrupted his path, there were his chip marks on the gray and black stone, arrows scratched sloppily, but he didn't need to consult them. He carried his pack and his ax and went along, his throat saying "Unh," his mouth saying nothing, and soon he was over the rock bed and walking up a steeper section of the track he had marked with his feet.

The pine forest to which he came was thinner than the ones below, and more sunlight fell through the treetops to make the floor of brown needles glow. Here, fifty feet in, was L'Ordinet's extracurricular project—a structure of felled saplings and dragged rotten trunks, half of a lean-to, something of a fort.

L'Ordinet threw his knapsack inside the three walls, each several feet high, made of propped notched heavy wood. Laying the ax on top of the pack, he took his blue woolen vest off, rolled up the sleeves of his blue woolen shirt, and stood in his personal clearing with his hands on his hips to look at the sun splatters on shiny pine, on bright-brown needles, on the shelter he'd begun. Then, from the knapsack, he took a bottle of Rhone wine, a plastic folding cup, and a sandwich made of spiced meat and mayonnaise. Standing, filling his mouth, smearing his chin, letting wine spill from his lips as he drank, L'Ordinet had a picnic before starting to work.

He walked from the clearing into denser forest, where heavy limbs had fallen, and small trees, and he dragged some back. He reentered the darker parts and chopped, with economy and expertise, a young evergreen, and hauled it to the fort. He skimmed the small branches off with easy horizontal strokes of the ax, then, setting one length of wood atop another, at right angles, he chopped and sawed—measuring only with his eye, and quickly—until he had much of the fourth wall complete. From sections of the larger lopped branches, he made long pegs that reinforced what he had forced erect. And it was later, not dark, but with a dimness diluting the hard light of April afternoon, that he stood with bark shreds on his shirt and splinters on his woolen sleeves, the knapsack inside his fort, and he outside it, looking—eyes little and steady, nostrils flared—as if he had made some place safe.

He carried the ax and saw and wine over the wall and lay back, his shoulders on his knapsack, sometimes drinking the water he'd carried with him, and sometimes the wine, looking up at the lessening brightness of the sky. Later, when there still was a little light left, he took a small thick magazine, a quarterly, from the knapsack and lay on his side, one arm propping his head, and stared in, leaning close, to look at a poem by Philip Sorenson, written six years before, that spoke of children jumping from a bridge to swim—

> each child, from the highest
> piling, electric with the wish
> to have the burning over with

—and he tapped the journal as if to offer praise. He took a flashlight from the pack and shone it, in the orange and purple wash that entered the grayness of dusk, and looked once more at the poem, then put the book and light away. He rubbed himself with insect repellent, replaced the bottle in a pocket of the knapsack, settled himself on his back, hands clasped beneath his head, and looked up.

It wasn't a dream in L'Ordinet's mind, because he didn't sleep and because the voices were his, spoken from outside his brain and by him—his own hard Middlewestern twang, each statement rising slightly with the tone of question, saying Sorenson got a kid in the middle of no place, like that, like you get a baby by snapping your fingers instead of loving and waiting a while. Elizabeth Bean has a baby by a man who shall remain nameless if she can help it, and all of a sudden the thumbless poet in disguise who'd rather sweat and box shows up with baby vomit on his shoulders and a wife who smiles and something in the cradle that is definitely not a kangaroo. My baby in a sterile house. H. L'Ordinet, deprived of child.

L'Ordinet curled upward, his legs not moving, his body bending forward and up. From his sitting position, he leaned his head toward the ground, teetered from the Indian squat, and was on his feet, packing the knapsack, tying the saw and water bottle on. He shoved his vest through the top of the pack in spite of the deepening chill, got the pack onto his back. In his left hand he carried the ax, in his right the flashlight. Its weak yellow light was diffused by the glowings of dusk, but he shone it at the ground and, stepping over the wall of his unroofed house or grown boy's fort, walked down the trail toward the rock bed. And when he came to the scratchings he had made as trailmarkers, he looked toward where he had been and, with the ax blade, gouged the markers out, so that his light caught only wide white scuffs on the stone, pointing nowhere. Then, his light brighter in the purer darkness, he carried everything down the narrow track, through black forest and across the silver stream and back to the world.

Lizzie didn't act surprised when she answered the door and found Mead Weeks II, in his open raincoat and new orange track shoes, smiling his white teeth and moving his soiled eyeglasses under her door light. She held her face as if it gave off signals which had to be concealed from Weeks in order that he neither snarl nor bite. And when Weeks II said, "That's a highly attractive bathrobe, Mizz Bean," she only thanked him and waited.

"I am here," he said, "to consult with you."

"Who's helping who?"

"If I may: *whom.*"

"Thank you."

He shrugged and said, "I should know, huh? The language runs in our family. So does correcting people. Could I come in to see you?"

"How about in the office, Mead? Tomorrow? I'm a little busy."

"Mizz Bean, from that glass on the table and the book beside it, I would guess that you're settling down to relax. I apologize for unsettling your evening, but you aren't really *that* busy, and there is a need."

"There is a need? What? Mead—what are we talking about?"

"Consultation, ma'am. My father would appreciate it."

"I'm sure he would. Ten minutes, all right? You have to promise. There are things I want to do."

"Everybody has things—"

"Mead!"

"—he wants to do. Yes, ma'am. Ten minutes, and we are all grateful."

Inside, Lizzie moved in the room while Weeks II sat on the sofa and looked at the cover of her book. Each time he looked up, she moved a foot or hand, changed her posture or her place in the room.

"This isn't what you had in mind for your Thursday evening off, I understand," he said. "I wanted to—what? About eight minutes left, would you say? I wanted to tell you that there is a clear and present danger, ma'am. I would say: Fly, the game is afoot."

"Thank you, Mead."

"Professor L'Ordinet has become unbalanced, I'm sorry to report."

"Thank you, Mead. It's time for you to leave now."

"He's not stable, and I think you, of all, must know."

"And good night," she said, leaning against the mantel, her hands deep in the bathrobe pockets.

"You know," he said, "I am a person of weak sexual impulse. It runs in my family. Shall I say: it's dried up in my family. But I want you to know, I can smell your breasts from across the room."

"Did you ever understand *anyone*, Mead? Anyone else? I don't want you to stay in my apartment any more."

"I'm not a rapist," he said. "It's entirely safe."

"And I'm not a rapee. Go away now, Mead."

"It was a compliment, ma'am. I can smell your fulsome breasts, the warmth from the valley between them, across the room."

"*That* is something you read in a book, kid. Good night."

Weeks stood and walked toward her. She made a fist and held it before her. "No," he said, "I'm not a threat."

"Out."

"It's Mr. L'Ordinet."

"*Out!*"

"See," Weeks said, "he and I are bound by oaths of fealty and chains of obligation. But I feel a stronger duty, though I have no intention of betraying the man I owe my life to, I have this extremely stronger feeling of obligation, it's only temporary with you, although it's a permanent tie with Mr. L'Ordinet, I owe him a tremendous amount, you see, it's a headlong stare of duty with him, whereas it's more of a peripheral though sincere glance, you might say, in your own case. If I can smell your breasts, then I'm in your thrall, but just a little. So I thought I'd tell you."

Lizzie opened the door, and he turned and walked through

it, carefully not touching her—she flinched anyway—as he went past her and down the stairs, smiling like someone who has performed immodestly effective deeds.

On the phone with Mead Weeks, the elder, she said, "Professor Weeks, your son came to my house tonight."

"Yes," he said, "and I want you to know how grateful I am for these counseling sessions you've arranged with Mead. I think they've been making a difference. I did, really, mean to phone first to thank you, but I have to confess I was embarrassed. I am. A father who doesn't understand his son."

"How long has Mead been coming here—did he tell you?"

"You mean—"

"How long, Mr. Weeks?"

"Well, I don't know, really. Is about two weeks accurate?"

"Mr. Weeks. Professor Weeks."

"Mister is fine. You can call me Mead, if you like, Elizabeth. May I call you Elizabeth?"

"Oh, Christ, Profes—Mr. Weeks. Your kid came here for the first time, ever, tonight."

"He did?"

"Cross my heart."

Weeks lost his tone of gratitude, of social correctness, of slightly goatish thirst. He said, "Elizabeth, my son is nutty as a fruitcake."

"Your son is a disturbed person, Mr. Weeks."

"He's taking drugs, you know, I'm sure of it."

"He sounds like he already took them all."

"And so. So."

"Mr. Weeks?"

"Can you tell me what I should do?"

"You should take him to a psychiatrist. Maybe at Upstate? Tomorrow morning, first thing. Sit there in the outpatient clinic with your son and *see* someone."

"I have a class tomorrow. A nine o'clock, and then an eleven-twenty. But I want to do the right thing, of course. Mead *should* be seen, you're right. I've started a correspondence, in a small way, with someone at that hospital, in fact. They seem —"

"Good night, sir."

"I beg your pardon?"

"I'm too tired to talk to you, Mr. Weeks, good night."

"Oh. Good night."

"Yes."

She stood at the phone, one finger disconnecting it; then, with her head hanging as if she couldn't stay awake, she dialed and waited for Eli Silver to answer.

But it was a woman who said, "Silver," as if she were an exhausted doctor.

Lizzie said, "Ah, Eli Silver's residence? Dr. Silver?"

The voice grew sharper. "Yes, it is."

"Oh. Are you Dr. Silver's nurse?"

"At ten o'clock at night? I don't allow him *that* kind of assistance."

"Oh."

"But I bet you I can tell who *you* are."

"I'm a patient," Lizzie said. "I was a patient of his a while back."

"His practice is limited to the treatment of infants and small children, lady."

Lizzie said, "Well, where were *you* when the lights went out?" She hung up hard.

L'Ordinet lived in a small apartment complex on the raw new road that ran above and parallel to University Drive. His flat was equipped with harsh-white, very smooth walls and synthetic tan shag carpeting and dark impervious furniture. It was as neat as a doctor's anteroom. L'Ordinet stood at his typewriter, holding on to the back of a chair, still dressed in dark-blue cloth, reading what he had written: *Somebody stole someone's person.*

When he answered the telephone at last, Mrs. DeAngelo asked if he was ill, and would he like her to get someone to teach his classes for a couple of days. L'Ordinet, his voice uninflected, insisted he was fine. Mrs. DeAngelo said that he had missed two days of classes already. L'Ordinet replied that he'd been thinking, and hung up. When the telephone rang again, he watched it until it stopped.

In the tiny kitchen, later, he unwrapped packages he had opened before; they contained envelopes of powdered milk, instant beef stew, dehydrated vegetables, pre-sweetened oatmeal. There was a small sealed plastic survival kit containing fish hooks and matches, a compass, a flare, a whistle, bouillon cubes, a compressed plastic emergency blanket. There was a small first-aid kit, an oblong rechargeable flashlight, a survey map of the state-owned lands above Route 12. He looked at them, laid them out on his counter, then replaced them in their mailing wrappers and put them back in the cupboard with the very clean glasses and plates.

In the alcove closet, with Joan Sutherland arias playing loud on his cassette recorder, L'Ordinet looked at new boot socks and his black rubber boots, at his blue woolen vest, at a pair of reinforced canvas duck-hunting pants, a heavy poncho with a brown and green camouflage pattern, a brown felt slouch hat. He whistled between his teeth, and then he sang the love of a courageous woman for a doomed political prisoner, no parody in his voice, but great off-key conviction.

The telephone tinkled under the music and the two committed voices, and he heard it. Shutting the closet door, looking at the phone on the living-room windowsill, holding the door-knob with one hand, gently rubbing his groin with the other, he sang on, but not in the language of Sutherland. He sang, "Somebody stole someone's *per*-son," holding the stressed first syllable strong and hard, as if he were not a man whose arms, despite his recent exercising, often felt weak, whose heart thudded slowly, painfully, when he took airplane rides or drove up mountain roads, and whose vision sometimes blurred, whose stomach sometimes emptied, at those altitudes. L'Ordinet was on his way to fainting, and he knew it, so he permitted himself to slide slowly down the length of the closet door until he sat against it. He drew his legs in and held them at the knee. He bent his head forward to rest atop his hands. He instructed himself in deep breathing, counseled himself control.

When the tape cassette stopped and the telephone was silent and he sat in his apartment breathing deeply and hearing only his breath, L'Ordinet looked up, across the room, and announced with surprise, "My shoulder still hurts."

Billie was whipping them in and Eli was whipping them out, because Billie's husband, a clerk for the sheriff's department, had to attend a bowling-league finals that Thursday night, and Billie wanted, she said, for once in the year, to be done on time. Underweight infants and overweight teenage boys, bedwetters, insomniacs, canker sores, unspecific stomach complaints, high fevers, two-week low-grade infections, and the usual run of sore throats and leaking sinuses—Eli, more or less cheerful to the parents, happy with the kids, sleeping while awake but functioning with some efficiency, walked his little corridor and visited his little examination rooms and gave prescriptions—Phenargan for coughs, Actifed for sinuses, sleep and liquids for colds, ease for the parents, Tootsie Pops for the children, joy to the world. He charged them $8 and $12 and $15 and nothing, and continued to move, his heavy shoes clopping, his long arms swinging, his knee pain making the calf muscle tremble by six-thirty, as the last mother of the day, the potato-fat wife of an Agway fuel-truck driver, carried out her two-year-old, whose lower face was bisected by wide bright-yellow streams of mucus from a sore red nose.

Eli called good night to Billie, and walked into his office, unbuttoning his long blue coat. When he shut the door, Elizabeth Bean, sitting on the sofa, said, "Am I still a patient?"

He sat behind his desk—it gave a little protection—and prodded with two fingers at an ashtray in the shape of a baby's footprint. He arranged the margins of the day's stacked mail. Lizzie said, "It could be the time has come for us to have a talk, Eli. Am I still a patient?"

"You're still a friend of mine," he said. "How are you?"

"I'm extremely well, thank you. I'm doing my job all right, and I think I was right to keep on living alone—without a baby to take care of. I'm an unstable person. I'm also a pretty intelligent person, that's why I do my job well. So I keep wondering, how much more stable would I have been if I'd kept it? Him."

"The baby's in good hands."

Lizzie said, "I'm not here to ask you who got it. Who got the baby."

"Him," Eli said.

"Him. I really shouldn't know. I'd prefer not to."

"I'm not going to tell you, Liz."

"I *said* I didn't want to know."

"So, how've you been?" Eli tried the old harried doctor's smile without knowing how not to try it, felt his eyes shifting to the telephone and mail and carton of starter samples on the rug near her feet, felt his hands wander on the desk, heard his feet scuff.

Lizzie sat up straight on the edge of the sofa, brought her legs together, clasped her hands on top of her thighs. She looked at his eyes and said, "Do you remember what we did together?"

Eli smiled the smile and nodded.

"Does that—do they embarrass you?"

He shook his head.

"And we were lovers, right? I mean, you remember the acts, but you also remember the condition? Something like being lovers?"

Eli said, "Lovers."

"Do you love me?"

Eli said, "I don't ever want you to think for a *second* that I was—that what happened to us was because of the baby. He was what was happening while *we* were happening."

"Eli, what in hell are you talking about?"

"It wasn't just to place a baby."

"*What?*"

"I didn't want you to think that."

"You thought I'd think that?" She stood up and kicked the front of his desk. It was dark hard wood, her face went white, and she fell backward to sit on the sofa. "Ow," she said. "Ow, look at me, you bastard: why does that idea even come *up?*"

Eli shook his head and spread his arms, shrugged his shoulders, tried to smile. "No," he said, "don't think that way, Liz. I was only worried about you. Just now, about that thing with the baby." He puffed his cheeks and blew out. "What I am trying to say is that in case that idea occurred to you, I didn't want you to believe it. Preventive medicine is all it was."

"Prophylaxis of the mind," she said. "Does that make you a scumbag or a prick?"

They sat in his office, doctor and patient, he behind the ostentatious desk, she on the tasteless orange leather sofa, and if someone had looked through his window they might have seemed, in the silence, to be dealing with matters of health.

"You know that my wife came home," he said. "Gwen."

"Darlin'."

"What?"

"Never mind. You did make love to me six ways from Sunday. To say the very least. And you took care of me and kept me straight and got my baby seen to, and thank you. And thank me. I would have preferred a couple of phone calls. Or a postcard: ALL'S WELL, BUT FORGET IT. Something along the lines of communication and dignity and affection and just possibly, but I don't really *think* I'd have done it, but *maybe*, some news of your divorce and your impending marriage to Elizabeth Bean, college shrink and one *hell* of a woman. But I don't think so. I mean, I've got a career going, there are some colleges I might go work at. I'm not anxious to give it all up just to live in a drag-ass town full of doctors. Thanks anyway. Isn't this humiliating?"

Eli stood and walked around the desk to where she sat. He leaned over, pulled her up—for a tall woman with broad shoulders and a heavy neck, she moved easily off the sofa—and he hugged her around the shoulders and the back of the neck, squeezed her into him, held on. "You probably saved my life," he said.

She said into the cloth of his shirt, "You know I didn't try to kill myself. You know how childish that was. I'd be embarrassed if you took that seriously."

"It was an honorable symptom," he said. "It was the same as a high temperature."

"I hope you and your wife make out okay," she said, walking toward the door. "I mean, it would be a great thing, considering everything. It'd be like seeing somebody get cured of cancer and making it all right and living to be ninety."

"She wants to have a baby."

"You could always adopt one, Eli. I'll drop you a line if, you know, if one comes up."

Lizzie smiled, and Eli smiled, and when she went out and he heard her car in his driveway, whining backward, he limped back to his desk chair and let himself fall into it, feeling his eyes begin to wander at the letters and journals, watching his hands open and close the top desk drawer, closing his eyes to force them still, but feeling them nevertheless on the move beneath the lids as the dark road gleamed with the lights of the truck that was taking the curve too quickly and as he took a hand from the wheel, despite their high speed, and held it back, past Gwen's face—he saw only her enormous eyes—to push at the boy, to push at—he said the name, finally: Chuck. *Chuck*— but feeling nothing as the weight went out of the car, as it hydroplaned on the wet road, as the rear end lost all traction, as *control*—what else are doctors supposed to have?—as control went and the truck, its air horn crying like an animal, turned as if directed there to cross in front of them, as he with one hand turned to get them away, Eli already hearing himself after the near-miss calming Gwen and joking with *Chuck* and driving slower the rest of the way, as the car, too easily, with insufficient warning that these things can happen to the happy and the innocent and those whose lives are not supposed to intersect with madness and calamity, began to roll.

It was the next part Eli always insisted on avoiding. But avoiding that was like avoiding the truck: after a while, it has to arrive, whistling its brakes and crying its horn and making the roar of locked wheels skidding. It arrived, and Eli, panting, saying terrible wordless vowels, having dragged the limp child out, went back on a swollen knee that wouldn't bend to pull Gwen up by the collar and long hair from the tangle of seat-belt webbing and sliced upholstery and matted shatterproof glass. He heard himself saying nothing reasonable and efficient. He saw himself, clenched like a movie monster, tall and limping and knotting with pain, unknotting himself, staggering at Chuck, his name was *Chuck*, to say, "Honey? Chuck? Okay, love? Daddy'll be right back." Because Chuck had moved a hand, and Eli had told himself to remember to say, later on, when they were saved, how tough Chuck was, how brave and casual he'd tried to be. And while the truck driver screamed from the cab, where the steering column had entered his chest —they would later cut the column apart and carry the man, twitching, into the ambulance, a part of the column wobbling in his sternum like a thick bloody arrow—and while car horns sounded and country men ran about with flashlights and flares, while others shouted into CB radios, while sirens and red lights entered and left his life, Eli kneeled over Gwen, sobbing, and pushed at her heart and breathed into her mouth, looking up only to see *Chuck*, it was, still move, but not seeing until later the blood in his ears and nose, thinking, *I'll be right there, love,* and telling Gwen in the language of his awful grunts that he knew he was in the center of the worst moment of his life and she had to be there to save him.

Daddy'll be right back, love.

But it wasn't the hand of a frightened state trooper that shook him, it was Gwen's, she was pushing him, it was his frightened wife, come back from Second City, Texas, possibly to save him, surely to get saved, roughly pushing his shoulder, saying, "Darlin'? Eli, come *back.*"

"Hey," he said, rubbing his face with his hands, "hey, Gwen. I was sleeping."

"Sure," she said. She stood between his legs, watching him as he sat up in the desk chair and his eyes began to move from under cover. "I know what you were doing."

"You do," he said.

"You come to the house now," she said, "and you have some bad meat loaf and some of your Château How-do-you-do and tell me all about how you spent the day saving heathen lives.

And I'll tell you how I applied to take the Graduate Record Exams and then my M.A. You think I'd be a good Master of Arts?"

"Mistress."

"Don't start me on that, Eli. I'm being decorous tonight."

"*You* be my mistress."

"I intend to be whatever I can."

"Do we have to eat meat loaf?"

"Unless you want to make something better?"

"You."

"Oh, my my."

"You stay here," he said.

Phil poured water from a green Fiesta pitcher into Mike's vaporizer, plugged it in again, and stood by the crib until a plume of steam caught the light from the hallway as it eddied over Mike's face. Annie in the hall outside the door said, "You look terrific as a father. You look just right."

"Shh."

"No, it has to be *good* for him to hear us, don't you think? He knows we're in his life, or he's in ours. That has to be good. What a great way to sleep."

Phil, with the empty pitcher hanging from his hand, said, "Sometimes, when I check him, late at night, I take my sunglasses with me. I hold them in front of his mouth."

"To see if they fog up?"

"Yeah. I have this weird idea he may not be breathing."

"I use a mirror."

"You do?"

"You're the terrific father, but I'm the terrific mother, dumbo. Of course."

"What else don't I know about you?"

"Nothing, maybe."

"This is okay," Phil said, pointing with his thumbless hand at the crib in its mist of steam.

"I thought you might think so. I knew you would. You're meant to be a father. I told you that."

"So what else don't you know about me?"

"Nothing."

"So here we are, then."

"This is it," Annie said.

"Except it's almost May and then the term ends. I get paid in June and July, and then we're on unemployment or something. Do I get unemployment if I'm a teacher?"

"We'll be all right," Annie said. "Mike's our good luck."

Phil turned his head without moving his feet, he was looking, moving a hand partly out from his body. Then, his trunk twisted, he pushed his hand into the lighted mist around Mike's crib and gently knocked three times on the wood he had splintered, then later bandaged with masking tape.

Annie said, "Cut it out."

In the apartment they now shared, Turner wrote short papers for I. R. Demby, and I.R. made him correct misspelled words and get his semicolons right. Phil's class wrote shorter sentences, with greater confidence and no more skill than when they'd begun. Mike Sorenson had recurrent spring colds, and Phil and Annie used the vaporizer until it became so caked with minerals from their hard water they had to soak the heating element in vinegar to clean it. Mead Weeks II saw a psychiatrist at Upstate every Tuesday. L'Ordinet missed morning classes more than Mead Weeks liked. Mead Weeks

II walked in the woods and tried not to make fires, spent hours in the library increasing his knowledge of mandala and racial memory. Candidates for Phil's job arrived on campus in hard new suits and bright new high-heeled shoes and talked with senior professors about methods of teaching composition. No one, according to Leicester, looked very good. Phil stopped drinking coffee in the office. His journal remained in his desk. Elizabeth Bean notified the college that she was talking with Bennington and Hampshire about becoming a Dean of Students. Horace L'Ordinet, with his shoulder aching from his work at the fort, with shortness of breath and nausea increasing, stalked Lizzie Bean to her apartment and stood there, often, at night, outside, unsure of his mission, but feeling right to be where he was. In his own apartment, he packed Weeks II's knapsack with care and studied maps. Gwen Silver prepared for the Graduate Record Exams. Anne Sorenson planted a vegetable garden and made sketches of Mike and hung them on the wall of the kitchen with finishing nails. The days were warm, the swamp was bright and full of motion, May rose before them all like morning sun, and Eli Silver took care of babies.

10 | Sickle

Behind the diving of birds over the swamp, and the blatting of frogs upon it, there was the flat hummed buzz of insect wings that sounded, by late afternoon, permanent; should the birds stop and the frogs go silent, the insects' rattling whisper would hang in the air over shimmers of heat baking upward from the earth. Phil was a few hundred feet downhill from their house, wearing shorts and sneakers, stripped to the waist, scything brush at the marshy edges of the road. He had cut the high timothy and redtop growing around their house, scything all day the day before, and now he had worked his way downhill, cutting in a slow regular rhythm, forcing himself as close as he could come to the small tight strokes of farmers, who could work without panting and mean it. He chopped at weeds that made Mike cough and redden at the eyes and leak pus down his throat and get sick, requiring that the vaporizer run all night and much of the day. He scythed at land that wasn't his because of his baby, although Annie insisted that nothing would prevent the pollen from drifting invisibly into Mike, making him gag on his juices.

That was why he was on the road, away from the house, and that was why Annie had come down, too, carrying a couple of cans of beer. That was why they stood in the dust of the road in the early spring afternoon and, saying nothing, watched the dark-gray or faded black or dirty dark-green Chevrolet drift slowly around the bend from near their house—they could not quite see their porch steps—and then, coming downhill toward them, pick up speed and bump past them in the dried ruts, scattering pebbles and blowing a plume of smoky dirt into the air. They saw a head and dark glasses, and then the fog of dust around the car. They bent away, Phil spitting, Annie swearing, and then faced downhill to watch the dark car turn right, away from Bailey, and go the back way toward Route 12, where it curved from the towns and paving, toward state lands.

They talked about jobs, and the pointlessness of what Phil had done—attacking a natural enemy outnumbering his muscles and strokes and his antique long-handled scythe from Maine—and Annie reported on Mike in his afternoon nap, sleeping in the playpen downstairs while music from the radio held him still. Then Annie went up the hill and Phil went back to standing in thigh-high brush, cutting in defiance more than usefulness.

He was doing that when Annie came down the hill again, keening—she sounded like an animal, a dog in pain. She made for Phil, but she called Mike's name, and Phil dropped the scythe and ran uphill like the man moving slowly in dreams. So he learned, the two of them standing breathless against the pull of the dirt road's slanting, that Mike, who could not walk, and whose playpen, barred and high, was proof against his escape, had been stolen from their house while they'd spoken of his health.

They spent minutes in the frost of emergency—fingers nearly numb, the palms and face cold, muscles clumsy and stiff. Phil telephoned the state police, who took his name and number and—because he insisted, only—a description of Mike. They promised to send an investigator if he didn't telephone in an hour to say they'd misplaced their child. They *wanted* to be helpful, he insisted to Annie, they just had their procedures. Their fucking procedures, she said, in the kitchen hung with Mike's face in charcoal and ink. Their fucking *procedures*. Neither of them wept, though each walked in circles on the kitchen floor.

Procedures, Annie said, in the house that was suddenly small on the crest of a hill above a swamp in land that was suddenly immense, under a sky that had grown high. And she went to the telephone and dialed the doctor, the one who had found their baby in an ocean of babies and who, in a county of procedures and infinite patience with detail, had placed the baby in her arms.

And while they waited for Silver to arrive, and while they waited for police procedures to be followed, Annie told Phil that Mike was sick. So they argued, then, about her exacerbation of the emergency with her own sudden fears, and about his unwillingness to hear the truth about Mike. Annie spoke of abdominal pain. Phil said *apparent* abdominal pain; he said *possible* pain and recited Silver's guess that the dripping mucus from allergies had irritated the stomach walls. Annie shouted of *real* pain, pain she *knew* about, her baby was sick, the police were waiting, Silver lived half an hour away at best, her husband was stumbling over his own helplessness, and a maniac, a child molester, a murderer, some crazy pederast had taken their baby from his bed in their house and no one wanted to *do* anything.

Silver drove the Hawk too quickly, with little control, and it staggered at the bends in the southern stretches of Route 12. Gwen, beside him because he was silent with fear for another woman's baby, a strange baby in a strange woman's house in another town, talked about seat belts. Silver snarled that the

Hawk was built before seat belts were required by law. Gwen stuck her hand between the seats and backrest to pull the seat belts out and to nag him into letting her lean over to buckle him in. Silver said no words, but made angry noises that drove her back to lean against her door, while she told him that if he insisted on killing himself in the car, he could kill her, too. So she left their seat belts off and, some miles later, told him how fitting it would be if the entire family could be destroyed by cars. He pulled over, halfway there, the Hawk shuddering at its brakes and skidding to a stop against the shoulder of the road. He buckled his seat belt while she fastened hers, then he punched the accelerator all the way down, and pulled out and drove the rest of the way doing 75, then 80, slowing only for acute bends, passing in no-passing zones and up hills, driving with his lights on and his horn often down, telling her that doctors were allowed to drive like this. When Gwen asked if doctors were inoculated against death, Silver simply said, Yes, unfortunately they were.

L'Ordinet used his seat belt too, to strap the crying infant in his white cotton blanket against the dirty upholstery of his Chevrolet as he drove in low gear slowly up the spur off Route 12, a nameless road that climbed steeply through the snow-mobilers' hills at the foot of the state forest. He didn't speak to the child, who cried mostly for hunger and sleep, and per-haps a little for the cramping in his legs and the pressure in his abdomen. L'Ordinet said only, Shh, and said it gently; he had no wish to be cruel, he told himself; a man who questions the morality of others, he instructed himself, has no call to be cruel. In spite of the heat, he shut his window so that none of the fine drifting dust of the single-track road would blow in to unsettle his child.

The forests, even in the sun and heat of an unseasonable May in the north-central reaches of New York, were dark. They seemed large now to L'Ordinet, who had known the lands, from his survey map, to look small against the surrounding countryside. The forests had looked small, and the county had looked small, and the roads had looked narrow. But everything now was larger than he was. The world is some surprise, he warned himself.

For the first time that day, he spoke. He said to the screaming baby, "We're really safe. Shh."

Phil phoned Mead Weeks, who had lived in Bailey for twenty-three years and who knew everyone, and surely the police. Weeks was away from the house, away from the office, but Mrs. DeAngelo, moaning for the Sorensons, took a message. And Mead Weeks II saying, "No shit," took the message at home. Weeks II ran out to his moped and, saying it again, "No shit," took off.

At the Sorensons' house, Eli Silver introduced his wife and offered Annie a sedative. She cursed at him until Phil hugged her into silence. Then Silver walked wide circles in the house —they might have been cartographer's contour lines. Suddenly snapping his fingers, clapping his hands together, frightening the rest of them, smiling the way a dog bares his fangs, Silver telephoned Lizzie Bean, while Gwen said to Silver, who didn't listen, and to Annie, who barely knew, "Who in the hell *is* she?"

Phil told her Elizabeth Bean was a psychologist.

Gwen said, "I believe that isn't all she is."

And Silver said, "Shut up." Then, "Not you, Lizzie. You understand? The Sorensons' recently *adopted* baby has been stolen? I'm here at their house. Are you listening to me? *Some*body stole him. Somebody, can you help us guess who? Do you think he'd *do* that?" When Lizzie hung up without answering him, he shook the receiver in the air before him.

"Pardon me," Weeks II said, at the screen door. "Pardon me. I believe I understand the nature of the problem and the locus of the, you know, the nexus. The nexus is this."

Phil went for him, his hand cocked, his eyes small, a mustache end in his mouth. Silver stood between them, saying, "I think we can do this, Phil. I think we're going to handle this. Phil?"

But it was the spattering of gravel outside and the slamming of doors that stopped Phil. Mead Weeks II simply smiled and shrugged his shoulders, said, "I'm telling you, sirs and mesdames, I genuinely *know*. You owe a guy, you keep your eyes on him. I have been to the *mountain.*"

"Is that a place, you fucking drug addict, or one of your trips you're talking about?" Phil said, his fist still up.

Eli said, "It's the police. I told them—"

Annie said, "Thank you. Thank you."

A man in a trim brown leisure suit, wearing white beads beneath his open-necked shirt, very broad and short, said, "Is this where the trouble is?"

Weeks II, without looking over his shoulder, said, "That is the voice of order and the codes."

Elizabeth Bean arrived twenty minutes later, her face red and sweaty, her eyes very large. The policeman stared at her. She looked away from Phil and Annie, and when Gwen stepped toward the door as if to greet or question her, Lizzie stepped backward and waited for Eli on the porch.

"The *last* place you should be is here," he said.

"I thought maybe I could help."

"Not by being here, Liz. I wanted you to *tell* me, on the phone, whether L'Ordinet might have done this."

"I know you won't believe I'm being generous about this," she said.

"Oh, Liz, you really aren't. Are you?"

"If that baby's father is involved, maybe I should be around," she said.

Eli shook his head.

"I should have stayed away," she said. "All right. All right. *Next* time I will."

They stepped back as everyone left following the policeman, who looked at his notebook, the open page of which was mostly blank because no one had spoken to him. He said, "The kid knows where to go."

Eli said, "Where?"

Gwen, pulling at his hand, said, "Hurry, please? It's their *baby.*"

Lizzie walked to her car as Phil pushed Weeks II out the door and toward the green truck, saying, "Remember, if you don't take me to the right place, my baby—our *baby*, damn it. Do this *right!*" Annie and Phil left first, followed by Lizzie's white Volvo, then Silver and Gwen in the Hawk. The unmarked police car came behind them.

L'Ordinet worked methodically, with a calm he found commendable. "This is my first father-and-son hike," he said, forcing a little chuckle so that his child could hear the humor, even irony, in his voice, and not be afraid. The baby, exhausted from crying, snuffled and whimpered a little, but mostly was silent. L'Ordinet put the knapsack on—it thudded and clanked because of the canteen and musette bag and long brush knife strapped onto it—and then, lifting the baby tenderly, he walked away from the car he had left half a mile above the old trail to his fort, and, stopping sometimes to look at a compass and up, through the roof of pines toward the sun, he bushwhacked through the woods. Sometimes snaky boughs whipped back to strike him in the face, and once a small one struck his child and made him cry again. But L'Ordinet hushed him breathlessly and rocked him on his rocking chest, and went ahead through the darker parts of the forest, west of the fort and above it. "Think of it as an outing," he whispered, worrying about his breathlessness and the tight feeling high in his head that made him hear a shrill, steady whistle. When he spoke to soothe his child, the child began to cry again. L'Ordinet shook him against his chest and went on.

When they came to the mile of Route 12 off which small

roads went toward the state forests, each about a quarter of a mile apart, Phil shouted at Weeks II and Weeks II replied. The green truck turned through the oncoming lane, its high beams on, and the police car pulled out too, but was forced back into line by a yellow Toyota pickup that had missed by six inches crumpling itself against the Sorensons' Travelall. The trooper spoke on his radio the rest of the way, following the Hawk that followed the Volvo into the green truck's dust. They went, more slowly, up the small road Weeks II had pointed out. By the time they were a mile into the forests, the Piper had taken off from the state strip in Oneida and was waggling toward the forest preserve, the pilot telling the plainclothes trooper the time of his arrival. Three miles into the state lands, Weeks II told Phil that maybe this was the wrong road. Phil made a very short statement: he was going to kill Weeks II if this was the wrong road. Annie looked up at Phil, because he meant it. Then they came to the Chevrolet.

It was late afternoon, and the cloudless sky was sucking up heat. They all stood at the green truck, waiting. Annie said, "He's sick. He'll get sick if it gets cold."

Silver, holding his black bag while he took his belt off, said, "Whatever's wrong with him, I'll make it better. I promise."

"How can you promise that?" Annie said. "Look at what else you promised."

Gwen told her, "Because he's good. He always tries to keep his promises and he's good."

Silver threaded the belt through the handles of his bag and buckled it. Then he put the belt over his neck so that it hung from his shoulder and across his chest. "Which way?" he asked Weeks II.

"This isn't the same place," Weeks II said. "I mean, it's *around* the same place, but it isn't the *same* same place. Do you know what I mean? But it's *almost* the same. I think."

Phil went for him then, and because Silver was adjusting his belt and the policeman was examining the locked Chevrolet and Lizzie was standing away from them to avoid Gwen and Annie, who were looking at one another, Phil reached him this time. He cocked his thumbless hand and shot a short right cross into his face. Weeks II, who couldn't box or begin to defend himself, started too late to throw his hands up in fear. The motion carried his chin away from Phil, but moved his shoulder in. Phil's punch landed high on the chest, and the shoulder muscle tore. The policeman looked up, touched his belt holster, then dropped his hand and continued to study the Chevrolet. Weeks II sat on the ground and held his arm against his stomach. Phil turned away.

Then Lizzie said, "It's a *baby!*"

Annie said, "Where?"

Lizzie, in her high heels and tan skirt and sleeveless blouse, cut up into the woods, stumbling in the caked pine needles but pulling herself along by holding on to boughs, climbing just to move. Gwen followed her, and then they all went, leaving Weeks II to sit on the ground, saying nothing, looking over his glasses, as the policeman, following, said, "Stay there."

A dove called, then stopped, and so did the other birds. The insects went on, diminished as they passed, then their hum climbed in pitch. The light lessened. The state police airplane circled overhead, driving two drifting hawks away. In single file, with Lizzie leading out of fear and embarrassment, Eli and Lizzie and Gwen in city clothes, Phil in shorts and sneakers, Annie in loose cotton drawstring trousers and a man's white T-shirt, sandals lined with mud and needles, they climbed the dark pitch and made for the crest far above them because they didn't know where else to go.

L'Ordinet, his chest swelling for proper breath but still unable to take one or keep it, had set his child inside the fort. Because he, too, felt the upward thermal leak, he set a match to the fire he had laid days before. The smoke eddied and made the baby cough. L'Ordinet fanned the smoke away with a quarterly magazine he'd brought in Weeks II's knapsack. The breeze of his fanning made the baby cry, though, so he stopped. The baby stopped too, though his shivering didn't. "Shh," L'Ordinet said, "don't you go and give us away, now."

Sitting near his fire, pouring water from the canteen into a small pot, stirring in pre-sweetened oatmeal, then setting it on a metal grill he'd propped over the fire, L'Ordinet panted and said, "I understand." The baby wheezed and shivered under its cotton blanket. "I'm responsible for you."

When they reached the crest, no less dense than the land below, but with more gray sky above them, it was darker. Annie shook, but insisted she wasn't cold. Phil hugged her with one arm until she pulled away from him and went to lean on a shaggy yellowing birch. Eli rubbed his knee and watched. The policeman, who had said nothing to them since they'd started the climb, spoke into a small transceiver, giving instructions for an ambulance to find their cars, and asking for more men. The airplane had left, to be replaced by a circling helicopter.

"It's in the wrong place," Phil told the policeman.

"So are we," the policeman said. But he spoke again into the transceiver. Lizzie started walking west along the hill, and Gwen followed her. The policeman turned east, waved them on, and went out of sight.

The oatmeal was too hot and it burned his baby's mouth. L'Ordinet propped his flashlight on some kindling in the fort and spooned cold water onto the stretched lips. The little tongue came out for it.

L'Ordinet heard footsteps. He said, "Don't be frightened. Your old man knows the woods."

Weeks II, his eyes bulging with pain, but smiling as always, looked over the edge of the chinked log wall and said, "Hey, baby."

L'Ordinet howled and Weeks II slipped back from the wall.

As Weeks II's footsteps went back and down, L'Ordinet, saying, "Right back," took the long wide-bladed brush knife from its scabbard, and then the flashlight, and he climbed his wall and went downhill in pursuit.

The smoke diminished as the fire died, and insects clustered over Michael Sorenson's mouth and eyes. He vibrated, and his closed eyes rolled in their sockets; he shook and made small gasping cries. The arms and legs, as if each received a separate electrical charge, jumped and relaxed, then jumped more. His cries were low and almost like the sounds a baby makes when it murmurs in its sleep, but he wasn't sleeping.

Lizzie, in the darkness, swearing at the branches that cut her forehead and the gnats that settled on her face, heard footsteps and shouted, "There?"

It was Gwen, close behind her.

Silver went ahead of them, and Phil hung back to hold Annie's hand, slowing her. She said, "I want to *see.*"

"You don't know that," Phil said.

She pulled her hand away and went, tripping, falling, moving on, to be with Silver and Lizzie and Gwen. Phil went slowly, watching the small flashlight beam of the policeman as he intersected their trail, too tired to speak, only shaking his head, then cutting in front of Phil to follow the others.

Below them, farther east, they heard a high hard voice call in the outer ranges of hysteria: "You fucking *spy!*"

The policeman turned off toward the noise and Phil went after him. Lizzie went ahead and so did Gwen. Silver stood where he was, watching the bright-blue beam of the helicopter searchlight as it lighted the tops of the trees, threw a rainbow that spilled like water down trunks and branches, leaving the ground they stumbled on still dark. Then Silver followed Gwen and Lizzie. Like a wide sideways V, the two parties went on, leaving the fort and Mike, who shook in its dark delta.

Demby and Turner drove their car, with Mead Weeks and

Mrs. DeAngelo, who had summoned Demby and Weeks from a long conference, in the back seat; they followed the state police cars on Route 12. Behind them, the ambulance, its lights winking for emergency, but going slowly, followed so closely that Demby had to bend into the wheel and squint from its bright lights in order to keep them on the road. Mrs. DeAngelo blew cigarette smoke in Weeks's face and he coughed, but said nothing. She said she *knew* L'Ordinet was a pervert, she'd always known. Mead Weeks studied Turner, and the back of Demby's brown neck. Watching his eyes, Mrs. DeAngelo told Weeks to lay off.

Then the helicopter circled over the road, the two trooper cars slowed, the helicopter climbed again, and a small bright light near the side mirror of the lead police car picked out the entrance to the road. The car wheeled and bucked into the mouth of the road, the other police car followed, and so did Demby. The ambulance behind them put more lights on and its siren started. Weeks asked Demby, "Shouldn't we pull over?"

"Now where in Christ would we pull, Mead?" Mrs. DeAngelo said.

The police cars had their sirens going too, and all their lights on, and Demby leaned on his horn and blinked his high beams as he followed. Weeks, sitting back, said, "I hope everything's all right."

Turner said, "That's my man."

Gwen was on her knees beside Lizzie, who sat with her legs pointing downhill and who worked for breath. Silver stood behind them, looking up the hill while Phil and the policeman, his radio to his ear, continued past them, following the beam of the small flashlight. The crashing below them and away had stopped. Gwen went up, then, and Lizzie climbed to her feet and followed.

Mike's shuddering had become a slow rhythmic pulsing of

the skin and the limb muscles, insufficient for frightening off the insects which hung on him at the eyes and ears and nostrils. He sputtered when he breathed one in, but didn't open his eyes or brush at his face. The skin of his cheeks and eyelids and neck was mottled with red bites. L'Ordinet climbed back over the wall of the fort and threw the heavy brush knife down onto the packed and needle-cushioned floor. "How's the boy?" he said. "I told you I'd be back. Were you scared? This is kind of a scary business. But you weren't scared, were you? That crazy addict was. He escaped me."

He leaned closer and then made a sudden little noise in his throat and smacked his baby's face, brushing the insects away. A chigger had burrowed under one of Mike's ears and L'Ordinet repeated boyhood wisdom to himself: "You never pull a chigger or a tick, or they leave their stomachs or something behind them. You never want bugs leaving their stomachs behind them." From the fire, he took a partly burned twig, and blowing on it to make its cool end glow, he brought it close to Mike's ear, forcing the bug to withdraw.

"No!" called Mead Weeks II, one arm hanging over the wall, his face looking blue in the darkness, his eyes wide enough to look as if they glowed. "We made a promise about fires, remember? There is *no* unnecessary use of any form of combustion or combustible. We *promised.*"

L'Ordinet threw the stick at Weeks II, who ducked away, groaning for his collarbone. Mike shook. L'Ordinet, on his hands and knees, feeling for his brush knife, shouted, "Who took my flashlight?"

"That's what happens," called Weeks II, moving to the forest below. "You play with fire and you lose your light. It's a parable about emotional blindness. The flashlight's a symbol, see."

L'Ordinet went over the wall after him again, the knife clanging on the logs he'd done his building with. He stopped to step on the stick he'd thrown, which was burning in the soft pine needles. He stamped, missed, stamped again, crushed the unburned end of the stick, then went downhill after Weeks II. The insects settled on Mike's face again, the fire in the fort made less smoke, and the fire outside the fort, smoldering needles and a burning stick that the nighttime breezes blew, began to grow.

Turner strutted in the road, walking close to the groups of troopers, three in one cluster, two in another, all of them listening to their radios and looking up the hill. In the first police car, parked behind the Hawk, its red lights spinning and clicking, a lieutenant spoke into his microphone to the helicopter pilot and the policeman who ran in the darkness with Eli and Phil. Mrs. DeAngelo, standing beside Mead Weeks, smoked cigarettes. Weeks told Demby that they'd have to continue their talk, back at school, when everything was settled. Demby, looking away, his teeth nearly touching, said he could always find another job.

As two of the troopers, each carrying a heavy flashlight, one with a shotgun in his hand, began to walk up the hill, and as Turner and Demby talked in the darkness, shaking their heads, Lizzie, three miles away from them and fifty feet in front of Eli and Phil, looked over the four-foot side of a shelter lighted by a patch of forest that roared as it burned. *"Eli!"* she screamed, and screamed it again before she climbed in and picked up someone else's baby, blowing at the insects dense on its face.

Phil ran into the fort, dragged the baby from her hands. Lizzie sat down. Eli called out to the rest of them that the woods were starting to burn. He forced Phil to let the baby go, and he set him on the floor of the clearing, in the smoke. Gwen and the policeman, then Lizzie too, stamped at the fire; the policeman whipped with his suit jacket, change and metal devices flying from the pockets as he tried to beat the fire out.

Eli listened to the heart and lungs, said, "Sweet Jesus," and picked the baby up and started down the hill. He kept a hand under the head and wrapped his other arm around him. "My bag," he called back, and Gwen, shaking a burned hand, stuffed his stethoscope inside and carried the bag down, running to catch him, hitting Annie, who stood looking after Eli and her baby. Then Phil came down, stopped, put his hand on her shoulder, took it away as if she and not the forest were burning, and they both ran back, after Eli and Gwen. The policeman and Lizzie came too, and the fire at the fort jumped into the crowns of the trees, pushed by winds, exploding from one tree to its neighbor, soon spreading to drop burning branches onto lower ones, and onto the forest floor. The helicopter drifted up, then away.

Eli, descending, met the policemen coming up. One of them struggled to aim his shotgun, but Eli was past, and then Gwen, carrying the medical bag. The roaring of the fire covered the sound of Mike's convulsing. Then Phil and Annie came, and then Lizzie and the policeman, who shouted over the sound of the fire.

Weeks II, higher up, and half a mile away, held his arm hard against his stomach and with the other arm pulled a prone L'Ordinet by his shirt collar. He tugged downhill a few steps, then stopped. Then he tugged downhill, then rested again. The fire was going faster than he was, but hadn't caught him yet. He walked and pulled, rested and pulled, leaving a trail, which was invisible in the darkness, of Horace L'Ordinet's blood, leaking slowly from a gash in the dark-trousered thigh he'd torn with his brush knife while falling downhill after Mead Weeks II. "All will be well," Weeks II said, during a rest pause, "and all manner of things will be well."

L'Ordinet, who was also bleeding from the head wound he'd suffered while gripping his thigh and curling forward into a sheet of glacial rock, said, mumbling, "This is very fine of you."

Weeks II said, "You should walk if you can, brother. There's an element of danger here."

L'Ordinet, holding his hand on his thigh, dripping blood from his head, falling forward, rose again and put his hand on Weeks II's shoulder. The troopers ranging out from the path, this time with the shotgun ready, heard Weeks II scream when the weight went onto his torn muscle, and the man with the pump-action 12-gauge fired off two rounds before Weeks II had a chance to speak. The first one took him in the shoulder and the side of the neck, but didn't kill him. The second round missed entirely, because the trooper had been frightened by the recoil of a gun he'd never shot before. They tied off what was left of Weeks II's arm, and one carried him down and away from the fire, while the other, kicking and cursing, prodding with the back of his flashlight, drove L'Ordinet down the hill.

Eli and Gwen and Annie rode in the back of the ambulance with Mike, Eli holding the oxygen mask on his face and telling Annie that he'd make her child better. Lizzie and Phil sat in front with the driver. The second attendant had stayed behind with a small valise of splints and IVs and burn dressings, waiting for the problems the troopers on their radio had signaled they were bringing in.

"Will he?" Annie asked. "Will he?"

"I'm taking care of him," Eli said. "I'll take good care of him."

"Will he?"

"I'm taking care of him, I'm doing everything, you'll see."

Annie wailed, "Can you save his *life?*"

Eli said, "I'm going to take good care, you'll see. I'll take better—good, better than my own."

That was when Gwen, sitting on the foot of Mike's litter, started to weep.

In the small county hospital where Eli Silver worked, the

rescuers were silent. Exhausted beyond emotion, running now on reserves of sugar and protein, sitting often because lactic acid flooded their muscles and made the tissue jerk, awake because they had to be, because they shivered with adrenalin, sometimes saying nonsense because emergency prodded them just beneath the skin and hair and eyeballs, they stood, then sat, grimaced and talked, then looked in silence for long minutes at wall tiles or water fountains, waited for word.

Silver walked on a leg as straight as a two-by-four, the knee swollen with gout by the trauma of running and jumping on the grains of uric-acid crystal in the joint. He never told anyone to hurry or take care, though Ada, whom he'd told the night operator to summon, swore at the staff, Silver included, and begged herself to have the patience of Gregory of Macedonia.

Silver, adjusting the plastic-topped croupette through which they watched Michael receive a steady flow of oxygen and sonic steam, asked her, "Who in hell is Gregory of Macedonia?"

"A perfect Pope," Ada said. "I made him up. He's the one to burn the Lutheran churches and bring our meatless Fridays back."

Silver told a night nurse, "Aren't we lucky she lets us live," then dictated what he was doing so that the nurse had a record for the staff coming on in the morning. "We're starting this male Caucasian infant, five months old, on an IV of penicillin, 250 milligrams Q6H. He's receiving oxygen because we suspect an aggravated sinusitis has become—this is just possible, now. We're treating for a pneumococcal pneumonia because the child presented us with icy hands and feet, profound coughing, a temp that went from 101 to 104 in the last half hour. His irritability has increased and we find wheezing. You got all that? We have—would you take this down too, please? We have taken a blood smear for a CBC, and we suspect the analysis will show us an increased white count, which is—"

"Expectable," Ada said.

"Which is, thank you, expectable, in a child who looks anemic and who presents the symptoms recorded."

Downstairs, in the corridor outside the Emergency Room, Phil wore a borrowed doctor's coat and sat on a plastic sofa with his hands on his legs. Annie and Gwen, carrying torn sandals and shoes, their faces filthy, their hands full of pine resin and blood, left for Silver's house to get clean clothes from Gwen's closet. In the Emergency Room, Dr. Elden, who had been on call, was cleaning pellets and cloth and wood chips from Mead Weeks II's shattered arm, and was waiting for X rays to help him decide whether enough of the blood vessels and ligaments and tendons were left for him to request help in repairing the arm, or to telephone for an operating room where he would cut the arm away. He told his nurse not to worry about the shoulder separation yet, because that was the least of Weeks II's problems. Weeks II was awake, though drugged, and was not speaking. In the corridor, his father was silent. Lizzie Bean walked on shredded stockings and a skirt that hung in three parts, half a blouse, a blue emergency-room blanket over her shoulders like a shawl.

When Lizzie crossed in front of Phil, who still sat with his hands on his bare thighs, he reached out—his arms were red with bites, and blood ran back along them as if blown by a spray gun—and he gently took her wrist. She stopped at once, looked at his face, and smiled.

"Who are you?" he said.

Lizzie said, "You know *me*, Phil."

"I mean, who are you in *this?*" He raised his hand as if to point at something near them, then dropped it. The doctor's coat over his shoulders fell away, and she saw the blue-black bump of a bruised or broken rib that made him bite his lip, and the swelling of his right biceps, which made the dark-blue upper arm half again as large as the one that still extended to hold her wrist.

"Oh," she said, "I'm someone who knows Horace pretty well. I guess we all know Horace pretty well now, don't we? But I used to know him better before he got sick. Is that the best way to say it? He was a nice person. He was never a generous man, but he was very sexy and very smart. Does that tell you?"

Phil nibbled on his mustache and looked at her and tried to smile. "Thank you for coming along," he said.

Lizzie opened his fingers with her free hand and stepped back, bowed from the waist like a performer, said, not smiling, "You're very welcome for everything."

Policemen walked along the corridor, carrying radios, being treated for burns of the hand and arm and face. A volunteer from one of three companies fighting the fire was rolled by his wife in a wheelchair. "He's all right," she announced to everyone, though no one had asked. His foot was in an elastic bandage. The woman in tight black slacks and black slippers told Phil, "He's fine."

Phil said, "What?"

Turner bought a Coke for Demby, and they shared it. Mead Weeks watched. Kessler, the radiologist, walked slowly down the corridor, carrying X rays, but Weeks didn't see him. Lizzie watched them both, then looked at Demby and Turner, and as they noticed, she waved, and they waved back. Turner called, "You one hell of a woman, Mizz Bean."

She called, "Turner—enough," and he laughed, put his hands out, palm-up, to be slapped in joy by Demby. But Demby, tall and wide and serious, was staring at Weeks until Weeks looked down. Turner withdrew his hands, put them in his pockets, then walked a few feet away from Demby.

Kessler and Elden came out of the Emergency Room doors and called Weeks in, and they disappeared. Then Weeks came out, whiter than before, his face streaked, his feet undirected. He leaned against the wall, said, "His arm."

"Fucking *shit,*" Phil said. "Mead, he's the hero of this.

Mead? If Mike gets out of this." Phil stopped and opened his mouth as if to breathe without gagging. "If he gets out of this, your kid's the hero. All right?"

"He only has one arm left," Weeks said.

Lizzie whispered, "He was once a very nice man."

Weeks said, "Who?" as Phil said, "Sure, he probably was. He must have been, if you liked him."

"You're being kind," she said, "thank you."

"No, I mean it," Phil said.

"Who?" Weeks asked them.

Gwen and Annie returned, Annie in Gwen's sneakers and dungarees and green sweater, Gwen in a white shirt and jeans. They stood at the top of the hall off the entrance as if they were shy, as if the feeling in the group down the hall were exclusive, or frightening.

Weeks II came out of the ER, an intravenous drip wobbling at the head of his litter, and Weeks held his face in his hands and shuddered. Elden and a nurse pushed the litter while Kessler, standing at the door, looked at Weeks. Demby walked over to him and put a hand on Weeks's shoulder. Weeks looked up and said, "If you please, I don't want you to touch me."

Phil slid to his feet and walked in short weak steps to Demby and put his hand on the back of Demby's neck. "I.R.," he said.

Demby said, "Hey, Phil," then walked back down the corridor and left. Turner followed him. Weeks walked in the other direction, after his son.

That was when Annie saw the nurse, walking quickly down the hall with a long pink lab report slip. Annie came to Phil and put her hands around his upper arm and squeezed. He sucked his breath in and leaned his forehead against the green wall tiles. She held on. Gwen went to Liz and said, "We don't need to be cruel to each other, do we?"

Lizzie said, "Mrs. Silver, I don't think I've ever been *cruel* to you."

Gwen said, "I think I was warning myself." She leaned in as if to sniff at Liz or study her skin, kissed her cheek.

Liz stepped backward suddenly and bumped into the wall, her head struck. "I'm sorry," she said. "You took me by surprise."

Liz slid along the wall until she was clear of Gwen, then walked to the vending machines and, without putting money in, pushed buttons. Gwen studied Annie and Phil, and said nothing more.

Ada, in the ward, handed the slip to Silver and said, "I don't understand this."

"A count of 18,000 whites?" Eli said. "No, neither do I. Look at this! Bands and polys. Are you kidding me? *Bands?* Oh, I *do.* I'll be damned, I'll be damned, I'll be damned, Ada —call downstairs, right away, call down and ask them to look for hooked red cells, do that stat, *tell* them stat. Because I'm ready to bet—do that, honey, will you?"

Eli opened the tunnels into the croupette, and, inserting his hands into fresh gloves, reached in to palpate Mike's spleen. He probed, the baby jerked but didn't open his eyes. "I can feel the spleen," he called. The night nurse wrote. "The spleen is enlarged." He withdrew his hands and sealed the oxygen tent. "I'm betting—see, they didn't even *think* to study the shape of the erythrocytes, or maybe they didn't notice, I don't know."

Eli limped to a metal stool and sat, his leg protruding stiffly in front of him, his lips pale with the pain. He looked at Ada, who was holding the telephone.

"Thank you," she was saying into the phone. "The erythrocytes are sickled," she told Silver. "You know what that means?"

"Yeah," he said, "I believe I do."

11 | Matters of Sickness and Health

Arnold Partse, asked by Eli Silver to represent H. L'Ordinet at his preliminary hearing—there were more charges to answer for than anyone but Partse and Annie Sorenson could recite—instructed L'Ordinet, sequestered now in federal facilities at Watertown, to write his own version of why he had stolen a baby. The document, forwarded by Partse to a psychiatrist at Cornell's medical college, in hopes that it provided a basis for a plea of temporary insanity, was titled, in heavy capitals, in black ink, on canary-yellow copy paper, THE MORAL STATEMENT OF AN AMERICAN MAN. The text, in a small tight slanting hand:

Well, friends, it has been a long and not unexciting journey. We were engaged, each of us, in one another's lives, and surely such an often wordless, but always intimate, communication is never wasted. Apparently, I made plans and did deeds of which I have little memory. I do not plead forgetfulness, for I do not wish us to forget. I do plead difficulties, obstacles, hardships, and disbelief—my own, perhaps naïve, disbelief in baby theft. For my child was taken from me by a woman with whom I had participated in its creation. Two thefts, then, are factors in our briefly mutual lives. To the parents I must state this: Never did I wish to cause harm to you or to our child. I wanted only what was partly mine. I beg for your compassionate understanding. I am not without sympathy for my own cause, but I wish one point to be made clear: I apologize. According to Dr. Silver, the child, named Michael by his surrogate parents, suffers from a disease called sickle-cell anemia. It is a disease of hemoglobin. I cannot tell you awfully much about it, although I am certain that Dr. Silver, who can be competent, though dour, would be willing to offer further technical data. It is claimed by some that only people of the Negro race, carrying certain genes, can transmit this disease. If such an assumption were accepted, one would then conclude that I, the father, or Ms. Elizabeth Bean, the biological mother, was a Negro person. According to Dr. Silver, in fact, the incidence of sickle-cell anemia is 1 in 100,000 for non-Negroes, 3 in 2,000 for Negroes. Matters of sickness and health prove less than we may think. It is suggested by Dr. Silver, who, in a time of great stress, violated my civil rights by taking a blood sample from my finger with a needle (and who is to say that this instrument was properly sterilized?), that it is I, the biological father, who carries and thus transmits the disease in question. The allegation, if founded, only proves that people cannot always control their lives. I did not wish, in the first place, to create a child. Furthermore, disease was never a part of my plans. My life was meant to take a different turn.

I should only, at this juncture, like to say that I have every hope for the full and lifelong recovery of my son. And I would like to thank Mr. Mead Weeks II, without whose help, although he is a disturbed person, I would not be here today. I happily acknowledge his assistance, while reserving for myself responsibility for certain mistakes that, in such a troubled time, are inevitable.

H. L'Ordinet
Assistant Professor

A month after Mike had been stolen, Eli Silver, at the county hospital, limped from the desk, where he had read charts and dictated ward reports. He went from bed to bed. He examined a twelve-year-old girl whose cervix was swollen and painful. His assumption, and Ada's, was that the girl, checked in for admission by her mother, had been molested by her father, famous in the town for brutalities against his other children. The girl would not speak to either of them, nor would she submit to examination. Silver dictated orders for her discharge from the ward, and telephoned Don Beverly, admitting physician, to arrange for a surprise visit to the girl's home from someone in the social-services department. He examined a college boy, in the teenage wing of the ward, rushed to the hospital by a dormitory director; Sarota, the college physician, had diagnosed meningitis. Silver found a strep throat, ordered home rest and antibiotics, and arranged for the boy to be driven to his dorm. A small boy, in the hospital for circumcision, was progressing satisfactorily. And Ada's nephew's daughter, her deafness seen by Silver as little more than plugged ears, was jollied and chucked and laved by the ENT woman who consulted with the hospital twice a week.

Silver limped out of the ward and didn't wave goodbye to anyone. Downstairs, in his mailbox, he found a postcard that read

> Elizabeth Bean
> Bennington College
> Bennington, Vermont

and he held it close to his face, looking for something—signature? a message?—and then decided that her name was signature enough for the occasion, that her name was the occasion, that the message was Elizabeth Bean. He folded the card twice and put it in the currency section of his wallet. He drove to his clinic slowly, wincing when he had to use the clutch.

Mead Weeks wore blue jeans and a suede sportcoat to work, and the collar of his shirt was open. Mrs. DeAngelo, drinking coffee and smoking cigarettes, whistled, but Weeks didn't smile. She said, "How's your boy?"

"He wants a hook instead of a prosthetic hand," Weeks said, tucking his blond hair behind his collar and rubbing at the blackened pouches under his eyes. He walked away, into his office with its gray steel desk and its books, its window overlooking the hot green quadrangle off the burgemeister's vision of a chapel. He composed two memoranda. One, to I. R. Demby, attached to a carbon of a letter from the Dean of Faculty and annotated by the campus head of the American Association of University Professors, discussed dismissal on grounds of moral turpitude. The other, to Philip Sorenson, Instructor in English, announced the department's wish to engage him on a one-year contract as replacement for Mr. Demby, whose departure was sudden and sad, but inevitable, given the circumstances. We know, he told Sorenson, that your personal acquaintance with people of unusual racial extraction will make for a heightened sympathy with our minority students, and that our course in Afro-American literature will benefit from your instruction. Although this offer may come as a surprise, we hope that you will accept the appointment. Finally, Weeks composed an advertisement for the MLA job list, and for certain magazines, offering an opening for an assistant professor of modern literature who would replace a colleague struck suddenly by severe illness. Surveying his morning's work, he signed the note to Sorenson with his first name only, Mead, because now they were colleagues, almost kin.

Phil had carried the rockers out to the porch again, and he and Annie sat there, moving slowly in place, while Mike, in his playpen, also on the porch, sucked at toys as he lay on his back to study the mobile Annie had made, which hung from the ceiling above him. The mobile moved as the wind off the swamp blew the smell of rotting vegetation and cut weed and evergreens to the house. Each figure spun in its separate dance, while the whole structure slowly turned. They didn't speak. They looked down the hill at the swamp near the house they had come to from Vermont and New Hampshire and Maine. Annie smoked cigarettes, the first time since they'd been married; the smoke carried up to the mobile and plucked at the characters who moved on their strings. Mike watched them and smiled.

When she lit another cigarette, Phil, his hands folded in his lap, said, "I always thought it would be great to get old and sit in a rocking chair on a porch and say, Okay, this is where we got to and it's all right."

Annie, in her Southern Comfort sweatshirt, said, "Except we had to have a baby. Adopt a baby."

"Oh, we had him. This kid was *delivered*, believe me. This is our baby. And what kind of *except?* Look at him."

"Because probably *he* won't get old and sit on a porch and rock back and forth and say, whatever that was. He won't get old."

Phil ate his mustache and his eyes became small. He looked at the swamp as a heron lifted up, seeming not to climb.

"Phil?"

"Maybe he will," he said. "Silver said you can't tell."

"But to grow up like that. He can't get sick, you know that. He gets sick, and they'll have to change his blood, transfuse him, whatever the hell it is. He can't get sick. And Silver hardly knows it all, pal."

"We won't let him get sick."

"Sure. We won't let him get stolen either, right? Wouldn't we have said that? So what's all this *we won't let*. We'll pray, is what we'll do. Or you'll spend the rest of your life knocking on wood like some kind of peasant in Bulgaria."

"Nothing wrong with Bulgaria," Phil said. "Or peasants. Or knocking on wood."

"It's so vulnerable," she said. "Every time you do that, I keep remembering how anything can happen."

"A lot of things can happen, all right. Sure. So what?"

"No: *anything.*"

"You want to trade him in for something that won't break? Hey, Mike, you think you're worth a Lancia with a thirty-thousand-mile guarantee?"

"Fuck you, Sorenson."

"I wish you would."

"I'd rather complain."

"It doesn't have to be fatal."

"No."

"It *doesn't.*"

"I know. I heard what Eli said. I know how wrong he can be. I heard what you said. Thank you all very much. I *heard.*"

"But you want something perfect."

"Eli didn't come close."

She threw her cigarette onto the grass in front of the porch. Phil pushed forward and out of the rocker and went down to retrieve the butt. Holding it like a teenager, as if it might burn him, he sucked in smoke and blew it out, coughed, suppressed the cough, then let it come. He stepped on the butt and smiled his foolishness to her, the gift without words he happened to have.

"You're perfect," she said.

"That's me." He waggled his four-fingered hand at her. "I'm even fun in bed."

"No. Michael doesn't leave my sight, and you know it."

"But when he's sleeping."

She said, "We'll see."

"I told you," Phil said. "Nothing comes with a guarantee."

Annie said, "I want him to be all right. I really do. I do. I want him to be healthy and all right and not to be sick all the time. I don't want him to die. You know, that's so fucking little to want for a funny little baby like that. It isn't fair. It isn't."

Phil said, "I vote we ought to take what we can get." He looked at her, but she continued to stare into the playpen.

Annie said, "Aren't you tired of talking about it? Aren't you just weary?"

"Remember, though, all right? Think about it—we take what we get."

"I'm not talking about him like that."

"No," he said.

"Please."

He said, "I won't either."

D‌emby's car was washed and hot-waxed for the trip; its overinflated tires made the car look more than ready —eager. They carried Turner's record player and carton of records from the empty dormitory out to the car, then a black camp trunk, a small box of paperback books, several cartons of shirts and sweaters and shoes. Turner's eyes were large and moist and his face was clenched into muscle knots, the tautness of being on the verge. When Turner slammed the trunk shut and sat in the front of the car, away from Demby, Demby started the motor, told Turner to fasten his seat belt.

"Don't mother me," Turner grumbled.

"Don't child me," Demby said, putting the car into gear and letting it roll. "You know, I'll help you get home if you decide that's where you should be. I'm not stealing you from anything, am I? Or am I wrong that we made some plans?"

And Turner, in the old voice, said, "I ain't but a *child.*"

Demby laughed as they went down the drive that led to the

street that would take them to Route 12 and then Route 17 and then, in five hours, New York. He reached his hand out, missed, leaned to reach further, and banged on Turner's shoulder. "Listen, son," he said, "you can always go home. And at least you won't get pregnant."

Weeks II, walking the campus lawns and drives, saw Turner and Demby leave. He stood on the edge of the college grounds and waved his only arm.

Lizzie Bean in shorts and a halter was cold, walking the rows of the air-conditioned twenty-four-hour Price Chopper near Bennington. She didn't shake, but she did rub her arms and shoulders, prodding the shopping cart forward with her pelvis, steering with her hips, hugging herself and puffing air from rounded cheeks; past religious books and bananas, then mayonnaise and diet dressings, then several salamis, and then around the aisle and into the first row of frozen foods, no problems but the chill and the hum of high fluorescent strips. It was in the second aisle that she noticed them—Cornish game hens, Long Island ducks, self-basting turkeys, a small section of geese, and the flock, as advertised in the newspaper, of hundreds and hundreds of roasters. Not in the meat section, among packets of red and yellow giblets and necks, not hanging upside down on aluminum racks, but here, where she stood shivering from the air conditioning and thigh-high freezer compartments, before her in the neatest rows, a couple of hundred fowl in hard plastic wrappers, all frosted and pale under the humming lights, their wings and legs tucked, looking like nothing special, cold and hard and arranged, and yet—goose and game hen, turkey, roaster—all of them looking at once like babies, three deep and three wide and repeated and repeated, lying in wait twenty-four hours a day: babies.

She knew what was happening, she simply didn't know its name. She released her shoulders and held to her red-handled cart and closed her eyes. She felt her head lean back, and then a hand beneath her shoulder blades. She heard herself gasp. A woman's voice, old and hoarse, asked, "Are you all right? Do you want a doctor?"

Lizzie kept her eyes shut, but she smiled. She was certain that she presented her professional counselor's smile. She said, "No, thank you. No. The last thing I need is a doctor. No."

Eli Silver did his afternoon rounds, saying hello to the staff, looking into the waiting room to wave at parents, at infants playing with toys, sick older children sitting in the dream of fever and mild constant pain. In room 1, he re-weighed a baby whose lips were severely swollen. He cross-examined the mother, dressed up in light-colored summer slacks and blouse as if for something special, and he learned that the child had been fed orange juice—"It's healthy, isn't it?" she asked—because there wasn't any milk in the house. He told her of allergies to orange juice, and gave her a list of new foods to try, one at a time, a week apiece.

In room 2, a mother and an eleven-year-old daughter, each very short, discussed with Eli the problem of breasts. Two girls in her class, the girl said, wore training bras, and she thought that if she wore one, something might appear to justify the wearing. Eli, while the mother fought back smiles, explained that breasts were not requisite in the fifth grade. He predicted bosoms beginning in a year or two, then told the girl that her mother—he knew this, he said, as a matter of fact—had not worn a bra until she was twenty-two, but look at her *now*. The girl blushed, her mother laughed, and Silver nodded at the girl, as if he and she agreed that breasts were legitimate business.

A child in room 3 had shown a positive reaction to a tuberculosis tine test, and the parents were afraid, the father's father, in Pennsylvania, had died of TB, or so they thought. Silver examined the three-year-old, hushed them while he bent to listen a second time to the lungs, said he heard nothing but perfect organs working well. He suggested a second test, promised X rays if this test, in three days, showed a positive reaction. Pressing the tiny spikes of the administering ring to the boy's arm, Silver, as the child teetered on the edge of crying, drew a huge heart with red ballpoint pen around the test patch; the child leaned to watch, and forgot to weep as Silver told him the heart meant he loved his mother awfully much. The boy nodded, very seriously, the father's eyes were wet, the mother wrote down Silver's instructions for a three-day regimen to keep the test area dry.

Silver looked at his mail—a free bottle of chewable vitamins with fluoride, an ad for grapefruit-extract diet tablets, a flier on pediatric enema kits, half a dozen drug protocols, a letter from HEW warning of the side effects of medication given to hyperactive children, and no postcards from New England, nothing from Arnold Partse—and he went back to work. He measured babies and weighed babies and dosed babies and kissed their sweet heads and listened to their bodies squeeze and work on schedule.

And at ten minutes of six, after an easy day, he took off his long blue coat, then his tie, and went outside—but not to the entrance to his house. Carrying his medical kit, he limped to the car, and opening the trunk to see if his equipment bags were there, he drove away from home, north, along Route 12, toward Bailey, toward the college, but beyond them, in the direction of Bear's Pass and the long fields.

He didn't drive repentantly slow, but he didn't speed, and in an hour he was there, parked at the side of the field which in fair weather, on Wednesdays, he dug. It wasn't Wednesday. And though it was nearly night, there was a glow in the sky and light enough to walk by. He hobbled across the wide and high-grown meadow, mariposa and toothwort and May apple up to his knees, the ground hard but springy, the calls of robins and distant crows blowing across the mile of field from the distant island of forest growing dark.

At the dig, he dropped his bags and walked slowly, unevenly, taking care with his knee, around the longhouse. He looked at the squares dividing it, a body laid out with its arms spread wide, the squares like a surgeon's painted-on guides for a complex operation. With his sore knee stiffening, he stooped to dig and scrape; he didn't bend his legs, he kept his head down, a feeding giraffe, and he worked the perimeter of a square, then dug into its center, sifting, prodding into softened earth with his fingers, letting the soil drop from his hand through the dusk winds back into place. He straightened, then moved to a second square as the darkness became solid, working by feel and not with his eyes, though sometimes he held stones to his face to peer at them. He found two battered points and put them into his bag, then told himself to dig one more, and he moved to it, scooping and sifting from the outside to the center, shaking the earth and dropping it, digging blind.

Later, the moon appeared, dull yellow, striped by clouds, throwing weak light for him to work by. But he had stopped. He had straightened and now he stood in the center of the black field. He had packed his bag, he held it, but he stayed where he was, looking. Niemann-Pick disease, tuberculoma, interstitial keratitis and nephritis, and he was thinking of babies too skinny and parents too fat, and German-measle blindness and hepatic cirrhosis, the stigmata of inherited syphilis, anorectal fistula, and babies danced above him and inside, they were too ill to cry and too weak to gasp, some saw pinpoints of light and others stared, seeing nothing, and parents wept and nurses muttered and the names of doctors were called on the hospital intercom, wives flew off in airplanes and mothers without babies drove old cars to Vermont, the woods caught fire and babies shivered on the edge of convulsion, the hemoglobin-F count of an infant increased, erythrocytes under dropping oxygen tension bent to the shapes of sickles, a thousand mouths that frowned or smiled up the barrel of a microscope and stayed on the eye and were printed on the barred moon.

Though wives returned. Never forget that, Silver prescribed. They did return. Above a house gone into the ground eight hundred years before, Silver reminded himself, not of Chuck in whose blood he waded every morning and night, but of the small airplane roosting. Need that was lucky for him, perhaps, and history between them maybe as strong as loss, and the airplane like a creature coming wounded back to a place that was safer than someplace else.

Was it Chuck's replacement he had prized from Lizzie Bean? Was it haste to add a life to the lives of parents that would, some morning or night, as they watched their baby laugh as if well, cause Anne Sorenson to say, "I hate him. He should have known. I hate him."

And Phil to say, "He's mostly a good doctor, though."

And Anne to say, "Yeah, but a little sloppy on some of the details, huh?"

Above the longhouse, Silver thought: Chuck, and now Mike Sorenson. The boy on the highway, the girl in the river, Dolores and Lizzie Bean and even L'Ordinet, Phil and Annie Sorenson, Gwen. Yes. But you're healthy, Silver told himself. You get loony, but you're blighted by health. You can't sustain being crazy, you keep getting well. You steal your health from them. Sorenson, puzzled and incapable of holding hate. Lizzie Bean, your baby machine. You drink their blood and get well, and there isn't any way to hide it. You're cursed with health, and all you can do, Herr Doktor, is live with your survival. That disease.

This would be worth telling, Silver said, in the black field off Bear's Pass, talking over clay and bones. Because if you can't stay crazy and if you have to live, then someone must be told. He was embarrassed by his pleasure. He knew a person to tell. Wives returned. Right back. And women in Vermont did have children they could nurse, sometime, if they wished, with luck and calculation. No, you're so easy on yourself. But wives did return, and husbands did, throwing the Hawk into gear and turning around on the outskirts of Oneida, New York, driving slowly into the high beams, following a trail cast ahead on the dark roads. And people who lived without children in their lives adopted them, though *adoption* was the wrong word, *marriage* the right one. And cells that went mad, flesh that edged closer to death in certain small bodies, could nevertheless be nursed —could be *doctored*—could be pleasured and coaxed into months of living, years, and people in the darkness of a nursery could bend to smell the milky breath at night and could be married to the future in its small risked skin.

Driving south into lighted towns and then out again into the darkness of country roads, Eli turned the radio on and leaned against the music. He downshifted at the bridge near New Sherburne, hit the accelerator as he shifted up, and he belted through the county, driving unwisely, not looking into his mirror or toward the mouths of junctions, going, in the small bubble of light, toward the mortgaged building that housed his medicine samples and sterilized instruments and incubating cultures and the house that he and Gwen continued to find and lose and find.

He turned the radio off. In the garage, he got slowly from

the car and puckered his lips against the ache in his knee. Holding his equipment bag in one hand and his medical bag in the other, he went to his doorway and kicked, banging again and again with his good leg, until Gwen turned on the light and opened the door.

In the flagstone foyer, wearing his old gray sweater, she studied his face, looked up and down. Then she walked back toward the kitchen. He dropped his bags inside and shut the door, followed her, limping.

"I already ate," she said, looking at him again, waiting.

"How's the studying?"

"I am not meant to understand numbers, math."

"You want me to explain some stuff?"

"What would you like to explain?"

He pointed at the open books and the scribbled papers on the kitchen table.

"Did you have an emergency?" she said. "Did the hospital call you?"

He shook his head, shifting the weight from the gouty leg. He moved to the refrigerator, opened a bottle of German beer, leaned against the refrigerator door, and drank.

"Did *you* run away?" she said.

He took the bottle from his lips and shook his head again, smiled a little, said, "No. Nothing dramatic."

"That's refreshing," she said. "Do you have some intention of explaining anything to me? You know, is something *up?*"

"You're too old to have a kid."

"Thank you. And who asked?"

"You know damned good and well who asked, and the answer is no, you're too old to do it safely, and we can't do it. *That* particular tango takes two, as—"

"—the song says. We've been married too long."

"No, we haven't. But you *could* be a mother and do the M.A. if I cut the practice back a little, you know, take fewer patients on and have shorter hours, something—a little arranging is all it would take, maybe. Maybe. If you wanted to do something like that. We could take turns at home. It wouldn't work out fair to you. It would still be tough, but we could do it. You'd work too hard, doing the degree and everything else."

"What *are* you proposing, darlin'?"

"Well, you think about it."

"You plan on impregnating some lonely lady in a nearby town?" She was smiling, then stopping herself, then adjusting the glasses on her nose and smiling again.

"There's a woman named Mrs. Podolak—"

"I know Mrs. Podolak, darlin'. I wasn't gone that long, you recall."

"Okay," he said. "Okay." He drank more beer, wiped his mouth, leaned harder at the refrigerator. "Listen, now. She's got a house filled with kids. They are—"

"Old children," Gwen said.

"Younger than we are. Young enough to be kids."

"Old children," she said, moving the glasses up her nose.

"Okay. Older children."

"Eli, what would we *do?*"

"With one or without one?" he said.

"And what about *Chuck*, Eli?"

"We remember him."

She started to cry, she pinched her nose and closed her eyes, then opened them. "And how can we—how do you propose we *do* it again? What if something happened again? How could we lose another child?"

He snapped his fingers. "As easy as that."

She pulled the sleeves of his sweater up her forearms and he stared at the skin, its pucker under the cuffs.

"Why don't we talk about it for a while?" he said. "Or later. Why don't we just talk about it sometime?"

She nodded. He watched her neck crease. Then it stiffened

as she pulled her head back, took her glasses off, moved in the kitchen, saying the names of food and drink, banging implements, staying away from the refrigerator, where he leaned to watch.

"Gwen," he said, "stop moving."

"Look who's talking," she said, standing in front of the empty oven, holding the door partly open. "Where *were* you?"

"I was thinking," he said. "I went to the dig and I was thinking."

"Well, so was I."

"Well, stop."

"Eli, I don't know what we should *do.*"

Daddy'll be right back.

"Let's go upstairs."

She slammed the oven door and pushed her sleeves. "That's not the answer," she said.

Right back.

"I didn't mean it to be."